TIME HAD RUN OUT

Abandoning stealth, Pam ran forward and jumped up on a platform with a thump. Before she could reach the engineer, however, he swiveled in his chair at the sound.

"Hey! Who are—"

Pam leaped forward, bringing down the butt of the Sherman sharply. She aimed for the engineer's head, but he dodged to one side, swinging one hand to block the blow. He missed, but she hit the top of his shoulder. His flailing hand slapped her helmet slightly ajar.

"Don't move and you won't be hurt," she said coldly, sliding one arm expertly around his neck. She tightened her grip slowly and held the Sherman in front of his eyes where he could see it clearly.

The engineer froze. His face flushed as she tightened her hold. As he strained for breath, he began to struggle, but she held him firmly. However, before he lost consciousness, she released her grip and eased him to the floor.

"Cancel order to prepare for manufacturing," Pam instructed the compute-

"Cancelled," the voic

MU
CHRONICLES

ROC

SCIENCE FICTION AND FANTASY

☐ **THE STALK by Janet and Chris Morris.** The Unity had made its offer, stated its terms. Now the United Nations of Earth must respond. But how could Mickey Croft make an unbiased decision for all humankind, when his own direct contact with the Interpreter had left him uncertain whether he himself was still completely human? (453077—$4.99)

☐ **DOWN AMONG THE DEAD MEN by Simon R. Green.** It was the most ancient of evils—and it was about to wake—in this sequel to *Blue Moon Rising*. "This one really stands out from the crowd."—*Science Fiction Chronicle* (453018—$4.50)

☐ **RED BRIDE by Christopher Fowler.** A horror is on the loose, savagely killing again and again. The police are powerless to stop the slaughter. The finest detectives cannot unmask the killer. Only one man suspects the secret. (452933—$4.99)

☐ **STALKER ANALOG by Mel Odom.** Bethany Shay was a cop on a serial killer's trail—a trail that led from the Church to the cybernet and into the heart of madness. (452577—$5.50)

☐ **THE MISTS FROM BEYOND** *20 Ghost Stories & Tales From the Other Side* **by Peter Straub, Clive Barker, Joyce Carol Oates and 17 others.** Twenty of the most haunting ghost tales ever created . . . all of them certain to transport you, if only for a brief time, from our everyday world to one in which even the faintest of shadows takes on a ghostly life of its own. (452399—$20.00)

*Prices slightly higher in Canada

Buy them at your local bookstore or use this convenient coupon for ordering.

PENGUIN USA
P.O. Box 999 — Dept. #17109
Bergenfield, New Jersey 07621

Please send me the books I have checked above.
I am enclosing $_____ (please add $2.00 to cover postage and handling). Send check or money order (no cash or C.O.D.'s) or charge by Mastercard or VISA (with a $15.00 minimum). Prices and numbers are subject to change without notice.

Card #_____ Exp. Date _____
Signature_____
Name_____
Address_____
City _____ State _____ Zip Code _____

For faster service when ordering by credit card call **1-800-253-6476**

Allow a minimum of 4-6 weeks for delivery. This offer is subject to change without notice.

MUTANT CHRONICLES

THE APOSTLE OF INSANITY TRILOGY

VOLUME ONE
IN LUNACY

by

William F. Wu

A ROC BOOK

ROC
Published by the Penguin Group
Penguin Books USA Inc., 375 Hudson Street,
New York, New York 10014, U.S.A.
Penguin Books Ltd, 27 Wrights Lane,
London W8 5TZ, England
Penguin Books Australia Ltd, Ringwood,
Victoria, Australia
Penguin Books Canada Ltd, 10 Alcorn Avenue,
Toronto, Ontario, Canada M4V 3B2
Penguin Books (N.Z.) Ltd, 182–190 Wairau Road,
Auckland 10, New Zealand

Penguin Books Ltd, Registered Offices:
Harmondsworth, Middlesex, England

First published by Roc, an imprint of Dutton Signet,
a division of Penguin Books USA Inc.

First Printing, December, 1993
10 9 8 7 6 5 4 3 2 1

This novel is dedicated to

Michael A. Stackpole,

with thanks for introducing
chaos and mutations into my life.
(I think.)

ACKNOWLEDGMENTS

Special thanks are due in writing this novel to John-Allen Price, Christopher Schelling, Fredrik Malmberg, Nils Gulliksson and the staff at Target Games, and Ricia Mainhardt; Bridgett and Marty Marquardt; also to my parents, Dr. William Q. Wu and Cecile F. Wu, and Michael D. Toman.

CHAPTER 1

Pam Afton slipped silently through the shadows on the third floor of Bauhaus Manufacturing Center Six. Unusually tall for a woman, she had to bend low to remain hidden by the robotic machinery around her. The factory arms and dies were not moving now, but their motors hummed quietly in readiness. She did not have much time.

According to the briefing she had received, she knew that an engineer was setting the design specs in the factory computer console tonight. As soon as he had finished, he would activate the entire factory. When he did, this center would begin rolling out a new shipment of Bauhaus MP-105s, their standard side arm, by the thousands.

Bright light at the far end of the floor told her where to find the engineering console. She felt a familiar surge of adrenaline as she worked her way toward it. In all likelihood, she would find only engineers and technical staff on this level, but she could not be certain. On her way in, she had evaded normal Bauhaus security.

As she worked her way forward, she stayed close to an interior wall. Tall vertical windows, looking out over one of the many underground levels comprising Luna City here on the moon, lined the opposite wall. The finest level of the city was on the terraformed surface, but the industrial centers and most of the ordinary residences and businesses lay here underground. Since the time was near 11:00 P.M., the windows opened on artificial night. If she had moved under them, her reflection might have shown in the windows and could attract the engineer's attention.

Pam felt the sweat running freely inside her light composite armor and helmet. She was slender and kept herself in excellent condition, freeing her now to slip through narrow spaces among the motionless factory robots. Shoulder straps crossed her back, holding a small backpack, and ran between her legs, then up to her shoulders again; a small metal box with a narrow hole through the middle hung from them in front of her waist. She might need that to escape later.

A beeping tone up ahead, followed by a man clearing his throat, helped her place the console more precisely, though it remained out of sight.

She hoped she would not have to kill the engineer. As a free-lance operative, she had been hired by a representative of her old employer, the Capitol megacorporation, specifically to sabotage the manufacture of weapons on this level of this Bauhaus manufacturing center; Bauhaus was one of their major competitors. She respected the weapon, but she knew nothing and cared nothing about the business. Of course she realized that it must have been competing effectively with a Capitol product.

Unlike most free-lancers, however, and most other people here on Luna, for that matter, she took pride in her own code of conduct. Part of her code required that she do exactly the job she had accepted. She would fight her way through the task if necessary, and fight her way out of trouble if it developed. In the past she had accepted and carried out assassination assignments. However, killing and injuring others without reason and random destruction of property were outside her personal code.

Pam had worked her way up through the length of the floor, ducking low and clinging to the shadows. Now she had reached the edge of the pool of bright light. At this end of the floor a single engineer sat before a large computer console on a raised platform. His back was turned to her, but she could see that he was unarmed.

She paused for a moment, listening. The motors hummed up and down the floor, but she heard no sign of anyone else approaching. She drew her Sherman .74 M13 Bolter, a light, oversized automatic handgun. Made of a hard composite similar to her armor, it doubled as a sap.

Holding it close, with the barrel upward, she crept quietly into the light toward him.

The Bauhaus engineer seated at the console had short, light brown hair. He looked intently at the design on his computer screen, speaking quietly into the mouthpiece to make changes. Then he nodded to himself and sat back in his chair, letting out a deep breath.

"All right," the engineer muttered. "That's it, then. Computer, prepare to activate the manufacturing sequence of Bauhaus MP-105."

Pam realized that she had run out of time. She could no longer move slowly. Abandoning stealth, she ran forward and jumped up on the platform with a thump. Before she could reach him, however, he swiveled in his chair at the sound.

"Hey! Who are—"

Pam leaped forward, bringing down the butt of the Sherman sharply. She aimed for the engineer's head, but he dodged to one side, swinging one hand to block the blow. He missed, but she hit the top of his shoulder instead of his head. His flailing hand slapped her helmet slightly ajar.

"Don't move and you won't be hurt," she said coldly, sliding one arm expertly around his neck. She tightened her grip slowly and held the Sherman in front of his eyes where he could see it clearly.

The engineer froze. His face flushed as she tightened her hold. As he strained for breath, he began to struggle, but she held him firmly. However, before he lost consciousness, she released her grip and eased him to the floor.

"Remember what I said." She sat down in his chair and put one foot lightly on his neck as he gasped for breath.

Pam was no computer expert, but she could use a terminal. "Cancel order to prepare for manufacturing."

"Canceled," said the computer.

Pam had already thought out her assignment. She had been hired to sabotage the weapon, which was the standard side arm for Bauhaus troops and was popular with many other people. If she simply turned off or damaged the manufacturing order, someone would eventually just fix it and turn it back on, whether it was this engineer or someone else. What she had to do was force Bauhaus to make a major expense that could not bring any profit in return.

That meant manufacturing flawed guns. However, her personal code would not allow her to endanger the anonymous soldiers and civilians who would use them. She could not make guns that would backfire or explode.

"Computer," she said. "Solidify the barrel and chamber completely."

"With what substance?"

"With the same composite of the surrounding surfaces."

In front of her the design altered. Now the ammunition could not move out of the magazine. The product was not a gun at all anymore.

"Prepare to manufacture. Then commence manufacturing of the full complement, however many that was."

"Acknowledged."

"Where is the manual override on this system located?"

"Manual controls are located here." The computer put specs of this level on the screen. An arrow pointed to the cabinet underneath the console.

Pam slid the chair back and opened the cabinet door. Behind it she found a smaller console with a tiny screen. She backed up again and aimed her Sherman at the controls. She fired twice, the sharp retort echoing up and down the floor. Then she slammed the cabinet shut.

"Manufacturing commences," said the computer. Up and down the floor, the robotic arms began to move, making the inoperative guns.

The engineer could not stop the manufacture now. By the time anyone else figured what had happened and disabled the factory some other way, the sequence would already be finished. Now she just had to get out of here.

Her helmet was still askew. She straightened it. Under the helmet, her straight blond hair had been cut short and blunt so that it would not get in her eyes under any circumstances. She was ready to go.

Pam lifted her foot from the neck of the engineer and

looked at him. He was still gasping for breath, but he would be fine. She got up, moving quickly, and stepped over him. Her shots would bring security personnel here quickly.

She ran down the main aisle in the center of the floor this time, toward the doors at the far end. Shouts and pounding footsteps sounded beyond the door, however, and she slid to a stop on the hard floor. She would need her shoulder harness and backpack after all.

Pam threw herself to one side, under a moving robot arm, sliding toward the exterior wall beneath one of the vertical windows. Still flat on the floor, she reached back over her shoulder and unfastened the backpack. In the same moment, the doors burst open and a Bauhaus security detail ran inside, weapons forward.

Sweat soaked her, inside her armor; excitement burned in her gut and in her fingertips. This was the critical moment.

In the shadows the Bauhaus detail would not see her immediately, off to one side on the floor among all the moving machinery. As they fanned out and advanced slowly, she pulled a roll of thin, sturdy wire and a pair of tough, skin-thin gloves from her pack. She slipped one end of the wire through the narrow hole in the box at her waist and then looped it around a leg of machinery bolted to the floor and secured it.

"The engineer!" Someone shouted from about halfway up the main aisle. "Move up! Check the computer."

Footsteps ran up the remainder of the floor.

Pam pulled her gloves on, then moved up into a crouch. Taking careful aim, she fired in a quick line from the top center of the window all the way down the center in quick succession. The broken glass flew outward, instead of inward on top of her.

"Over there! Fire! Fire!" a man screamed.

Pam sprang up on the sill among the remaining shards and simply jumped out the window.

Bauhaus weapons blazed behind her and chewed chunks out of the wall as she fell through the darkness toward the street.

* * *

Lane Chung walked through the steam clouds leaking from the street in the free-lancer's neighborhood where he lived. Filthy buildings of gray stone rose up on each side of the street, with scowling gargoyles staring down at him over hooked beaks or long fangs. In the distance gunfire rattled on another block; the sound was so routine that at this distance, he hardly noticed.

Streetlights that worked threw small pools of yellowish illumination across the crowd of people walking up and down the street around Lane; many streetlights were out, leaving irregular spots of darkness. The mood of the crowd was hostile and suspicious of strangers, as always.

Lane arrived at the small, unassuming doorway of the Midnight Star at midnight, as he usually did. Like any inhabitant of Luna City, and especially the free-lancers who habituated the Midnight Star, he paused just inside to glance around the crowd, with the steam of leaking street ventilation clouding around him. The other free-lancers were loud and raucous, but he saw no sign of trouble. Of average height and weight, Lane slipped unnoticed through the jostling people and ordered a drink at the bar. Then he found a couple of empty stools by the counter along one wall and worked his way to them.

Lane sat quietly, as he normally did, looking around. Most of the people here were unemployed free-lancers, as he was, hoping a prospective employer would come in with an assignment just right for them. The competition was fierce, but anyone seeking a free-lancer would come to this part of Luna City, so Lane hung out here with all the rest.

Every free-lancer had a different history, of course, though most had served at one time in the military of one of the megacorporations in space. Mishima, Bauhaus, and Capitol provided most of them. Very few people ever left the service of Cybertronic, because once they became cyborgs, life in mainstream society left them permanent outsiders. The Brotherhood, the religious organization dedicated to fighting heresy and the Dark Legion of aliens, also maintained the loyalty of its members.

Lane drank slowly. If someone with a job offer came in, Lane wanted to present himself in a professional way.

Most free-lancers were not as particular. However, as he surveyed the crowd, he saw none of the hiring agents, legitimate or otherwise, whom he knew.

After Lane had sat alone for about an hour, he spotted Pam Afton's short, straight blond hair in the doorway. Her sharp blue eyes spotted him. First she stopped at the bar for a drink; then she began working her way through the crowd in his direction. She wore a skintight gray jumpsuit and merely a handgun in a holster, but Lane saw that she had a freshly scrubbed look, as though she had just showered. He suspected she had just finished a job.

"Hiya, blue eyes." Lane grinned and patted the stool next to him.

"Hello, Chung." She grinned impishly and slid her taut, lithe figure onto the stool.

They had been colleagues and friends for seven years, never romantically involved. She had joined his unit in the Capitol Special Forces during his second tour, serving in the Martian Banshees. They had fought troops from the Mishima megacorporation with short-term successes but never a final one.

"You look cheerful," said Lane, looking up at her; she was a little taller. "I think I know what that means. Want to tell me about it?"

"Sure. It was great." She lowered her voice and leaned close to him. "An entire shipment of Bauhaus MP-105s that won't fire and can't even be fixed."

Lane laughed. "Really? So they have the entire expense of making and shipping them."

"And they'll take a hit on their famous reputation for making quality weapons."

"They sure will. Everybody I know in Bauhaus likes the MP-105."

"And I got away clean."

"You didn't have to shoot anyone?"

"No. Blasted my way out a window and used a pressure belt pack to slide down a wire."

"A wire? How high up were you?"

"Only the third level." She paused to sip her drink and winced at its strength. "That's low enough for the belt pack to stop my momentum."

"Just barely. Put too much friction against the wire and it'll cut it."

"I know, I know." Pam let out a breath and glanced around the crowd. "I'm just glad I got a paying job again, Chung. Look at these poor drunks. There are just too many of us. Most of them are as desperate as I was yesterday. Now I have a few months to find another job."

"Well, I don't. Don't take this wrong, but I'm as desperate for money as anyone here."

"Oops, sorry." Her lighthearted tone turned serious. "Unless we make it into very top-level jobs, we'll never know how long a payment will have to last. But look, Chung, I can stake you for a while if—"

"Not necessary. At least, not yet." Lane sighed. "Two tours in the Martian Banshees and this is the best I can do. Scuttlebutt is, as veterans of the Banshees, you and I are among the best soldiers within the forces of the megacorporations. So why aren't we doing any better?"

CHAPTER 2

"Ease up, Chung. We *are* doing better ... than most of them." Pam gestured toward the crowd with her free hand, smiling wryly. "We get the jobs we do here in Luna City because Capitol Special Forces *are* often used for clandestine operations. And our various employers know it."

"Yeah, all right." Lane grinned. "Sure, I remember all those old assignments with the Banshees where no prisoners could be taken—and the nature of the attacker had to be kept secret for political reasons."

"We did more than a few of those together, Captain." She smiled wryly.

He laughed at the use of former rank. "That's right, Lieutenant. We sure did. But in Capitol Special Forces we always had the latest military technology. We're both out of the loop now."

"That's true, but ..." Pam shrugged. "You really think it matters? All that use of combat analysis with integrated computers and laser technology works fine on a battlefield, but it's not very useful for the kind of work we do here in Luna City."

"You're right about the battlefield work," said Lane. "But when we've been out a few more years, we'll have definitely been left behind in hand weapons and explosives, too. The black market only provides equipment, not training. For now, we're still using all the hand weapons we smuggled out of the service when our hitches ended."

"I took what I could." She frowned. "Not as much as you. I didn't like the price that black market guy demanded." Her face tightened.

Lane waited to see if she would go on. He suspected

the demand had required more than money, but she had never mentioned it before. When she said nothing more about it, he let it go. They had remained friends in part by respecting each other's privacy.

"I used my old Bolter tonight," Pam said casually. "I hope they don't replace the Sherman .74 M13 Bolter. It's my most personal tie to the Banshees, except for you." She laughed lightly and sipped her drink again.

"Same here." Lane tapped his own Sherman at his belt. "You and the Bolter, like night and day."

He looked at her blue eyes awkwardly for a moment. Usually their talk avoided direct expressions of feeling like this. Then he glanced away, reaching for his own drink. "I like my old Capitol CAR-24, too."

"The old standby light machine gun and grenade launcher. Yeah, I cleaned mine last night. I almost took it with me today, but I decided it was too bulky."

"You didn't have to launch any grenades tonight, eh?" He grinned and relaxed, more comfortable now that they were talking shop again.

"No," said Pam. "For this job, that would have been overkill."

"A stealth job."

"That's right."

"Did you use a disguise? Or did your classic Anglo-Saxon looks fit right in?"

"Don't forget my Scots ancestors, Chung; they wouldn't like to be left out. But in this case, I didn't bother. The engineer saw my face, but I'm not worried about him. For Bauhaus, this was a routine job. They won't prioritize hunting me down when so many of us do this kind of work."

"Yeah, that's true. Personally, I hate disguises. They just get in the way."

"Murasaki would have been good at the work we do now," Lane said quietly. An old Banshee comrade of theirs, Greg Murasaki had fallen fighting Mishima megacorporation troops on Mars during Lane's second tour. "He enjoyed special ops. His enthusiasm showed up in how good he was."

"I know," Pam said slowly. "But he really hated Mishima. On Mars he could fight them all the time. Here in Luna City, with the Pax Luna making this a neutral zone, he'd have to watch the Mishima logo go by every day. I think it would have driven him crazy."

"Yeah. Maybe so." Lane shook his head wearily. "For all I know, he's better off. At least he isn't worried about his next job."

Pam paused. "He didn't want eternal rest. He wanted to send Mishima troops to *their* eternal rest."

Lane looked out over the crowd again. Some of the people around them were talking loudly and laughing; others, their faces tense and serious, pushed their way around the bar, anxiously looking for someone who might help them somehow. A few, like Lane and Pam, sat quietly.

"You ever wonder if this is worth it?" Lane asked. "I didn't become a Banshee to wind up this way."

"No one ever did," said Pam, looking at the crowd with him. "I don't know which I like least—fighting with the Banshees, knowing I could killed any second by Mishima, or hanging out here, begging for jobs."

"Not much of a choice, is it?" Lane sighed. "The last really high-paying job I had took place last year."

"Which one?"

"I had to root out some terrorists hiding in the old lunar mines under the city."

"I remember now." Pam looked at him sympathetically. "You're right, this life doesn't give us a decent choice at all. It's not much of a society, for that matter. No one really wants to live this way."

"So what do you think, blue eyes—can you think of a reason that makes this life even worth living?"

Pam looked out over the crowd and said nothing.

Lane sighed. "I can't, either."

Capitol trooper Carter Harrent squatted under a tree with his partner, Moore Romano, in the humid, terraformed Venusian jungle, poking at the bowl of village stew that was his lunch. Carter's Capitol M606 light machine gun lay on the ground next to him, Capitol's logo of the shield of stars and stripes overlaid with an attacking eagle shining on the stock in the sunlight. His squad of six troopers was assigned to the little Capitol village here called Fairview. They acted as an observer outpost and also policed the small village, resolving disputes among the farm families.

It was dull duty, but it had never been dangerous. The squad ate lunch in rotating pairs; now their four comrades remained on duty, watching the villagers form their little plots of land. Every day was like this.

Idly, Carter wondered what the planet had been like before Capitol had terraformed it. He had heard the place had been uninhabitable for humans, but that was a long time ago. As far as he was concerned, it was too hot and humid for humans right now.

"What do you think is worse?" Moore looked up from his own lunch. "Fighting here in the jungle against the other megacorporations like Mishima and Bauhaus, or fighting elsewhere on Venus with the Brotherhood against the Dark Legion in the Venusian Crusade?"

"I hate the jungle," said Carter. "But at least Mishima troops are human." He had heard that the Dark Legion was comprised of monstrous aliens, but that was all he knew. Here at Fairview, the Dark Legion hardly even seemed real. Some people didn't even believe it existed at all. "Where did the Dark Legion come from, anyway? You know?"

"Yeah," said Moore. "My old lieutenant used to fight them when he was a Capital liaison to the Brotherhood. He told me about them. The first humans who got to Nero, the tenth planet, discovered them."

"They're from Nero? I thought that was a little planet. How can there be so many of them?"

"He said they aren't really from Nero. Some weird seals and other formations were there and some kind of influence on the minds of the first humans there forced them to destroy the seals. The Dark Legion came out of another dimension. Nero just held the portal they passed through."

"Another dimension?"

"That's why they're so monstrous-looking." Moore nodded, munching the stew.

Carter felt a chill up his back, even in the heat and humidity of the jungle. "Why didn't anybody ever tell me this? I just thought they were . . . oh, I don't know." He hesitated. "What else do you know about them?"

"I know the lord of the Dark Legion is a monster called a Dark Apostle, named Algeroth." Moore ran a hand through his curly black hair, casually as though none of this meant anything to him. "There are lots of lesser monsters called nepharites. I think they're the generals of the Dark Legion. But the one who rules the Dark Legion is Algeroth."

"Really?"

"And I heard that they have a dark power that can turn you—that is, pervert you into one of their own. The lieutenant told me that most of their troops are perverted souls from other dimensions. But they can turn humans, too."

"How do they do that?" Carter asked quietly.

"I'm not sure, exactly. But apparently the Brotherhood says the Dark Legion's creatures can offer certain powers, and a human who can't resist the temptation accepts the power in exchange for undergoing an initiation rite. Then the human becomes a heretic."

"I'd rather stay in the jungle and fight Mishima," said Carter. "Not that we're anywhere near the front here, of course—" A rumble out of the sky got his attention, and he looked up into a ceiling of thick white clouds.

"Sounds like a Capitol troop carrier," said Moore. He grinned. "Hey, maybe we'll have some company around here for a change."

"Doesn't sound quite right," said Carter, still looking up at the sky.

A couple of the villagers came out of their huts to look. The other troopers came out of the trees. No one spoke as the roar grew louder.

Suddenly, Carter saw a large, black troop carrier descending straight down out of the clouds on vertical jets. It had been a Capitol ship once; he recognized the design and the old, faded insignia. Carter had ridden in this type himself; its fuselage was forty meters in length and twenty meters in diameter. It flew on two jets hung from narrow delta wings. However, its usual straight, sleek lines and jungle camouflage of green, khaki, and black were gone. The ship was completely black and looked as though it had half melted and then froze into position again. Weird, unidentifiable mechanical shapes grew out of its sides like cancerous growths, ruining its aerodynamic shape.

"Something's wrong," said Carter, fumbling on his belt for his communicator. "I got to get their I.D."

The black troop carrier came down swiftly in the nearby jungle, blasting and burning away the trees and underbrush with vertical jets. It landed with a rough thump. Before Carter could make any contact on his communicator, the big doors of the troop carrier opened. He froze, staring.

The troops who came running out of the carrier bore no resemblance to anything ever human. Thousands of huge, twisted, grotesque shapes wearing armor and bearing gigantic weapons ran out of the jungle toward the village, firing in all directions. Behind him Carter heard villagers scream. His own comrades shouted alarms and began to fire.

As if in a dream, Carter's arms felt slow and clumsy as he swung his Capitol M606 light machine gun up from the ground. Action was pointless, anyway. He might as well flip a light switch while the sun went nova.

Momoko Watanabe, a Mishima Army trooper, sat in the top of an observation tower, at a Mishima outpost, overlooking the Venusian jungle. Her job, done at an immense communications console, was to control robotic observation drones assigned to the front against Capitol. Today, though, one of her drones spotted a fast-moving troop carrier flying on the edge of her territory out of another part of Venus toward Capitol territory.

"Computer, run identification analysis of unidentified ship," she ordered.

When her computer reported a fifty-percent likelihood that the carrier was a Capitol ship, she assigned the observation drone to follow it. She had never seen a ship with exactly that appearance, but her colleagues had told her about the black technology of the Dark Legion. It physically altered human technology into something more efficient and powerful, though sometimes less reliable.

She suspected that she had located a Dark Legion ship moving into a Capitol section of Venus. While she personally did not care what happened to Capitol, she would have to report what she found to her superiors. If the Dark Legion was opening a new front on Venus, top Mishima strategists would want to know about it.

Momoko watched as the drone followed the mystery ship from a much higher altitude. When the black ship descended suddenly into the clouds, the drone shifted to infrared sensors and maintained the image. As the other ship landed, Momoko watched as a horde of figures charged out and overwhelmed a small village.

"Computer, run analysis of individual troops." Body weight, height, girth, and heat came up in front of her, with the computer's conclusion. As she had expected, the fighters from the mystery ship were not human. They were too big, too monstrous, too alien.

As she watched her console, the handful of troopers at the village were slaughtered where they stood. The villagers threw themselves on the ground in terrified surrender, but they were executed on the spot, with one exception. A single young woman was grabbed by a large enemy trooper and carried back to the black ship. The others burned the village and the small tilled area near it.

In moments the attackers had returned to their ship. It took off with a roar, leaving behind a blazing ruin. The attack had been completed within a few minutes.

"Drone Yamamoto, maintain observation at a safe distance." While the drone followed the Dark Legion ship back to the Dark Legion territory on Venus from where it had come, she ran a combat analysis on her computer. It agreed with her own observation, that this probe had nothing to do with the minimal importance of the village itself.

The Dark Legion was conducting some sort of test, either of its tactics, weapons, or troops. It might also be probing in order to observe the response by Capitol. She had not gathered enough information for a more detailed conclusion.

When the drone veered away at the edge of Dark Legion territory, following its instructions to remain safe, it had gathered all it could. Momoko entered her personal observations into the report with the visual record and transmitted it to her superiors. In combination with their other information, they might be able to make more sense of it.

CHAPTER 3

Momoko leaned back in her command seat, studying the information in front of her. She knew that Mishima computers were fairly sure, from circumstantial evidence, that a nepharite commanded the Dark Legion beachhead on Venus. After a moment she leaned forward and punched up satellite reconnaissance of the central site.

The image that came up on her screen showed her a Citadel, but it appeared modest: a few towers and basic launch and landing facilities. She felt certain that terrible mysteries lay somewhere below ground, though she had no direct evidence of that. In her own opinion, it was a much greater danger to Mishima than Capitol, but of course no one at the strategic level asked for a mere trooper's judgment.

Drone Yamamoto hovered near the edge of the Dark Legion beachhead, out of observation distance of the Citadel, awaiting further instructions.

Momoko left it there for a while, trying to decide what to do next. "Drone Yamamoto, maintain random search pattern at a safe distance. Transmit alarm at first sight of further activity in enemy territory."

She checked the position of her other drones and sent two more to observe the Dark Legion beachhead at different altitudes and from varying directions. This beachhead was not, technically, within her range of orders, which instructed her to observe the Capitol front. However, since the Dark Legion had just raided Capitol and had taken a prisoner, she decided she could justify the action, if necessary. Her real reason was that the situation was too unusual for her to ignore.

Thirty-two minutes later, all three drones transmitted

the alarms she had ordered. On three screens receiving transmissions from the drones and one showing the satellite recon, she saw a single ship taking off from the Dark Legion beachhead. Like the other ship, it was a dark technology perversion of a Capitol ship. Unlike the other one, this was a fast courier ship, headed straight into space.

"Computer, track the Dark Legion ship until a trajectory in space has been established. Then plot the likely destination and report."

While she waited, she studied the ship. Originally, this craft had been a small space plane of a Capitol type that she had often observed on the Capitol front through her drones. It was fifteen meters long with a single jet in the fuselage and stubby delta wings to fly in and out of an atmosphere. From past experience and computer analysis, she knew it also possessed the structural strength and proper seals to survive the vacuum of space. Small jets positioned at intervals around its body facilitated its docking in space when necessary. Like the troop carrier, however, it was completely black, not camouflage, and its shape was distorted by mechanical additions that neither she nor her computer could identify.

A few minutes later, the computer put up the trajectory it had plotted on one of the screens in front of her. Momoko was startled, but she knew her duty, which was simple enough. She immediately transmitted this report up the line to Mishima Venus command, too. After a moment of thought, she added a purely personal guess, that the single woman who had been taken alive from the Capitol village was probably on that courier.

The Dark Legion courier was heading for Luna.

On Level Four of Luna City, Kenji Hayashi sweated in the back of a small restaurant. The front of the restaurant was bustling, and the kitchen was busy, but he was alone back here in the filthy, cramped cubicle to the rear. His job was to oversee the cleanup and keep all the old machinery functioning.

Now he had worked open the back of the dishwasher, which was supposed to vaporize food particles while leaving the dishes and glasses untouched. Apparently the power had gone totally out of control. The unit had vaporized every dish and glass he had just placed inside.

This job was a long way from his training as a Mishima Elite soldier. However, Kenji felt that his personal commitment to Bushido, long outdated in this time, required that he do every job with absolute dedication. Firearms and *kenjitsu* were his strong suit; however, he would defeat this dishwasher, too, no matter what it took. Enemies within Mishima had set him up to be framed for improper behavior and shamed out of the Mishima service, but he would not allow his spirit to be broken.

Suddenly, the rear door of the cubicle was yanked open. The Whiz Kid, a nineteen-year-old who shared Kenji's Japanese ancestry but would not reveal his real name, stuck his head inside from the dirty, narrow alley. His black hair was mussed and his face tense.

"Hey, Major!"

"Not anymore, Whiz Kid," Kenji said gently. "You know that. But what is wrong?"

The Whiz Kid glanced around the dank cubicle and lowered his voice. "Can I talk freely in here?"

Kenji nodded authoritatively. He acted as an informal mentor to the Whiz Kid, a brilliant but socially inept teenager heavily into cyberspace. In fact he spent most of his time on his computer, almost living in cyberspace.

The Whiz Kid was a friend and protégé on the street, though his closest friends were the other young people in his cyberspace gang. He was a fully modern kid, though, with no sense of Bushido. Someday Kenji hoped to instill in him a sense of *giri,* the belief in personal obligation that drove Kenji, whether he was fighting Capitol troops on Mars and Venus or trying to fix a dishwasher.

The Whiz Kid slipped his skinny frame inside and closed the door. He wore his customary black satin jacket. "You interested in some cyberspace street talk about Mishima?"

"My formal ties to Mishima have ended," said Kenji, a little puzzled. "You know that. But if you wish to talk with me, I have no objection."

"My cyberspace gang got word that Lord Mishima is going to be assassinated some time today! Triple zowee!"

Kenji straightened, studying his face. Lord Mishima owned and led Mishima megacorporation, but that was only the beginning. A man of immense privacy and reserve, he commanded an almost mystical presence, not only within Mishima, but throughout all the human worlds. Kenji respected him as a man of the old values. While he had never met Lord Mishima, he understood implicitly that the man shared his own belief in Bushido.

"Exactly what did you hear?" Kenji asked.

"Word is, the Brotherhood has sent a couple of their mortificators to assassinate Lord Mishima right here in Luna City."

"How? All of Lord Mishima's movements are confidential. Everything he does remains highly classified at all times."

"I guess that's why this is different," said Whiz Kid, shrugging. "The gang says Lord Mishima's going out to dinner with a few top colleagues or something. Anyhow, supposedly, the mortificators know exactly where to find him about an hour from now."

"I have never heard of this much private information being available before. Maybe this is all phony. Or they are all simply mistaken."

"One of the guys in the gang told me that the original source is an employee of the restaurant. All the regular workers were cleared out so that only Mishima staff will work there, except for the chef."

Kenji nodded. When he had been in Mishima's military service, he had heard that this was the way Lord Mishima moved around Luna City. Usually silence was either bought or enforced at gunpoint until Lord Mishima had finished his business, but no policy could be completely reliable. This assassination attempt could be genuine.

Ever since Kenji had left the Mishima Elite, he had privately considered himself a *ronin*. Originally, in the ancient days on Earth, they had been samurai without masters. Here in Luna City, a certain class of people sometimes called themselves *ronin*. That group was comprised of various mercenaries, private investigators, bodyguards, hired swords, and other assassins. However, they believed in none of the old, traditional values of the samurai, such as loyalty and honor. Kenji felt he had much in common with the true *ronin* of ages past, precisely because of his sense of these values.

"All right, Whiz Kid. I am coming." He paused. "You were cleaning my armor and weapons for me. They are still in your home."

"That's right. I'll help you get ready."

With careful but deliberate speed, Kenji disabled the dishwasher so that no more dishes could be vaporized. Then he called his superior to report that a personal emergency had occurred; he could not say explicitly that his obligation to Lord Mishima overrode his obligation to clean dishes. While his boss shouted angrily that he had to remain on the job, Kenji hung up on him and hurried out with the Whiz Kid.

Kenji and the Whiz Kid ran up the narrow, dark alley, jumping over garbage and puddles of water. They both lived in cellar apartments nearby, with doors that stood adjacent to each other. Now the Whiz Kid let Kenji into his small, one-room home to help him prepare.

The room was a crowded mess. An elaborate computer station filled one corner. The only other furniture were a couch and a couple of chairs, all covered with dirty clothes. It was a sharp contrast to Kenji's own tidy, spare apartment across the small porch that separated their doors.

First Kenji put on his armor. Dark blue and trimmed with thin red lines, his armor was light, but large and exaggerated in shape to deflect blades and slow down rounds of ammunition. The flared shoulder blades, skirting, and shinguards all were reminiscent of ancient samurai gowns and armor; so was his helmet, which featured stylized wings sweeping back from his forehead and a chartreuse eyeshield. The logo of Mishima, a circle with a block "M" against the red and white rays of the rising sun, still lay on both shoulders and on the center of his breastplate.

They worked quickly, neither of them speaking. Kenji had shown off his armor and weapons to the Whiz Kid before at the youngster's request, and the Whiz Kid had volunteered to help care for them. Now the Whiz Kid worked with tense determination, eager to participate.

After the Whiz Kid had helped Kenji fasten his armor, Kenji pointed to his samurai sword, hanging by its silken sash on the wall. The Whiz Kid brought it and secured it to Kenji's waist. Kenji also pointed to a smaller sword and accepted it. Last, he pointed to his Mishima-manufactured Tambu no.4 Windrider light machine gun in a rack inside a wall case. It fired a ten-millimeter slug, with thirty rounds to a magazine. The Whiz Kid handed it to him.

Kenji checked the weapon and loaded it. "Where is this restaurant where Lord Mishima will be attacked?"

"The White Swan. It's on this level of Luna City, about six blocks away."

"The White Swan," Kenji repeated. "I have heard of it. I am surprised that Lord Mishima would come down to the inner levels. I believe he usually stays on the surface, among all the towers of the megacorporations and the Brotherhood's Cathedral." He thought a moment. "Do I recall that the White Swan is on the top floor of a four-story building?"

"Not exactly. All four stories are the White Swan restaurant. But the private banquet room makes up the top floor."

"How much time remains before the moment of the planned attack?"

"Uh, forty-one minutes, but that was just street talk . . . a guess."

"I understand. Remain home." Kenji strode out without looking back, knowing that the Whiz Kid would cooperate.

Forty-one minutes would have been plenty of time to hike the distance of six blocks on old Earth or even the jungles of Venus. Here on the jammed streets of Luna City, he still should make it. If the approximated time of the assassination was inaccurate, however, he could do nothing about that.

Kenji moved with determination through the crowded streets. For the short distance he had to cover, walking would be the fastest mode of travel. At one point the crowd was so dense that he could not move forward at all; when he managed to continue, he saw that a crew from Imperial megacorporation was cleaning up some dead bodies in Imperial uniforms.

He finally reached the main doors of the White Swan with seven minutes to spare. However, the doors were locked. That was consistent with Mishima policy regarding Lord Mishima's excursions, but it did not help Kenji.

Now feeling anxious, he pushed past other pedestrians to circle around the building. If Mishima guards were nearby, they were in plainclothes; that was not impossible, since Lord Mishima's presence was a secret. However, if they revealed themselves by trying to stop Kenji, then he could enlist their aid.

By the time Kenji had worked his way around to the rear alley, he was surprised that no one had approached him. Since Kenji was wearing his full Mishima armor, they should at least give him a fair hearing, though he would freely admit he had left Mishima service. Then he saw several pools of blood on the filthy pavement of the alley. The rear door of the building stood ajar.

Kenji slung his Windrider forward and advanced carefully. Through the sliver of light inside, he saw a man in Mishima security clothing, standard gray shirt over black pants. This one lay facedown with a long slash in the center of his back, in a pool of blood. He still wore a Harker communication headset and his own Windrider lay on the floor next to him.

After listening carefully, and hearing only silence inside, Kenji slowly leaned his shoulder against the door, his Windrider aimed inside. He found two more Mishima security guards, also killed by sword wounds. Kenji understood; the Brotherhood mortificators had required silence and stealth at this stage of their attack. Mortificators routinely carried a double-edged mortis sword.

When he stepped all the way inside, he found two Brotherhood mortificators, also dead, in their traditional black clothing and black cloaks, now soaked with red. They had been killed with the short swords carried by Mishima guards, as he judged by the appearance of the wounds. Somehow, the mortificators had managed to sneak up close enough to kill the Mishima security guards before the guards could either fire their Windriders or report upstairs through their Harker communicators; otherwise, Kenji would be able to hear gunfire right now. Also, at least some of the dead had fallen outside and had been dragged inside to hide their presence from passersby in the alley.

No one else was in sight; because these men were still bleeding, he knew that the mortificators had been here only moments before.

Kenji moved quickly, but kept his footsteps light to minimize the sound. Down the short hall he found the lift, but decided that if the mortificators heard it coming, they would be waiting for him up above when the doors opened. He had to try several hall doors before he found the back stairs. Then, moving faster, he hurried up the stairs.

As Kenji turned the corner from the second floor to the third, he heard the chattering of gunfire above him. Shouts followed, with thumps and crashes, then return fire. He raced up the remaining stairs, swinging his Windrider into position as an open doorway came into view on the top floor.

Kenji's trained eye took in the entire tableau in an instant. All over the private room, tables and chairs had been overturned, dishes of food thrown in all directions. Ten or twelve Mishima security guards lay dead, caught by surprise. At a long table against the far wall, another four well-dressed men lay facedown in their food, shot as they sat; two more had been blasted out of their seats. Three Brotherhood mortificators had fallen by return fire.

Now Lord Mishima, calm and motionless in a plain gray kimono, stood at his place of honor at the long table, his back to the wall but not pinned against it. His face, lined yet ageless, remained expressionless as he watched his last two security guards stand in front of the table with drawn swords against six mortificators. They had drawn their twin-edged mortis swords. All had emptied their firearms and in the close quarters here, no one had a chance to reload.

Since Kenji had come in behind the mortificators, he

could not spray them without hitting Lord Mishima and
his surviving guards. Instead, he switched his Windrider
to single-shot fire and sprang to one side, where he could
fire safely. His entrance caught everyone's attention, and
the Mishima logos on his armor told them where his loyalty belonged.

As four of the mortificators closed with the two Mishima guards, the other two mortificators swung toward
Kenji in a clearly suicidal move to preserve their comrades' attack on Lord Mishima.

One mortificator ran toward Kenji, his mortis raised;
Kenji fired repeatedly into his chest. He fell forward, in-
terfering with Kenji's line of fire to the second man. The
mortificator behind the first came charging in the same
moment, slashing down with his own mortis.

Kenji stepped back, but the blade knocked the Windrider loose in his hands. Rather than fumble for his grip,
Kenji dropped the Windrider. He danced backward again,
using the additional time to draw his samurai sword.

Across the room Lord Mishima had remained where he
stood, observing the events without reaction. His two
guards fought defensively, parrying the mortis blows of
their four attackers and slowly retreating, always blocking
the way to Lord Mishima. In a moment they would be
pinned against the table, however, and unable to parry indefinitely.

CHAPTER 4

Kenji knew he had only moments. He blocked his enemy's mortis, then without drawing back his blade, he slipped to the side and slashed lightly across the mortificator's eyebrows, drawing blood. As the blood ran down into his eyes, he blinked frantically and swung his mortis hard down toward Kenji's shoulder.

In response, Kenji stepped laterally again, allowing the mortis to chop into the flared shoulder of his armor. Because he had not bothered to parry the stroke, he now had the mortificator's arm extended, his body defenseless. Kenji slashed his enemy's neck, bringing blood spurting. Then, with an upward stroke, he knocked the mortis from the man's hand as he staggered forward, helplessly grabbing his neck.

Kenji did not have any more time to worry about him. Two of the other mortificators turned and advanced on him, leaving two to hold down the Mishima guards. Now, however, the guards faced equal odds and could fight more aggressively.

Now that Kenji no longer faced gunfire, he had equalized the odds with his two opponents. None of the mortificators wore armor, probably having sacrificed protection for agility and stealth. Kenji's own armor equalized their weaponry.

Holding his sword vertically, hands close to his chest, he moved forward carefully. The mortificators in front of him separated slightly, feinting; now they were on the defensive, buying time for their companions to kill the Mishima guards and move on to Lord Mishima.

Kenji would have to use his advantage of armor to go on the attack. He feinted to his left; when the mortificator raised his sword to parry, Kenji had already turned and slashed down at the other man on his right. As that man blocked his stroke, Kenji spun in between them, his shoulder flares pushing them aside; he felt a blow on the side of his helmet, knocking it askew to his left.

Ignoring the blow, Kenji advanced past them and impaled one of the other mortificators in the lower back, as he fought with a Mishima guard.

Kenji yanked his blade free and spun again, already swinging his sword in a horizontal parry to catch the two mortises slashing down behind him. He knocked them both aside. As the two Mishima guards now advanced on the lone mortificator still in front of the table, Kenji blocked the way of the two mortificators who had been facing him.

Now time was on the side of Kenji and the Mishima guards. Once the two guards finished off the single mortificator they faced, the odds would finally swing in their favor, with the two guards and Kenji against the last two mortificators. Since their goal was to defend Lord Mishima, they could fight defensively indefinitely, and Kenji did not doubt that an emergency call for help had already gone out for Mishima reinforcements.

Kenji held his defensive position, his sword in front of him. He waited, knowing the mortificators would have to make the offensive moves. If they chose to flee, that would serve his purpose, but he knew better than to expect flight.

The two mortificators spread out, to move against his sides. Kenji parried tentatively in both directions, aware that he would need to rely on his armor again to survive a two-pronged attack by trained assassins now that he could not move freely—most important of all was to block their access to Lord Mishima, even if Kenji fell.

The mortificator on Kenji's left feinted. Instead of parrying reflexively, Kenji ignored it and blocked a serious lunge from the man on his right. Then, twisting, he parried the next stroke from the mortificator on his left.

In that moment the man on his right slashed horizontally at his neck, in the crack below his helmet.

Kenji chose not to turn back toward him. He merely

feinted to his right, inviting the man on his left to strike. Kenji then raised his right shoulder, taking the blow intended for his neck on his armor, and whirled left again.

He had caught the mortificator on his left in a backstroke. Before the man could swing his sword forward again, Kenji ran his abdomen through, then yanked his blade free. He spun, ducking, and parried an overhand stroke from the other man just in time.,

Kenji glanced at the surviving Mishima guards. They were driving their opponent back, inexorably. Kenji advanced on the lone mortificator in front of him.

At this point, Kenji's armor gave him a tremendous advantage against a single unarmored opponent. He would not have thought less of the man if he had chosen to retreat with his companion and escape. Neither mortificator made a move to withdraw, however, and Kenji understood that they had probably never come this close to assassinating Lord Mishima; most likely, they had never even seen him in person before. They still hoped to succeed somehow.

Suddenly, moving aggressively, Kenji advanced, feinting and lunging. The mortificator knew he could not get through Kenji's armor easily, so he began shifting laterally, still hoping to move around Kenji to reach Lord Mishima. Kenji also stepped to the side, countering him.

The mortificator suddenly jabbed his sword forward, forcing Kenji to parry; however, in the same motion, the mortificator flung himself sideways past Kenji, rolling over the table. He landed on the far side, only a few steps from Lord Mishima, and drew a slim dagger from somewhere in his clothes.

Startled, Kenji whirled late. However, the mortificator had to run behind Kenji on the other side of the table to reach Lord Mishima. Kenji leaned across the table and, as the mortificator flung himself through the air toward Lord Mishima, Kenji slashed off his head.

The headless body fell at the feet of Lord Mishima, who glanced at it impassively.

In the same moment the two Mishima guards simultaneously impaled the last mortificator before them.

Both guards turned, their swords dripping blood, and looked at Kenji.

"Leave us," Lord Mishima said quietly.

The two guards bowed deeply. One of them glanced out a window.

"The reinforcement security detail has arrived in force," said one of the guards. "We will secure the building." He and his companion hurried out.

Kenji, nervous in the presence of Lord Mishima, sheathed his sword and took off his helmet. Holding his helmet under one arm, he bowed deeply and held the position for a moment. Then he straightened enough to look up.

Lord Mishima nodded slightly, allowing Kenji to stand erect again.

"You are a Mishima Elite trooper," Lord Mishima said calmly. "You are not part of my personal entourage. How do you come to be here?"

"I am a former Elite trooper," Kenji said politely, understanding that Lord Mishima had merely recognized his armor. "A retired major. A friend learned of the movement of Brotherhood Mortificators and a rumor of their intentions. He alerted me. I apologize for arriving so late."

Lord Mishima remained formal and composed. "I stand in your debt. Tell me how I can express my gratitude."

Kenji felt a flood of excitement; to this point, he had not thought about a reward for his actions. Now he suddenly realized that he could ask for almost anything. Lord Mishima controlled one of the most powerful megacorporations; his wealth and power were incalculable. At the very least, Kenji could request to be reinstated in the Mishima military, possibly with a promotion. He could ask for a chance to explain the false accusations that had led to his leaving the Mishima Elite, and an opportunity to gain revenge against those who had set him up.

In the same instant that these thoughts ran through his mind, Kenji knew that he could not make any of these requests. He had come to save Lord Mishima because of his personal loyalty and respect for the man, driven by his sense of duty, of *giri*—obligation to be carried out for its own sake. Accepting a reward would give Lord Mishima the belief that Kenji had helped only for what he might gain by doing so.

Kenji bowed again. "I am honored to have served."

Lord Mishima studied him for a moment. "You may have your choice of positions within my organization. Tell me how I can express my gratitude."

"I am honored to have served," Kenji repeated formally. "I request nothing in return."

For the first time, then, Lord Mishima smiled slightly as he looked into Kenji's eyes. "You are *ronin*."

Kenji bowed his acknowledgment, knowing that Lord Mishima finally understood. He had used the old term in its original meaning of a samurai who had no master, Kenji felt certain, not for the modern class of unprincipled killers. In doing so, Lord Mishima had expressed his understanding that Kenji lived by the traditional values. Therefore he also understood why Kenji would not accept a reward for his actions, the way most Mishima employees or troopers would have. That acknowledgment was the true reward for Kenji; he had earned Lord Mishima's respect.

"What is your name?"

"Kenji Hayashi."

"I give you a new name. From now on, you will be known as Yojimbo."

Kenji bowed his acceptance, recognizing the name of a mythic samurai hero from the deep past on Earth.

Outside and downstairs voices barked orders. Footsteps ran throughout the building, but no one fired weapons. Kenji knew that Mishima reinforcements were securing the building without difficulty.

"Yojimbo," said Lord Mishima. "I must hire a man to perform a specific task. This is a personal matter, not a corporate one. I require a man I can trust. As a *ronin*, will you accept a contractual agreement, not as a company employee, but from me personally?"

Kenji felt a glow of pride. He understood the offer, and it was no less a compliment for his knowledge that Lord Mishima could simply not tolerate remaining in debt to a powerless stranger. Lord Mishima, like the *daimyo* of traditional Japan, had offered in modern terms to become his lord, at least for the duration of this job.

"I am honored to accept," said Kenji.

Lord Mishima nodded. Both were aware that Kenji had accepted without asking what the job would involve. It did not matter; the point was that Kenji would do his bidding as a loyal samurai.

"I have picked up certain rumors," said Lord Mishima. "Rumors, no more, but important ones. A presence from the Dark Legion may have infiltrated Luna City."

Kenji was startled, but merely waited for him to continue.

"A rogue Capitol ship, perverted by black technology, may have brought a woman to this presence."

"Who is she?"

"The identity and value of this woman to the Dark Legion are unknown."

"I see."

"These rumors may mean nothing. However, the danger cannot be ignored. You will find out if a Dark Legion presence is truly established in Luna City and who the woman is. You will not allow the mission to become common knowledge or acknowledge the identity of your lord."

Kenji bowed.

"I will arrange an open line of credit through Mishima for your budget. I care only about results. You have no limit on legitimate expenses."

"When I have my results, how will I communicate with you?"

"Make your request through your computerized credit line. Your new name will be your password."

"It will be done."

"You are dismissed, Yojimbo."

Kenji bowed deeply. When Lord Mishima responded with a brief nod, Kenji backed away from behind the table, then turned and hurried out of the banquet room. His mind was whirling with his new name and status. Best of all, he had just quit working as a dishwasher to become a samurai.

* * *

At home in his clean, tidy apartment, Kenji told the Whiz Kid only that all was well. The Whiz Kid understood the rest. The blood on Kenji's armor and the damage to its composite material told him that Kenji had arrived in time to meet the mortificators. If Lord Mishima had been assassinated, Kenji would have either died defending him or at the very least would have gone hunting his killers and told the Whiz Kid about it all.

Instead, Kenji simply asked the Whiz Kid to help him set aside his weapons and take off his armor. When Kenji had changed into normal street clothes, he drew his sword to clean it. The Whiz Kid eyed the bloodstains on the blade.

"You needed your sword? Wasn't your Windrider enough?"

"No."

"Why not?"

Kenji smiled indulgently. The Whiz Kid was the opposite of Lord Mishima. Where Kenji and Lord Mishima had understood each other with very few words spoken, the Whiz Kid understood very little about Kenji at all.

"When you fight alone, you must prepare for every contingency. Two suicidal mortificators attacked me in close quarters. I shot the first one, but he knocked my Windrider aside. Also, they had to use their swords because they did not have time to reload."

The Whiz Kid nodded, a shock of his black hair swaying over his forehead.

Kenji wiped his blade carefully with a clean cloth. He had to choose his words precisely. "I have accepted an assignment."

"Really? You signed with Mishima Megacorporation? That's great!"

Kenji looked sternly into his eyes. "No, I did not. I have accepted a personal contract."

CHAPTER 5

The Whiz Kid looked at him, puzzled.

"My employer and the conditions of my employment must remain private, but I wish to hire you to help. Are you willing?"

"Well . . . sure!" The Whiz Kid's eyes widened, but he said nothing more.

Kenji suspected he had just realized who had hired Kenji, but as long as Kenji did not actually tell him, this situation would suffice. "I want you to go back into cyberspace and see if you can get any leads on a rogue Capitol ship that landed here in the last day or two."

"A rogue ship? What does that mean?"

"It may have been converted to black technology."

"You mean the Dark Legion?" The Whiz Kid's mouth dropped open. "Zowee—here on Luna?"

"Maybe. We are merely investigating a rumor."

"Got it! Come on!" The Whiz Kid turned and ran out the front door, across the porch to his own front door.

Kenji picked up his Windrider and his samurai sword before following him.

As the Whiz Kid leaned into his virtual reality hood and entered cyberspace, Kenji continued to clean his sword. Then he checked and reloaded his Windrider. As he worked, he considered the task ahead of him.

Finding a single individual woman, apparently someone's captive, on Luna City would be extremely difficult under any conditions. Luna City covered nearly all of the moon and was built many levels deep underground; its dense population was immense. He did not feel he could handle this task alone, but if he enlisted help, he would have to limit the information he shared with his colleagues.

The Whiz Kid leaned out of his hood. "I got something! Not too much, but that ship landed, all right."

"Yes? What else?"

"Nothing else. All anybody in the gang has picked up is that a mysterious Capitol ship landed and took off again after just a few minutes."

"Someone or something must have been picked up or dropped off."

"Yeah, but it's not in the docking port records. One of the gang members broke into the computer files for me. This landing and departure aren't even mentioned."

"Then how does anyone know a Capitol ship landed?" Kenji asked. "We must be sure of our information."

"It transmitted a Capitol registration number for docking permission to a Capitol port. The port computer read the insignia on the side of the ship as it hovered over Luna and okayed the number automatically. That's the only recorded contact in the computer files."

"I see." Kenji thought a moment. "This is enough confirmation of the rumor for me to proceed further. Are you willing to work for me over an extended period as a hired employee?"

"Doing what?"

"Primarily, seeking information through cyberspace," said Kenji.

"Zowee! That's perfect. And you're going to pay me, too?" The Whiz Kid grinned.

"I will pay you a professional rate. We can work out the details later."

"I'm in."

"Good. Also, are you willing to use your home here as a command center? I believe it will be safe. Those we seek have no way of knowing that we are searching for them—whoever they are."

"Sure. Anyhow, I'm already set up here."

"Excellent. Now, because of the difficulty of our task, I must consider forming a small team to work with us. I do not believe we can accomplish it alone."

"Who are you going to get?"

"I do not have specific names in mind yet. However, I need free-lance mercenaries, people with military skills and experience. And they must be trustworthy. Most mercenaries are no more loyal than their bank accounts will justify. I am seeking people with a higher standard."

"I'll go back into cyberspace and ask where to find them. People like that must be here on Luna somewhere. This town has everybody."

Kenji doubted he could find anyone with his own commitment to traditional honor. However, the job required colleagues who possessed many of his own personal characteristics. In short, no matter what their ancestry or precise values, he had to find *ronin* like himself.

Lane spent the day drifting from one free-lance hangout to another, hoping to get a line on work. As usual these days, he wore no armor and carried only his Sherman .74 M13 Bolter handgun on his belt and his Capitol CAR-24 light machine gun on a shoulder strap. He heard nothing new and saw only the same faces as yesterday, but that was normal. As usual, he saved the Midnight Star for the last, since it was his favorite place to spend the evening.

When Lane first glanced around the crowd in the Midnight Star, he spotted Pam's blond hair immediately. She stood in a far corner of the room talking to someone Lane had never seen before. As yesterday, Pam wore her tight gray jumpsuit and her own Sherman. The man, of Asian descent, wore the dark blue armor of the Mishima Elite, two swords at his waist, and a Windrider light machine gun slung casually over one shoulder; he held his winged helmet under one arm. His hair was short and bristly; his features were even and angular, and his expression reserved.

Lane moved toward them cautiously, not wanting to interrupt Pam in anything personal.

When Pam saw Lane, she waved for him to join them. Her face was serious, unsmiling, which told him that this was more than a social conversation. He drew in a deep breath, hoping some work would come of this.

"This is Lane Chung," said Pam. "The other free-lancer you asked about."

"I am Yojimbo," the man in the armor said formally, with a slight bow.

Lane nodded casually. "You asked about me? How do you know my name?"

"I have spent the day asking those who often employ people in your profession for free-lancers of unusual ability and commitment. Several names came up, but you two were mentioned most frequently."

Lane felt a surge of elation, but fought to hide it. He saw that Pam had also taken on a veneer of reserve. If they were about to dicker over their fees with a new employer, they did not want to act too eager to accept.

"What's your business with us?" Lane asked.

"I am assembling a small team of people who can maintain confidentiality. I need people with military experience, ideally special operations experience. My sources tell me you are both former Martian Banshees."

"That's right," said Pam.

"But what's the job?" Lane asked.

Yojimbo glanced around at the crowd. Most paid no attention to them, but those closest were listening. They obviously hoped to volunteer, too, if the work sounded good.

Lane pulled out a small hand-held sonic disruptor. He dialed a radius of one meter and switched it on. Those outside the radius would hear their voices only as a low-pitched buzz, the words unintelligible. The trio huddled close, turning their backs to everyone else so no one could read their lips.

"We will be hunting representatives of the Dark Legion," said Yojimbo grimly.

Lane tensed with anticipation. This was a job that would mean something to him. He glanced at Pam.

Pam's face hardened with resolve, too.

"Where will we go?" Lane asked.

"We seek a Dark presence right here on Luna."

Lane was shocked, but tried not to show it. He could hardly believe it. Yet he had seen too much of life with the Banshees and in Luna City not to know anything was possible. "Here? What kind of presence?"

Yojimbo looked back and forth between them for a moment, his face serious. "I must reserve further details for my team. Are you interested?"

"I am," said Pam.

"Hold it," said Lane. "Before we go on, I have some questions for you."

"Go ahead."

"You know we fought against Mishima when we were with the Banshees. Now you want to hire us to work with Mishima. How do you feel about hiring former Capitol veterans?"

"I am not with Mishima Megacorporation now. I am a former Mishima Elite, but no longer."

"Oh. Well, the same question stands. For all I know, we may have met in battle against each other."

"I have no problem with it. Surely you free-lancers have worked for many different employers since leaving the Martian Banshees."

"Yeah, but that's us, not you."

"I believe the Dark Legion constitutes the true threat to humanity. I will assemble a team of free-lancers who will work with me."

"I couldn't say that better myself," said Pam. "If you're comfortable with us, I'm willing."

"Who are you working for, then?" Lane asked. "If it's not Mishima? Yourself?"

"I have been hired by an individual who will not be named," said Yojimbo. "Those I hire are responsible directly and only to me."

"I don't like working in the dark," said Pam. "We have a right to know who our ultimate employer is."

"I am forbidden to share his identity," said Yojimbo. "This is a condition of employment for all of us."

"All right," said Lane. "I'm willing to fight the Dark Legion for anybody, I guess, as long as this isn't a swindle of some kind."

Yojimbo stiffened slightly. "I have told you all I can at this stage. If you are willing to join my team, tell me what your fee is."

Lane thought a moment, then quoted his last fee plus fifty percent.

Yojimbo raised his eyebrows slightly and turned to Pam, waiting.

Pam quoted the same amount, cocking her head to one side as she looked at him. Her blond hair swayed.

Yojimbo hesitated a moment. "Here is my offer. I will meet your fee, but you will be responsible for all your own equipment and weapons. At that price, you can afford it. If I choose to provide them, it will be my choice, not a requirement."

Lane grinned wryly. He had expected to bargain in the normal way, arguing over the amount of Cardinal's crowns as he usually did. However, Yojimbo had caught him off guard. Most likely, neither of them could know what new weapons might be required. Whether or not this agreement would cost Lane and Pam more than a lower fee with Yojimbo paying their expenses was impossible for any of them to know.

"I accept," said Lane, turning to Pam.

"I do, too," said Pam.

"Good. I believe that combining our experience with Mishima and Capitol will make us a strong team."

"I know the Capitol mortuary here in Luna City," Pam said, with a wry smile. "Some of our former Banshee vets work there now. If our team has casualties, we're all set."

Lane laughed lightly, but Yojimbo did not seem to get the joke.

"Let's get to particulars," said Pam. "What kind of presence are we looking for?"

"I have very little information. However, I know that a black technology ship, a perverted Capitol ship, apparently made a secret landing for a short time at a Capitol docking port. A woman may have been on it."

"Who is she?" Lane asked.

"I have no further information about her identity. From the brief stop the ship made, I surmise that either she was dropped off or someone or something else was picked up. This is all guesswork, however."

"She's a heretic?" Pam asked. "A human who has gone over to the Dark Legion?"

Yojimbo hesitated, then shook his head. "I was told she was a woman. If my source believed she was a heretic, that term would have been used."

Lane nodded. "Look, we need to get out of here and go somewhere secure. How about it?"

"I have a small command center already established," said Yojimbo. "We will walk."

Lane and Pam followed him out of the Midnight Star onto the crowded street. They said nothing, but exchanged satisfied glances when Yojimbo was not looking. Lane would have agreed to fight the Dark Legion for much less than he had asked; he felt certain that Pam would have, too.

The task Yojimbo had presented would inspire Lane for a change. Instead of fighting endlessly for soulless megacorporations or for commanders who considered them cannon fodder, they could protect the humans on Luna from the Dark Legion. For a while, at least, it might keep life worth living a little longer.

Lane and Pam followed Yojimbo to a residential neighborhood near the free-lancer hangouts, here on the same level. Down in an unkempt, jumbled one-room cellar apartment, Yojimbo introduced them to a teenager in a black satin jacket only as the Whiz Kid, in what was obviously the kid's home. The Whiz Kid had been in cyberspace, talking to his gang.

"Have you heard anything new?" Yojimbo asked the Whiz Kid, nodding toward the computer.

"I don't know. I picked up some rumors of heretics and necromutants in Luna City, but that's common."

"It is?" Yojimbo raised his eyebrows. "I have not been aware of rumors like this."

"Aw, I have," said the Whiz Kid. "In cyberspace people always have lots of rumors circulating. Trouble is, most of them come to nothing."

"We've heard rumors of that kind in the free-lancer bars," said Pam, glancing at Lane for confirmation. "Nobody takes them seriously, that I know."

"That's right," said Lane. "These rumors are always treated more or less as a joke."

"Maybe they should not be," said Yojimbo. He gestured toward the couch and chairs for them to sit. "The Dark Legion presence on Luna may have been here longer than anyone ever suspected. That would explain the rumors."

"Aw, throw that junk aside," said the Whiz Kid. "The clothes, I mean."

Lane grinned and carefully put some of the clothes on the floor. Pam did the same and sat next to him on the couch. As Yojimbo spoke, he picked up the clothes on a chair and idly began folding them.

"Please go back into cyberspace," said Yojimbo. "Ask everyone for as many of the rumors as you can gather. We might find some truth in some of them."

"All right." The Whiz Kid leaned back into the virtual reality hood over his computer.

"Heretics are people who have gone over to the other side," Lane said slowly. "But they still look like people. Has anybody here actually seen a necromutant? I haven't."

"No, I've never seen one," said Pam.

"I have never seen one, either," said Yojimbo as he folded a black satin jacket identical to the one the Whiz Kid wore now. "I never fought the Dark Legion as a Mishima Elite. We fought Capitol."

The Whiz Kid had leaned out of his hood and was listening again. "I have a description of necromutants on file. You want me to put it on the speaker?"

"Yes, please," said Yojimbo.

"Where did this description come from?" Pam asked, cocking her head to one side.

"Uh . . ." The Whiz Kid glanced back at his computer screen. "*The First Chronicle: The Arrival of the Darkness,* by Plinius Varro. But there isn't much."

His computer spoke in a clear, formal tone. "Then suddenly a gate into another dimension was opened and horrible monsters of metal and flesh, cogwheels and muscle, glass and tissue emerged and reaped their vengeance on the settlers. This was the first known confrontation with the Legions of Darkness.

"The evil from beyond had now found a way into our

solar system and on the tenth planet the hordes of evil unleashed their destructive potential. They fought down the settlers and twisted them into grotesque shapes, mocking the human body. The first necromutants were born."

"It goes on to say that more necromutants were made out of ordinary humans," said the Whiz Kid.

"What?" Lane sat up, startled.

"Just summarize it," said Yojimbo.

"Zowee—I'll give it a shot. It says that people are taken to chambers of black technology where their basic genetic code is reprogrammed. The result is a twisted, gigantic body with big muscles. Their skin turns a dull black, with the texture of leather, and their hair gets either black or silver. Sometimes their limbs are altered in shape to accommodate holding certain black technology weapons."

"They must be very powerful," said Yojimbo. "Physically, at any rate."

"What about their minds?" Lane asked. "Are they controlled in some way?"

"Their minds retain some personality," said the Whiz Kid. "According to my sources here, they can lead small groups of Dark Legionnaires and take enough initiative to think. But they aren't the people they used to be anymore."

"I see," said Yojimbo.

"That's all I have about necromutants," said the Whiz Kid with an apologetic shrug. "The rest of it is about the history of the outer planets."

CHAPTER 6

"So the necromutants were human once," said Pam. "That's what I always heard."

"But they don't look human anymore," said Lane. "If some of them are here in Luna City, then they have to stay hidden or disguised. That's the important part to us, if we're going to find them."

"We can chase down rumors later if we have to," said Pam. "I'd rather start with something solid."

"Like what?" Lane asked. "It doesn't sound to me like we have much."

"I know the Capitol docks fairly well; before I joined the Banshees, I worked on them. We should inspect the site where the mystery ship landed."

"I agree," said Yojimbo.

"So, what do we need to do?" Lane asked. "Do we need any preparation?"

"Not really," said Pam, with a shrug. She rested one hand on her Sherman, in its holster. "This is just recon of a landing site."

"So we'll put stealth over power," said Lane. "We don't need armor for that. I guess I'm ready."

"Me, too," said Pam.

"I will go as I am," said Yojimbo, glancing down at his armor. He turned to Pam. "You feel this is a good time? Early evening?"

"As good as any. Ships come and go all the time. We're just as likely to run into crowds in the middle of the night as we are now."

"All right. How long will it take? We are about two kilometers from the Capitol docks, I think. Walking will be best for that distance."

"The docks are one and a half kilometers from the Midnight Star," said Pam, with a little smile. "But we can make a fast trip. We don't need to fight the crowds on the street."

"Oh?" Yojimbo looked at her in surprise. "You mean the hike along the tubelink tunnels? I know it can be fast, but it can be quite dangerous, between the bandits who prowl in them to prey on the trains and the train crashes from poor maintenance. Is that what you mean?"

"No." Pam shook her head, sending her short hair swinging. "We might as well just ride the tubelink as hike along the tunnels."

"Then what do you suggest?"

"The maintenance tunnels that connect some of the tubelink tunnels and many of the main power stations."

"You do not mean the secured tunnels that lead out of the ports?" Yojimbo still looked puzzled.

"Not those, either," Lane said with a grin. "Those are heavily guarded. We'd never fight our way through; we need passes and we don't have any."

"The tunnels I know are largely a secret," said Pam. "Most of the people who do know about them don't bother to use them because none of the tunnels go in a straight line—you might as well travel on the street or on the tubelink in most cases. But I've used them in the past, and I know the route from here to the ports."

"So we can move fast without being noticed?" Yojimbo asked. "That sounds good."

"But we'll need lights," said Pam. "These tunnels are dark. Lane and I each have lamps on head straps back in our homes."

"I have a lamp imbedded in my helmet," said Yojimbo, picking it up. "Will one be enough?"

"In this case, I think so."

"Good enough for me." Lane stood up, adjusting his Capitol CAR-24 strap on his shoulder. "Blue eyes, Yojimbo—let's go. We're wasting time."

Pam started by leading them to a nearby tubelink station. Lane had used the tunnels a few times with her, but he had not memorized much of the complicated maze. With Yojimbo bringing up the rear, they wrestled through the crowd waiting for the train and moved up the far end of the platform.

There Pam lifted a small access lid and climbed down a rusted ladder. Steam drifted out, rising around her. Lane followed her down.

Lane found himself descending into darkness as he moved hand under hand on the damp metal. He heard Pam's footsteps below on a hard floor, then joined her. Above him, Yojimbo switched on his helmet lamp and closed the hatch over them. His beam of light angled into the darkness as he joined them.

By Yojimbo's light Lane saw that they stood in a narrow tunnel only a meter wide. In contrast to the noise of the bustling tubelink station above, or the streets, this tunnel was absolutely silent. Ahead, Lane saw other ladders leading down from above and also more access hatches in the floor. Narrow passages to intersecting tunnels opened on the tunnel at irregular intervals.

"Come on," said Pam. "Not all the tunnels are so claustrophobic."

She led the trio, with Yojimbo walking in the rear. The beam of his lamp shone forward over Lane's shoulder, throwing Pam's shadow down the tunnel ahead of them. As the light moved forward, rats and some sort of scaled bugs vanished into the shadows. Pam turned at the first corner, leading them down an identical tunnel.

No one spoke as they moved through the maze. Lane saw no landmarks other than occasional water stains or bullet holes; Pam had clearly memorized the route. He saw no sign that anyone had been here recently, though the rats, bugs, and other unrecognizable vermin continued to scurry away from them around every corner.

Some of the passageways were much wider than others; not all intersected at right angles. They entered some passages large enough for small military vehicles, though Lane saw that anything of any size would have to be brought down in parts and assembled here. Yojimbo's light paused on several piles of human bones and tattered cloth. Anything of value had apparently been carried away long ago.

"We're getting close to the Capitol ports now," Pam said briefly.

In this area Lane saw that the passages here were about two meters wide and three high. Also, intersecting tunnels met theirs at right angles now. Finally, their tunnel came to a stop where it accessed a large intersecting tunnel. Ladders led upward on the back wall. As Lane looked to each side, he saw that all the parallel access tunnels ended against the same wall.

Pam picked a ladder and slowly climbed up, her Capitol CAR-24 swaying behind her on its strap. Lane followed her. From behind him, Yojimbo's lamp still lit their way with a tight, bouncing beam.

At the top of the ladder Pam glanced down and waved toward Yojimbo. The light went off soundlessly. With a small grating of metal on metal, Pam opened the access lid on its hinge. A narrow sliver of dim light angled down through the opening.

No sound came from the level above.

Pam swung her CAR-24 forward and moved up cautiously.

For a moment Lane could see nothing but her silhouette blocking the access hatch. Then she climbed all the way up. Lane followed her up the ladder, bringing his own CAR-24 into position.

When Lane moved his head up through the hatch, he saw Pam moving silently across the floor through faint light from above. In the shadows, he could not see where they were. Following her lead, he moved up to join her in securing the area. He heard Yojimbo follow him out and take a third direction.

The pale light came from a couple of overhead lamps that remained on, though most of them had been shot out. In fact, whatever this area had been, something had trashed the place. The walls were full of bullet holes, most of them large caliber, and long black burn streaks showed where incinerators had thrown directional flames. Several large holes in the walls had been blasted by small explosives. Lane saw no sign of human or necromutant remains.

Parts of two walls had collapsed. In some places the

ceiling had come down. Some steel beams had been heated to the point of melting slightly before they solidified again.

In a few minutes the three experienced veterans had policed the immediate area without a word. No one detected any sign of others nearby. They relaxed slightly, looking around in the mess.

"Where are we?" Lane asked.

"Just inside the docking port where the mystery ship landed," said Pam.

Yojimbo nodded, still studying their surroundings.

"Something weird sure happened here," Pam said quietly. She grinned slightly. "I guess that's an understatement, eh? But still . . ." She shook her head.

"What was this place?" Yojimbo asked.

"It's a foyer leading to a cargo bay." Pam pointed to a collapsed wall of rubble. "The warehouse is that way." She swung her arm around to another fallen wall. "The docking port is over there."

"Any idea what might have happened here?" Lane asked. "I mean, obviously somebody got into a fight. But why?"

"Maybe not," said Pam. "I don't see what anyone had to fight about."

"The Whiz Kid said the Capitol records mention only the arrival and departure of the mystery ship," said Yojimbo. "Capitol obviously kept this destruction a secret for some reason."

"The damage looks recent to me," said Pam, examining the broken edge of a steel rod.

Lane saw that the inner surface showed no rust.

"What do you think?"

"Yeah," said Lane, running a finger along another piece of broken steel. "Too much steam from heating vents leaks through the tunnels not to rust these surfaces over time. These beams haven't been broken very long at all."

"I agree," said Yojimbo. "We should look at the docking port itself."

This time Yojimbo walked point through the rubble, climbing over and through fallen chunks of wall. No sign of anyone else's presence appeared. On the other side of the fallen wall, the docking port was marked by the entrance to a large airlock, big enough to pass cargo. Instead of a normal door, however, the airlock had a big steel disk welded across its opening.

"That's a standard temporary patch," said Lane. "The airlock must have been blown up by the ship as it left."

"Why hasn't Capitol repaired this by now?" Yojimbo asked. "In the years that I fought Capitol as a Mishima Elite, they were very fast with logistical matters. Why would they leave a Luna docking port unrepaired?"

"They're probably even more puzzled than we are," said Pam. "I suppose they've left it so long to avoid destroying evidence of what happened."

"No crew is here to search for evidence," said Yojimbo. "Would they preserve it for such a long time?"

"It's only one docking port out of many," said Lane. "Maybe they finished their search and just haven't gotten around to the repairs. I'm sure they'll get to it before long."

A low whirring sound reached them from a short distance away. Lane heard a single voice shouting orders. He and his companions tensed.

"An outer door just opened automatically," said Pam. "I know the sound. Someone's coming this way—probably Capitol security."

"We must have triggered a silent alarm," said Lane. "Time to go—back the way we came?"

"*Now,*" said Pam, pointing.

Yojimbo led the way back through the rubble. Shouts and the pounding of running feet reached them, but the guards were still out of sight. Instead of starting down the hatch, however, Yojimbo crouched next to it with his Windrider positioned to give covering fire.

Lane came next. He started down the ladder into the hatch. "Aren't they going to follow us down here?"

"They may," Yojimbo said with quiet tension.

Lane descended the ladder quickly. The shouts overhead grew louder as Pam started down after him. At the bottom he stepped away from the ladder to give her room, holding his CAR-24 in ready position.

Pam jumped down the last few rungs and also swung up her CAR-24.

Yojimbo started down the ladder, but paused when Lane could still see only his legs. Then Yojimbo's Windrider chattered overhead, out of sight. Yojimbo, now holding the light machine gun high with one hand as he continued to fire, came farther down the ladder.

"Pull back," Yojimbo ordered firmly.

Lane and Pam hurried up the tunnel they had taken to get here, their weapons still ready. Yojimbo fired out the hatch as long as he could reach it, then yanked the heavy cover over his head with a clang. Nimble even in his armor, he hurried the rest of the way down the ladder. Then he backed up the tunnel, his Windrider trained on the closed hatch.

Soon the hatch was lost from sight in shadows straight behind them. When it was thrown aside again with a loud clang, all three of them angled fire up at the source of the dim light that shone down the opening. They continued to do so as they backed up the tunnel, the snapping of their three weapons reverberating off the walls of the narrow tunnel. No return fire came from the open hatch.

"No one is in any hurry to come down there," said Lane. "That's a very defensible bottleneck."

"They may know where to find other access hatches nearby," said Pam. "We can't afford to be outflanked."

"Lead us," Yojimbo said simply, turning on his helmet lamp. He took off his helmet and handed it to Pam. "If they follow us into the tunnels, we can find another defensible position. Since we must hurry, you should wear the lamp."

Pam put it on and jogged up the tunnel. As before, Lane followed Pam while Yojimbo brought up the rear. She turned the first two corners they reached, creating a zigzag that would block even residual light from the helmet lamp from leaving a glow behind them to reveal their route.

Lane heard muffled shouts and a couple of bursts of gunfire behind them, but the sounds did not come any closer. The security guards must have known how easily a trap could be laid for them down in these tunnels. After a moment the hatch closed again with a distant clank.

Even so, Pam did not slow down. Lane knew from their years together in the Martian Banshees that she was cautious yet decisive; she would not dawdle. She led them briskly up the tunnels, occasionally pausing to listen for pursuit. They heard none.

They reached the same tubelink station where they had first descended into the tunnels without incident. Now back in the normal crush of people waiting for the next train, they worked their way up to the street.

On the crowded street again, in the shadows of dark, stark edifices and their frowning gargoyles and other statues, Pam finally turned and returned Yojimbo's helmet. He turned off the lamp and held it under one arm. Lane let out a long breath.

"Well done, blue eyes." Lane grinned.

Pam lowered her voice, glancing around. No one in the press of passersby was paying any attention to them. "We didn't learn much, Chung. But I'm willing to believe that a Dark Legion ship landed there for some reason." Pam turned to Yojimbo. "What now?"

"Assuming we are right, what sort of fight took place?" Yojimbo asked. "What do you think happened there?"

"When the ship landed, the Capitol port authorities and security expected some sort of normal business to be conducted. The . . . visitors, I'll call them, probably killed them all to eliminate witnesses. Since the Capitol employees were caught by surprise, I doubt it was much of a battle."

"Then the visitors from the ship finished their business and left again." Lane nodded. "Okay, that holds up."

"It isn't much," said Pam. "I repeat, what now?"

CHAPTER 7

"Perhaps the Whiz Kid has learned more by now from his cyberspace gang," said Yojimbo. "We can return to the command center and ask."

"You two go back," said Lane slowly. "I have another idea. Maybe we can get some rumors off the street through the black market."

"You have someone in mind?" Pam asked. "Anyone I happen to know?"

"Cameron Glen."

"That weirdo?" Pam laughed lightly. "You sure you want to bother?"

"What is wrong?" Yojimbo asked.

"He's a strange guy," said Lane. "Always a little out of it. Sometimes getting information out of him is tough because his answers don't always make sense. But he works the black market and picks up information all the time."

"Maybe we should all go see him," said Yojimbo.

Lane shook his head. "I can't find him directly, but I know someone who can. I better not bring strangers until I've renewed my acquaintance with all concerned. This will work better if I go alone for now."

"All right," said Yojimbo. "We will wait for you at the command center."

Lane nodded and slipped away into the crowd, grinning. Calling the Whiz Kid's apartment a command center struck him as a little absurd, but that was Yojimbo's business. For that matter, the guy seemed to *be* all business.

As he started walking, he took a quick glance up at the skyline to get his bearings. A large, laughing gargoyle with long, curved fangs glared down at him from its perch over a large doorway. He glanced away and hurried up the street.

Lane hoped he could find Fay Fan without any delays. She was a cyborg veteran of Cybertronic megacorporation, the only one he had ever known who had left their service to become a free-lancer. Like Lane, she was of Chinese-American descent. Lane respected her independent spirit, especially knowing how high a price she paid for leaving.

She had once told him that Cybertronic no longer supplied her mechanical body parts directly. That made her a regular customer of Cameron Glen. Lane knew her, too, from hanging out in the Midnight Star, but not as well as he knew Pam. Lane and Fay had never served together or done a free-lance job together.

One night, however, Lane had walked her home. If she still lived there, he could find her again. She lived in a certain section of Luna City where cyborgs were common, near some Cybertronic barracks. Fay had told Lane that she felt more at home in that neighborhood.

Fay's block was lined with four-story apartment buildings, all a dingy gray. Each apartment was a flat that covered an entire floor, with an exterior door reached by a long staircase. Steam leaked from vents in the streets, clouding the buildings. Lane reached the building he sought and climbed the steps to the second-floor landing.

A statuette of a dead rat lay across the lintel of Fay's door. Real ones slept next to it, their tails hanging down. Lane knocked politely and waited. He saw no button for a bell, which in most Luna City buildings would not work anyway. After a moment he knocked more forcefully.

Still no one answered. He had heard no sounds from inside, either. However, he did not want to go back to the command center with nothing.

Lane decided that inside he might be able to find a clue to where Fay had gone today. If she no longer lived here, he could learn that inside, too. Deciding he could afford to reimburse her for the door out of his new salary, he stepped back and aimed his CAR-24 at the lock on the door.

The door was made of solid steel, but a sustained burst

of fire from the CAR-24 chewed the lock to pieces. Lane glanced back over his shoulder to see if anyone on the street showed interest. A few passersby glanced up, but gunfire was so common in Luna City that most did not even turn to look. He slung the light machine gun out of the way, pushed the door open, and slipped inside.

"Freeze!" A woman's voice was followed by the loud ratcheting of weapons being cocked.

Lane froze; he knew better than to take chances if someone already had thrown down on him.

He was standing in a cramped, cluttered living room, with clothes, weapons, and small mechanical parts he could not identify scattered everywhere. The voice had come from slightly to his left. Until he was allowed to unfreeze, he could not turn to look.

"Lane Chung?" It was Fay's voice, surprised. "What's the matter with you?"

"Sorry, Fay. Can I move now?"

"Slide the CAR-24 strap off your shoulder. And keep your hands away from the Sherman."

"You got it." Lane slid the strap off his shoulder, letting his CAR-24 fall with a thump. Then, holding his hands palm forward at his shoulders, he turned.

Fay Fan, short and petite, knelt just inside the end of a narrow hallway. She held a P1000, a Cybertronic handgun, aimed at him. Standing behind her, a short, slender man named Klaus Dahlen held a Bauhaus MP-105 on Lane. His narrow face was tense, his blond hair tousled.

"Kick the door closed. Keep your hands where they are." Fay had part of a sheet wrapped around her torso, but it did not look deliberate; more likely, she had leaped out of bed and simply caught the sheet when she grabbed her gun and ran up the hall. Her black hair was cut short and blunt around an oval face.

Her eyes did not blink. In the past she had told Lane that they were Cybertronic mechanicals, with multiple focusing distances and infrared heat sensing. They did not have to be remoisturized by blinking, to prevent breaking her concentration as she aimed.

Lane had never seen Fay undressed. He noted that her appearance was completely human at first glance. Her body looked even shorter and more petite than when she was dressed.

"What's the idea, Lane?" She kept her gun on him, but her voice had turned more conversational.

"I was in a hurry to find you. When I figured you weren't here, I wanted to see if you'd left a clue to where you'd gone." He paused. "I'll pay for your door."

"Count on it."

"That's a weak story," Klaus said sourly.

Lane had met him briefly a few times in the Midnight Star, not enough for them to have much rapport. Klaus had been a Bauhaus tank commander before turning free-lance. He had always been dour and unpleasant. Lane did not know how trigger-happy he might be.

Fay smiled wryly. "It sounds like him." She stood up, letting the sheet fall, and lowered her weapon. Cyborgs, after their many multiple surgeries and implants, rarely had the same modesty for their bodies that other people had. However, Fay had obviously not chosen the kind of implants that distorted bodies.

Klaus kept his MP-105 on Lane. "What do you want here?"

"I want a line on Cameron Glen." Lane still did not move, eyeing Klaus carefully.

"That's all?" She watched him carefully.

"Yeah."

"Why?"

Lane hesitated. He knew Yojimbo wanted to keep their mission quiet; panicking all of Luna City with talk of a Dark Legion presence here would make their job even more difficult. On the other hand, Fay did not sound very cooperative.

"Tell him to lower his gun." Lane did not look at Klaus, making clear that he considered Fay to be in charge. "I don't talk under these conditions."

"All right, Klaus. We know what he wants."

"I don't trust him."

"Shut up and do it."

Klaus, still scowling at Lane, lowered his MP-105 to his side, but did not relax.

"I'm following a rumor of heretics here on Luna," Lane said quietly.

"Hah!" Klaus laughed derisively. "You've fallen for that, eh?"

Fay watched Lane with her dark, slanted eyes, still ignoring the fact that she was nude. "Go on."

"Cameron Glen picks up rumors from sources I can't get anywhere else. I want to find out what he's heard." Lane lightened his tone a little. "Look, I messed up barging in here. But the Dark Legion won't wait. I can't, either."

"Klaus is right, you know," Fay said cautiously. "We've all heard rumors about heretics on Luna for years. None of them were ever true. Why would you believe one now?"

"I'll tell you why," muttered Klaus. "Someone hired him to do something—we don't know what—and this story about heretics is an easy cover-up. I know a lot of people who don't even believe the Dark Legion exists at all."

"Think it through yourself, Fay," said Lane. "You and I haven't been real close, but we've gotten along. Why would I come here after you?"

"You tell us," said Klaus, his face taut.

Lane ignored him. "Fay, all I want to do is find Cameron Glen. If you can tell me where to look, I'll just move on. He won't have to know how I found him."

She moved to a padded chair and sat down tentatively on the arm. "I'm inclined to believe you. And this is nothing to take lightly. If the Dark Legion has some sort of beachhead here on Luna, we're all in very big trouble."

"I don't expect we'll find a beachhead in the strict military sense," said Lane.

"Then what do you expect?" Klaus demanded.

Lane kept his eyes on Fay. "Maybe a special operations center, gathering intelligence. Or maybe a special ops team on a particular assignment."

"What kind of assignment?"

"I can't know at this stage. Sabotage, assassination, planting a heretic as a mole . . ." He shrugged.

"Are you on a job?" Fay asked. "Or just pursuing this on your own?"

"I'm on a job."

Fay glanced at Klaus, then studied Lane again thoughtfully. "So someone takes this seriously enough to pay real money for an investigation."

"That's right."

"The megacorporations have a poor record of cooperation against the Dark Legion," Fay said quietly.

"That's right. Too much deep-seated resentment and competition among them has always inhibited any real alliances."

"We free-lancers who have fought for different corporations probably hate that the most," said Fay. "You've said so, too, Klaus."

"Yeah. I have." Klaus's tone lightened for the first time.

Lane knew that soldiers with a certain independence of spirit were the ones who became free-lancers in the first place. Once in retirement, they had a lot in common. An understanding of the threat posed by the Dark Legion was part of what they shared.

"We'll take you to see Cameron," Fay said finally.

"Not necessary," said Lane. "You can just tell me where to find him."

"I want to hear it all," said Fay, standing up. "Wait while we get dressed."

Lane nodded. He still did not acknowledge Klaus, as Fay took her companion's arm and led him back down the hall. Then Lane sat down in a chair to wait.

Pam sat with Yojimbo in the Midnight Star. She was curious about him. Most people who employed free-lancers were either stuffy corporate types or loud, overbearing military veterans. Yojimbo had a calm determination that she had seen only in a few of the finest Martian Banshees.

The Whiz Kid had not picked up any more useful information today. Now Pam and Yojimbo sat over drinks, considering their situation. The crowd around them was dense, but calm.

"All I know about you is that you were a Mishima Elite," said Pam. "Where did you serve?"

Yojimbo looked at her slowly, a little startled. "Does it matter?"

"I usually work alone. Now that I'm part of a team, I'd like to know my commander."

Yojimbo nodded once in acknowledgment. "I served two tours, mainly on Mars."

"Really?" Pam smiled. "Is that why you never said? Because Lane and I were Martian Banshees, fighting Mishima?"

"In part. I did not want to distract any of us with old concerns."

"Well, I can understand that. Especially when we first met. But what else?"

"That part of my life is finished."

Pam shared that attitude herself. Most free-lancers, if they were healthy, had left the service of one of the megacorporations over one resentment or another. Few of them liked to talk about their reasons.

"I wonder if we faced each other," Pam said casually, watching for his reaction.

"Quite possibly." His manner remained all business. "The odds are good."

"Lane and I were involved in the Chilzone Campaign for four months. We fought Mishima Elite troops to a stalemate in the floor of the crevass."

Yojimbo turned and looked at her for a moment. "Yes, I was there, too. When the time came to withdraw, we made a night march up the pass between the Lynnet Hills to escape. Is that what you want to know?"

"Relax, will you?" Pam smiled and patted his shoulder. "When you hired Lane and me, you said it didn't matter to you that we had fought on opposite sides—that you had no problem with it. I'm not looking for grudges."

"Then what are you searching for with these questions?" His dark eyes met hers.

"I suppose I'm looking for a bond. Even if we were on opposite sides, we still have that experience in common. And we aren't in the services now."

"We may have killed each other's comrades and friends, or caused such deaths."

"That's the nature of war." Pam drew in a deep breath. "Maybe I've presumed too much here. Do you still feel a loyalty to the cause of Mishima?"

Yojimbo looked away and said nothing for a moment. "No. Not to the cause of Mishima Megacorporation, which is no better than the cause of any other megacorporation fighting for territory in which to sell its products."

"Then what's wrong?"

"I feel a personal loyalty to many of my former comrades and superiors. This is greater than the values of the corporation and its business goals. It is personal."

"I understand."

Yojimbo looked at her closely.

"Well, I do."

"What I am talking about comes from my ancestral Japanese culture. The values of Bushido."

"When you hired Lane and me, you said you were looking for people of unusual commitment."

"Yes."

"I have my own code. For instance, I kill only under specific circumstances. When I owe loyalty or favors, I keep them. I don't make excuses."

Yojimbo nodded. "It is not the same."

"Maybe not," said Pam. "Maybe it is."

When Yojimbo said nothing more, Pam let the matter drop. However, she had learned a little more about Yojimbo. She respected his old-fashioned values. As a Martian Banshee, she had been briefed about these concepts before facing the Mishima Elite, even though most of the Mishima Elite nowadays showed no sign of interest in the old value system. If she understood him, then he shared her disgust for most of the people around them, who accepted corruption and betrayal as a normal way of life.

CHAPTER 8

Lane followed Fay and Klaus through the dingy streets to a tubelink station. They stood jammed in the train with the usual crowd, not speaking. Lane felt this was just as well. He had always found Fay oddly attractive, despite her being a cyborg, but they had never been romantic. Considering Klaus's hostility toward Lane, they were all better off not making small talk.

Klaus took them to a lower level in Luna City, one devoted to industry. By the time they reached the blocks of warehouses, the dark streets were nearly deserted. Even the crowds of Luna City did not want to come here.

They stopped at a warehouse with the Bauhaus logo covering the front wall over the main door, a simple cog over a dark background. However, Klaus moved through a narrow alley down the side of the warehouse to a small door, where he rang a buzzer.

"You met Cameron Glen before?" Klaus muttered to Lane gruffly.

"Yeah. Fay introduced me some time back. I know he's a little weird."

"More than a little."

"I think he's getting worse," said Fay.

"What happened to him?" Lane asked. "Nobody ever said anything, in my presence."

"No one knows any details," said Fay. "He's a veteran of the Imperial Blood Berets."

"Blood Berets?" Lane frowned. "Don't they fight the Dark Legion?"

"That's right," Klaus said grimly. "In the jungles of Venus. If you ask me, Cameron had a little too much of it. But no one knows exactly what happened to him."

The heavy door opened suddenly. Some strangers, glancing suspiciously at the trio outside, slipped past wordlessly. They all wore armor, with Imperial and Bauhaus logos.

Lane stopped the door from closing and warily moved inside. Klaus and Fay followed him. Huge crates, stacked high, were silhouetted against faint light from the far end of the warehouse. Lane heard no sounds. Reflexively, he swung his weapon into position and moved forward.

From up ahead, Lane heard high-pitched giggling. He tensed, continuing to move forward, and tried to locate the source of the laughter. It came from the far side of the warehouse, off to one side of the main aisle down the center of the warehouse.

Suddenly, a man's voice came booming through a loudspeaker somewhere overhead. "Welcome, creepy friends. Come into the highlands of Luna where the jungle never grows."

Lane froze, glancing into the shadows in all directions, and spoke in a whisper. "Does he mean us?"

"I think so," Fay said quietly. "My infrared eyesight shows no one else hiding in the shadows, but a couple of security cameras up on the ceiling are following us. Don't make any sudden moves with your weapon."

Lane decided to let his CAR-24 swing down on the shoulder strap. He started forward again. "Hello!"

"Hi, Johnny Cope, are you walking yet?" The voice boomed again.

"It's Fay Fan and two friends," Fay called out. "Cameron, I'm bringing Klaus and Lane Chung. Remember? You've met them both before. I introduced you at the Midnight Star once, a year or two ago."

"All right, my bonnie moor hen. Come on up."

"What's he talking about?" Lane asked quietly as they walked forward.

"You got me," said Fay. "Nobody I know has ever figured it out."

When Lane turned the corner around the last stack of crates before the far wall, he found a small security station on a raised platform. The seats were surrounded by consoles full of control panels and screens. Clear security screens surrounded the station, but the door stood open.

A small, slender man with dark hair and a pointed face walked out of the doorway. He wore a plain jersey with the Imperial Blood Beret logo on it, a grinning skull with a sword driven through it from above. Below the jersey he sported a Scottish kilt in a green hunting tartan. Instead of demanding their business or greeting them normally, he folded his arms and leaned one narrow shoulder against the wall of the station.

"Hi, Cameron," said Fay cheerfully. "You know Lane and Klaus, right?"

"Seas between us great have roared," said Cameron, squinting at them. "Aye, I know them."

Lane felt relieved, but did not let down his guard. This situation made him very wary. Still, Cameron seemed to be alone and unarmed; that made him less dangerous.

"You work security here?" Lane asked politely, hoping to establish a rapport.

"As tall as Ben Lomond."

Lane had no idea what that meant, either, so he said nothing more.

"Your operation still running okay?" Klaus asked casually. "How's business?"

"Bonnie," said Cameron, with a grim look that seemed to belie the word.

"Your last customers didn't carry anything out," said Lane. At least Cameron had finally said something he understood. "Didn't they buy anything?"

"Aye." Cameron glared at Lane.

"That's not how it works here," said Fay. "May I tell him, Cameron?"

Cameron shrugged. "Flow gently, sweet."

"He has a good arrangement here," said Fay. "No one gets their goods here on the premises. He just alters the warehouse requisitions so that goods are sent to his customers with payment already recorded in the computer."

"And payment in cash, I suppose," said Klaus.

"I'm flexible," said Cameron. "But electronic payment goes into my personal account. And I take payment in information, sometimes, as well."

That was the first completely clear response Lane had heard from him.

"You do?" Klaus sounded surprised.

"The theme of my lays."

Lane studied Cameron carefully. The more Lane listened, the less crazy the guy sounded. Lane had a suspicion that everything he said made sense, at least in some way.

"We're looking for information," said Fay. "What will that cost us?"

"Depends on what it's about, my bonnie."

"The Dark Legion," said Lane. "I'm following up on a rumor of heretics here in Luna City."

Cameron tensed and straightened up from the wall. "Eh? You think you have word that's worth following? Most of those rumors are just nonsense."

"Yes, I know," said Lane.

"For instance, why would the Dark Legion send a presence here? On Mars and Venus they came with an invasion fleet." Suddenly Cameron sounded completely normal.

"I don't know why," said Lane. "I wish I knew their reason. But I have evidence that someone from the Dark Legion landed here recently."

"Coming through the rye." Cameron frowned. "Hm, well, so you're serious, eh? I make my living selling goods and information. I rarely give anything away, but today you have caught me just right. After all, if the Dark Legion brings war here, my business may not survive."

"You have something for us?" Fay asked.

"Maybe. This is only a few hours old, right off the streets."

"Go on."

"A mystic is wandering around Luna City."

"What do you mean, 'wandering'?" Fay asked. "He must be doing something."

"Searching for the purple heather, for all anyone knows." Cameron shrugged.

"Come on, who is he?" Klaus demanded.

"Easy, friend. His name is Honorius. Word from the bonnie braes is that he's a renegade, maybe insane."

"From the what?" Klaus muttered.

"Why would the Dark Legion care about him?" Lane asked. "What's one more crazy guy, more or less?"

"The Brotherhood is looking for him."

"Really?" Lane felt a sudden rush of interest. Fay and Klaus also became more alert. "What's so important about him?"

"No one from highland to moor seems to know," said Cameron. "But if the Brotherhood wants him, the Dark Legion might want him, too."

Lane did not know too much about the Brotherhood. Everyone knew it was led by the Cardinal, who lived in the tallest tower on the surface of Luna. The Cardinal ruled by the Book of Law and used his immense organization to combat evil in any form. That meant human temptation and corruption, but of course would apply even more to the Dark Legion. Since Lord Mishima had never joined the religion of the Cardinal, he was considered evil; everyone knew that was why the Brotherhood considered him to be their enemy. Lane could see by the state of Luna City in general that the Brotherhood had a lot of work to do.

"Who in the Brotherhood is looking for this Honorius guy?" Klaus asked.

Cameron shrugged.

"It's too big to tell," said Fay. "The Brotherhood bureaucracy is immense—the curiae, the directorates, their inquisitors, mortificators, troopers."

"Mystics are very important to the Brotherhood," said Klaus. "The order to find him did not originate down at the street level."

"I've never known much about the mystics," said Lane. "Just that they've got their heads in the sky or something. What are they, exactly?"

"I took a review of that question myself," said Cameron. "Come on into the station. I have a file up on the computer." He stood away from the entrance, gesturing.

Fay led the group inside. Lane stood behind Klaus, pressed against a counter in the cramped cubicle. Cameron stood in the doorway.

"Computer, quote the file's core description of a mystic," said Cameron. "Keep it brief."

The computer spoke in a calm, clearly enunciated woman's voice.

Under the guiding light of the Cardinals, the Brotherhood learned how to tap into ancient powers long lost to common man. A source of power was opened up, and the mystics devoted their lives to understanding and ultimately controlling this new force. Though several lifetimes have been spent studying this force of life, only a small part of the total power has been learned to date.

"Explain the part about why some people had to become mystics to do this," said Cameron.

The power can be controlled by beings pure of thought and soul and shaped into different forms, both for attack and defense.

"Now give us the part about mystics who have actually succeeded in achieving some of this power."

Mystics who have devoted their lives to the art of control have achieved powers of perception far beyond normal senses. They pry into the future, trying to predict the flow of time, and they search the minds of millions for the nearest trace of darkness and evil. They spy into the darkest chambers of the Dark Legions, trying to find the way of undoing the Dark Legions. The future is not the only domain of the mystics. The mystics also search the past, scribing the events that shaped our present age.

"That's the important part," said Cameron. "The file has lots of peripheral material about failed mystics of auld lang syne, that sort of thing."

"How accurate is it?" Lane asked.

"Well . . . it's from some fairly recent history volume." Cameron shrugged again.

"That part about mystics spying on the Dark Legion's darkest chambers doesn't sound right," said Lane. "If they could really do that, then the Brotherhood would always know what the enemy is planning and doing."

"I'm sure that's just overstatement from some historian," said Fay. "But I suppose the mystics are trying to do that sort of thing all the time."

"That could be our answer, then, about Honorius," said Lane. "Maybe he's mastered more of this power than usual. The Dark Legion would want him, and the Brotherhood wants him back. It makes sense."

"You never said why the Brotherhood has to find him," Klaus said to Cameron. "A mystic is part of the Brotherhood. Has he run out on them for some reason? Or did someone kidnap him, or what?"

"The rumors never mentioned that part," said Cameron. "I don't have any more for you. For that matter, I don't for sure know that the Dark Legion is even aware of him."

"Understood," said Lane. "That's only surmise. But it's worth investigating."

"Thanks, Cameron," said Fay. "We're in your debt. If we get something you can use, I'll get it to you."

"Don't bring the news of your own defeat so early in the morning."

Lane blinked in surprise.

"It's not morning," Klaus muttered. "Come on, let's get out of here."

Yojimbo spent the evening with Pam in the Midnight Star. Sometimes they sat together, getting acquainted; other times, Pam circulated through the crowd, making small talk with colleagues. Periodically, Yojimbo checked with the Whiz Kid to see if he had any new information, but he did not.

When Lane appeared in the doorway, he had two people with him. Pam returned to Yojimbo, who turned on his own sonic disruptor. Lane introduced him to Fay Fan and Klaus Dahlen and told Yojimbo and Pam that they had helped him find out that a renegade mystic had wandered away from the Brotherhood.

Yojimbo tensed and studied the faces of Fay and Klaus. Then he asked them to step outside the radius of the sonic disruptor for just a moment. When they did so, Yojimbo turned sternly to Lane.

"How much did you tell them?"

Lane looked straight into his eyes. "I told them I was following a rumor of a Dark Legion presence somewhere in Luna City."

"I made clear to you that I expect confidentiality in this matter."

"That's right."

"I hired you because I believed you could be trusted. You have violated my trust."

"No."

Yojimbo remembered very well that when he had been shamed out of Mishima Elite, he had not been given the opportunity to present his own case. He would not treat his own colleagues that way. "Explain yourself."

CHAPTER 9

"These rumors have been common for a long time," said Lane. "We've already discussed that. Following up this kind of rumor doesn't reveal anything of substance. I did not tell them about the damage at the docking port or any other details."

"You apparently told them you are part of a team. As soon as you arrived, you reported to me right in front of them. What else did you tell them?"

"They know I'm a free-lancer. They know I have an employer. This is nothing new, either."

"I think we ought to have them join us," said Pam. "If you can afford it, I mean."

Yojimbo turned to her. "Why?"

"We have two searches now. We need to follow up rumors about the Dark Legion and also this missing mystic. Five will be much more effective than three."

Yojimbo knew that was true. "Is that why you brought them here?"

"Yes," said Lane. "So you could meet them."

"How well do you know them?"

"Professionally, I know they're good. We aren't close as personal friends."

"You're both willing to rely on them in a fight with heretics, if necessary?"

"Yes," said Lane.

"Me, too," said Pam. "I worked with Klaus once. He's a grouch, but he can do the job."

"All right. And they're interested?"

"I didn't offer them anything," said Lane. "I just asked them to come with me. No promises made. But they're free to take a job."

Yojimbo nodded. Klaus and Fay stood just outside the sonic disruption radius, watching. Yojimbo gestured for them to step back inside it again. He offered them both jobs at the same fee he was paying Lane and Pam. After they accepted, Yojimbo adjourned the team for the night. They agreed to meet at the command center early the next morning.

When the team gathered in the morning, Yojimbo had already asked the Whiz Kid to go into cyberspace to seek the latest rumors.

"How long does this take?" Klaus asked, nodding toward the Whiz Kid at his computer station. "I'm ready to hit the streets and get to work."

"We have no way to tell," said Yojimbo. "But during the night, I decided to organize our communication."

"Yeah?" Lane looked at him in surprise. "Why? What's the problem?"

"If we do make contact with a Dark Legion presence, we will need to communicate through the city with some security. As soon as we leave here this morning, I will purchase belt computers with voice functions for everyone in which we can share our information. I have chosen two secret code words for us, and of course we will scramble our communications."

"What are the code words?" Pam asked.

"The first is this." Yojimbo wrote a Japanese character on a scrap of paper. "It is pronounced *sai* and represents a spear. This will verify any written communication between us. Memorize it and learn how to write it. I will arrange badges for us to wear."

"What's the other one?" Fay asked.

"Yojimbo," said Yojimbo. "We will use either term to verify spoken communication that is not face-to-face."

"We could call ourselves Team Yojimbo," said Lane. "But no one is supposed to know we exist as a team, so I guess we can't call ourselves anything."

Pam laughed.

Yojimbo smiled. "Formally, I declare us to be Team Yojimbo, whether or not we have the opportunity to use the name."

"Team Yojimbo it is," said Pam.

"Who cares?" Klaus muttered.

Fay glared at him.

The Whiz Kid leaned out of the hood in his computer station. "Half a zowee. I have something, but I can't say if it's worth very much. Just more rumors, but they're new."

"Go ahead," said Yojimbo.

"I put out the word yesterday that I wanted to hear anything about heretics. Three people heard of sightings on Level Four, near the old Imperial and Cybertronic warehouses."

"Nobody you know actually saw them?" Klaus asked, folding his arms.

"No. They only picked up rumors."

"That section is some of the worst in Luna City," said Fay. "I've been down there to pick up black market Cybertronic parts. Some of the factories down there are abandoned. The warehouses sometimes house terrorist gangs."

"It sounds like the kind of neighborhood where the Dark Legion might hide," said Yojimbo.

"It's also the kind of place where false rumors would start," said Klaus.

"You have more?" Yojimbo asked.

"One more," said the Whiz Kid. "A lot of people heard of a necromutant on this level, creeping around the Mishima warehouses."

"A necromutant?" Lane raised his eyebrows. "Wait a minute. Those are monsters. Heretics can pass as ordinary humans, but not a necromutant. Why hasn't more of an alarm been raised about this?"

The Whiz Kid shrugged. "Aw, how would I know? I'm just reporting what I heard."

"We will have to consider the problem as we investigate," said Yojimbo.

"There's black market activity there, too," said Pam.

"We can get started there," said Yojimbo. "We'll form two squads."

"I know that section of Level Four," said Fay. "Klaus and I can track down that rumor."

"Good," said Yojimbo. "I know the Mishima warehouses. Lane and Pam will come with me."

"What about the belt computers?" Lane asked.

"We'll stay together until I buy them. But remember, every call we make through the city can be picked up and unscrambled by anyone with enough desire and the right equipment. Prioritize face-to-face discussion. Let's go."

Yojimbo took them to a Mishima store and bought each team member one of the latest computers that could be clipped to their belts. The computers could also communicate with each other across five hundred meters, though in Luna City the signal would be cut off between levels by the lunar rock and soil. Still, they would be better than Harker headsets, which were too common; almost anyone could easily drop in on communications using them.

At the same location Yojimbo ordered badges produced for the team—a red circle with the character *sai* in white. Each member wore at least one.

While the badges were prepared, Fay programmed the code words into the belt computer, as well as the scrambling and descrambling codes. She called the Whiz Kid on an unsecured line to arrange for him to match his computer to theirs. After that, the two squads split up.

Yojimbo wore his armor, as usual, but the others did not. Like Lane and Pam, Fay and Klaus wore casual clothing and carried only a pistol and a light machine gun. He said nothing to them. So far, they were still trying to find out if a threat existed, and what it really was.

While Fay and Klaus picked their own route, Yojimbo took his squad on the tubelink to the Mishima warehouses. The shadowed, dingy streets in this industrial area were bustling with people doing business. However, the warehouses themselves were well lit and clean, maintained with usual Mishima care.

Pam, already jammed close to Yojimbo on the crowded sidewalk, spoke in his ear. "Got any ideas where to start?"

"I don't have a particular suggestion," said Yojimbo. "How about you two?"

"I think so," said Pam, turning to Lane. "Didn't a couple of guys we know hire on recently as enforcers over in this area? A couple of months ago?"

"Yeah, that's right," said Lane. "Uh ... that tall, heavy guy with the red beard and his friend. I can't remember their names."

"Enforcers?" Yojimbo said. "You mean Mishima guards for the warehouses?"

"No." Pam smiled, her blond hair bouncing as she turned to look at him. "Black market enforcers, working for the people who run the business in this neighborhood."

"I see."

"Eric Fano," said Lane. "That's the big guy's name. What's his friend's name?"

"You mean that short, stocky guy—the one with the scar across his forehead?"

"Yeah."

"Vince Marga."

"Right! We can start asking around for them."

"Who are they, exactly?" Yojimbo asked. "What did they do before they became black market enforcers?"

"They were free-lancers, like us." Lane grinned. "Not as good, but decent."

"I suggest you two take the lead," said Yojimbo. "At your convenience."

Lane pointed to a big, scowling man standing at the entrance to a narrow alley between two warehouses. He wore the Bauhaus gearwheel logo on his armor and a helmet, but at this distance the weapon he held was out of sight. "That guy looks like an enforcer, too. Let's ask him."

"Your call," said Pam. "Lead on."

Yojimbo brought up the rear as they worked their way through the press of pedestrians. The man at the front of the alley saw them coming. He warily raised a Bauhaus Panzerknacker AG-17 assault rifle.

Yojimbo saw Lane greet the stranger by showing that both his hands were empty. Behind him Pam and Yojimbo did the same. The other man relaxed slightly, but kept his Panzerknacker in position.

"Hello," Lane said amiably.

"This alley is closed, friend." The stranger spoke sternly, but civilly.

"I'm looking for Eric Fano or Vince Marga," said Lane. "They're enforcers in this neighborhood."

"Who's asking?"

"I'm Lane Chung. They'll know my name."

"I'm not promising anything, but where can you be found if someone wants to?"

"I'll be right here on the street today."

The stranger nodded. "Move on, then."

Lane walked on down the street, with Pam and Yojimbo following him. Then he stopped and turned. When Yojimbo glanced back, he saw that the man in the alley was still watching them, but was now out of hearing.

"Could you hear?" Lane asked. He was smiling.

"Yeah," said Pam.

"Was that a good response?" Yojimbo asked. "I could not read his meaning."

"I don't expect he'll go out of his way to find them," said Lane. "But he virtually said that he'll pass my name to them if he sees them."

"He expressed that when he asked where to find you?" Yojimbo asked.

"That's right."

"So, now what?" Pam asked.

Lane shrugged. "We look for Eric and Vince, anyway. And if we find more enforcers, we spread the word with them the same way. And we stay out on the street, where we can be found by anyone who's looking."

Since Fay knew Level Four better than Klaus, she led him out of the tubelike station. She swung her Cybertronic AR3000 assault rifle forward just because she always did so in this neighborhood. Half a step behind her, Klaus readied his Bauhaus Destroyer light machine gun.

The street here held only about half the pedestrians of most Luna City streets. Many of the lights had been shot out and never replaced, leaving the area dim and deeply shadowed. As usual, steam rose up from cracks in the city ventilation system.

Fay warily studied everyone she saw, and they looked back at her and Klaus the same way. No one made a suspicious move, however, and they all walked past each other. Klaus turned and watched the strangers over his shoulder.

"What do we do now?" Klaus asked quietly. "I don't think any of these people are going to like answering questions from us."

Fay pointed toward a factory that had lights in street-level windows. "We'll have to find someone who works here."

"You really think they'll be any more cooperative?" Klaus muttered sourly.

"One way to find out." Fay looked at the other buildings up and down the street. Most of them were dark and empty. A few others showed some light. Without a contact in the area, they would just have to take their chances.

"Everybody's coming the same way," said Klaus.

"What?"

"Look. Everyone on the street is coming toward us, back toward the tubelink station. No one is going in our direction or just walking across the street. Something weird must have happened up ahead somewhere."

As Fay approached the closed doors of the factory, she saw more pedestrians hurry past them, looking at them closely. For the first time, she realized that they were not hostile or even simply exercising normal caution. One young woman in a civilian jumpsuit with the Capitol logo looked panicked.

"What's down there?" Fay asked. "What's wrong?"

The young woman started to hurry past her.

"Please tell us," Fay urged gently. "Is it dangerous? We were going that way."

The woman stopped, her green eyes wide. "Somebody said a heretic was seen down there. Word is all over the street. He hurt someone. You know what I mean? A heretic."

"Has anyone reported it to your superiors? The

megacorporations could send troops down here." Fay's real reason for asking was to find out if such troops were already on the way.

"Of course people reported it. But nobody in the high offices cares what happens down here. No one believes the reports." She glanced back over her shoulder and then hurried on.

"That's good enough for a start," Fay said grimly. "Let's see what we can find."

"Maybe we should have brought heavier artillery, or armor or something."

"I don't think armor helps much against them," said Fay. "Their powers are a little strange—throwing blindness or disorienting people, that kind of thing."

"Yeah, that's right. But I wouldn't mind a little extra protection, anyway."

She moved off the street to a sidewalk. "We're going to stand out, moving against the flow of people. Try to stay in the shadows."

"Right behind you."

Fay assumed the attitude of walking point, magnifying the focus in her cybernetic eyes to see farther. She shifted to infrared vision every few seconds, seeking heat signatures in the shadows. She did not know if a heretic's heat would be different from a normal human's, but at least she would know when the darkness hid someone.

With Klaus right behind her, Fay moved down the street into deeper shadows. The crowd of people passing them had changed now. Instead of ordinary people in working-class megacorporate clothing, now ragged, unkempt individuals hurried up the street. Their filthy clothes sometimes bore old, tattered logos too worn to identify.

Fay would usually have been on the alert for these very people in this neighborhood. They were the desperate muggers and thieves and perhaps political terrorists who preyed on citizens in other parts of Luna City and fled to its darkest recesses to hide. Now something even worse had scared them away from their homes.

CHAPTER 10

Within a few minutes no one remained on the street ahead of Fay and Klaus. She advanced slowly, looking from side to side. When she looked back, she saw that the fleeing crowd had left them far behind as they neared the tubelink station. Then she glanced forward again.

A faint, quick flash of light between a couple of buildings reached her infrared sensors. She halted, watching, but it did not reappear. Without turning to Klaus, she pointed with one arm. Then, with the precision of long-established teamwork, she angled to the left of the alley and Klaus wordlessly angled to its right, their weapons ready.

Fay and Klaus crept up on the opening to the alley from each side, now in almost complete darkness. That meant Klaus could hardly see. Fay's infrared sight and her movements would have to lead him.

Fay hesitated, listening. She heard nothing in the alley. Moving quickly, she went into a crouch as she swung around the corner, her weapon forward, looking down into the darkness. Following her lead, Klaus swung around his corner in a standing position over her.

All she saw were a couple of fading heat spots on the broken pavement. They represented footsteps. Someone had fled from them.

"We have something," Fay whispered. "Somebody is running instead of joining the rest of the crowd at the tubelink station."

"Might just be a crazy guy. Someone who won't leave even if a heretic is around."

"Maybe. But we'll check."

"You decide how."

Fay considered her next move. The narrow alley was a perfect place for someone to lay a trap. On the other hand, all they had were the footprints leading forward down the alley. If they chose not to follow them, they would have nothing. By the time she hurried around one of the buildings to cut off their quarry, the heat from his footsteps would have dissipated and no track would be left.

She knew she would have to go first. Even worse, Klaus would not be able to see her in the shadows, so he could not give covering fire without the risk of hitting her. Still, she could see their prey better than a heretic could see her. That made the risk worth taking.

"Wait here. I'll wave if I can. I may have to tap the butt of my AR3000 on the pavement for you to come up." They had used this technique in similar situations before.

"Right."

Fay crept forward slowly, putting more effort into silence than speed. She heard and saw no sign of anyone up ahead. Toward the end of the alley, where it faced the wall of another building and ended in a T intersection with another alley, the tiny remaining heat spots turned right.

When she had been a Cybertronic trooper, Fay had chosen to enhance her eyesight, reflexes, and her strength to some degree. Because of her petite build, she had decided to avoid having oversize weapons and armor implanted. They were too heavy and awkward for her body. Even her strength had been increased only to a moderate degree since she had not wanted to look strange. In many cases, such as carrying a very large weapon, her small size and weight still limited what she could do. However, in this case she was now able to draw on her unnaturally quick reflexes as well as her infrared vision.

She hesitated at the corner, where she still heard nothing. Then she swung around it, crouching, her AR3000 up and ready. Nothing happened.

Up ahead, fading heat spots showed the track of her quarry behind columns of heat representing leaking steam vents. Whoever he was, he had moved up the next alley and turned a corner to the left. Here faint light leaked around another corner on the right.

Fay looked back at Klaus and tried waving silently for him to follow. As she had feared, he could not see her in the shadows. She tapped her AR300 twice on the hard pavement, and he jogged forward.

When he reached her, Fay pointed up the next alley and spoke in a whisper. "He went up and turned left. I haven't heard anything."

"You want to keep following him? We're just asking to walk into a trap."

"I think he's more interested in running than fighting. I'll move up to the next turn."

Klaus nodded.

As before, Fay advanced quietly, watching the heat spots as they slowly faded to nothing. She knew which corner her quarry had taken, so stealth was all that mattered now. At the next corner she paused as she had done earlier, then again swung around in a crouch.

Lane and Pam spent several hours moving up and down the streets of the Mishima warehouse district, while Yojimbo patrolled the same area singly, at a distance. They told anyone who would listen that they would like to speak with Eric Fano and Vince Marga. No one made any promises. Finally, as they took a break standing against the wall of a warehouse, a large, stocky man with short red hair and a bushy red beard stepped in front of Lane.

"Hello, Lane." Eric Fano's tone was casual, but his eyes studied Lane warily. "Everyone I've met this morning says you're looking for me."

"And me." Vince Marga stepped up from behind him. The short, heavy man had a horizontal scar across his forehead. "This is a real distraction. What do you two want?" He softened a little, looking at Pam.

"We're just checking out a rumor," said Lane. "We need to talk to someone we can believe."

"Is that all?" Eric relaxed. "I thought you wanted something important."

"It's important to us," said Pam. "We're checking out a rumor of a necromutant around here somewhere."

Vince sneered, then broke into a chuckle. "Yeah, like a necromutant could hide in this crowd?"

"What of it?" Eric demanded, glowering down at both Lane and Pam.

Lane let his face go expressionlessly cold. "You think there's anything to it? You guys are on the street here; aren't you keeping track of your turf?"

Eric stared back at him without answering.

Vince, still grinning, elbowed his partner. "Go on, Eric. Otherwise, we'll never get rid of them. They'll be pestering people here for days."

Finally Eric grinned slightly, too, and relaxed. "All right. All right. We might as well get rid of you two. No one ever saw any necromutant around here."

"How do you know?" Lane asked.

"It was my idea," said Eric. "Look, we were getting some black marketeers from other neighborhoods trying to muscle in on us. I created the rumors among their customers to undercut them. It hasn't cut down on the day traffic here, but it's kept out some of the trouble at night."

"You came up with it yourself?" Pam asked. "You know for sure this originated with you?"

"That's right," said Eric. "This rumor will serve its purpose for a while, then be forgotten. No different from a lot of other rumors that circulate from time to time. People will forget about it, and we'll have to handle turf wars the usual way." He nodded toward Pam's CAR-24.

"We won't say a word," said Lane.

Fay saw a wider alley this time, backlit from the street at the far end. Next to a small, roiling cloud of steam from a crack in the alley, a human figure was silhouetted halfway down the alley, also glowing with the heat signature of its form. Then, suddenly, the stranger turned toward her, and all her sight went black.

She threw herself on the ground to her left, firing blindly forward. Her AR3000 chattered and vibrated in her hand. When she hit the hard pavement with her left shoulder, she rolled once and came up firing again.

"Klaus, I'm blinded!" She had to warn him. Invoking blindness in others was one of the Dark Gifts that all heretics supposedly possessed.

A wave of sheer terror swept over her, disorienting her. She fumbled desperately for her AR3000, trying to scramble to her right in order to become a moving target. The effort was hopeless, of course, since she could not see her enemy. For all she knew, she was making herself an easier target.

"Get down!" Klaus shouted behind her.

As she let herself fall, she heard the chattering of his Bauhaus Destroyer just to her rear.

Instantly, the terror she felt vanished. She remembered, belatedly, that invoking extreme fear in an enemy was also a mystical ability of the heretics. Her vision returned in the same moment, and she looked forward.

The heretic lay twitching on the pavement up ahead in the near-darkness.

Klaus advanced slowly, his weapon held ready. "Were there more?"

"No. Just one." Fay got to her feet, angry now that her fear had subsided.

Fay followed Klaus to the heretic, who grimaced as he looked up at them. Now for the first time, she could see that he was wearing a hooded cloak, and the hood still framed his face. His torso was splattered with his own blood.

Steam drifted over her.

"You got me," the heretic said huskily. "But you'll never get my master. You'll never find him. And when he knows the future, he'll have you all."

"Who is your master?" Fay demanded.

The heretic made a face that was half grimace and half triumphant smile. He said nothing, but he still watched their faces. His legs jerked and kicked uncontrollably, and the bloodstains on his clothing continued to grow.

Klaus lowered his weapon and emptied the magazine into the heretic.

"Klaus!"

"He was practically dead, anyway."

"That's not what I mean. We have to search him. Now it's even a worse mess than before."

"Oh. Yeah."

"So *you* search him. I'll keep watch."

That evening, Lane sat impatiently on a couch between Pam and Yojimbo in the command center as the two squads exchanged their information. In a chair across from them, Klaus finished the reports by explaining that the heretic had carried no evidence of any sort about his identity or any other Dark Legion individuals. The Whiz Kid, at his computer station as usual, had not learned anything new, either.

"We have to sort out exactly what the heretic revealed," said Yojimbo.

"What do you mean?" Fay asked. She sat perched on the arm of Klaus's chair.

"For instance, he did not actually say what his master is, did he?"

"Not precisely," said Fay.

"You mean 'what' or 'who'?" Lane asked, frowning.

"I mean, 'what,' " said Yojimbo. "Human or . . . other."

"I see."

"Nor did he say that his master is present on Luna," said Yojimbo.

"No."

"Hold it," said Pam. "I'm no expert on the Dark Legion, but I know a little about it. Supposedly, new, low-level heretics follow more experienced heretics with greater psychic powers, but they all obey nepharites. I don't think a minor heretic would call a senior heretic his master."

"You think a nepharite is on Luna?" Yojimbo asked. "This is your conclusion?"

"Yes."

"Klaus told us the heretic had no further evidence of his identity or residence," said Yojimbo. "What do the rest of you think?"

"His behavior and words are only circumstantial evidence," said Lane. "But I'm betting Pam is right."

"That part about the heretic's master learning the future

might mean the mystic," said Fay. "I thought of that right away."

"It could be," Klaus said with his usual dour gruffness. "We'd better take the possibility seriously. Better to err on the side of readiness."

"I agree," said Yojimbo. "We will proceed on the assumption that a nepharite is on Luna somewhere. If the danger is less than that, we will not complain."

"We still don't have a real lead, though," said Lane. "What do we do now?"

"The nepharite is looking for that missing mystic," said Pam. "That's a lead."

"We don't know where he is, either," Fay said with a wry grin. "Some lead."

Everyone smiled. Yojimbo was glad; it showed him that his teammates had maintained their poise. This was a benefit of their experience as free-lancers.

"We know more about the mystic than the nepharite," said Lane.

"This is where we will start," said Yojimbo. "If we can find the mystic first, we can draw the nepharite to us. If the nepharite finds him first, maybe the trail to the mystic will lead us to the nepharite."

"Makes sense to me," said Fay.

"What are we going to do with the mystic if we get him?" Klaus asked.

"Maybe we'll learn about the future," Pam snickered. "We'll ask him if we're going to find the nepharite or not."

Everyone laughed.

"Come on, seriously," said Klaus. "The Brotherhood is already looking for him."

"That's a good point," said Pam. "Maybe at some point we can pick up the Brotherhood's investigators and follow them. They might know more about following their own mystic than we can ever figure out."

"We just don't want the Brotherhood to know that we're crossing into their business," said Klaus. "Their interference will just slow us down."

"If we get into a hassle with them, we can drop that approach, can't we?" Fay said, looking around at all of them. "We don't care about the mystic, except as a lead to the nepharite. So we can follow that lead if it's convenient and drop it if it becomes a bother."

"I agree," said Yojimbo. "Now, we have had a long day. We will break for the night and meet here in the morning. Team Yojimbo, you're dismissed."

CHAPTER 11

Ragathol the nepharite, follower of the Dark Apostle Algeroth, sat in his high, stone throne on its pedestal in the central chamber of his underground lair. It lay deep beneath the surface of Luna City in an abandoned mine. Around the chamber his twisted, misshapen lamps of black technology glowed yellow with a purplish corona to provide light.

The nepharites of Algeroth were devoted to the act of war. They were his generals, leading his forces in combat. Calm and serene on his throne of carved stone, Ragathol had come in secret to Luna many weeks before, bringing a handful of heretics and necromutants to do his bidding among the humans here. No one of the Dark Legion had ever penetrated so far into the realm of humanity.

Like all the nepharites of Algeroth, Ragathol towered over the former humans, the heretics, who now followed him. He stood four meters tall, heavily muscled with long, sharp spikes growing out of his shoulders and the sides of his head. One long spike grew at a forward angle from the top of his head. His forehead was low and a heavy brow ridge protected his deep-set eyes. Below his short, pointed nose his jaw was long, opening wide to reveal long, shiny teeth when he shouted his battle cries against the armies of humans.

Here on Luna, the need for stealth prevented him from going to the streets of Luna City to direct a charge of his minions, but he hoped that time would come eventually.

Ragathol heard the sharp footsteps of one of his followers approaching on the hard stone floor outside the entrance to this chamber. He shifted his position on his throne, waiting. One of his heretics entered the chamber and bowed smartly.

"Yes, Boroth?" Ragathol's low voice rumbled against the rock walls of the chamber.

"A heretic has arrived from his lordship the Dark Apostle Algeroth, to see you."

"What is his name?"

"He calls himself Kyno."

"Bring him in."

Boroth turned and gestured. Another man, wearing a plain gray tunic, walked inside the chamber and also bowed, but less deeply. He had rather ordinary human features and short brown hair.

Ragathol glowered sternly at the heretic. If Ragathol had been near a military front, then a message from Algeroth would be good, maybe even an order to attack. Here, in this setting, Ragathol did not know what business Algeroth would have with him.

"What does the Dark Apostle want with me?" Ragathol demanded. "From where has he sent you? Has he come forward toward the center of this solar system?"

"No," said Kyno. "His lordship still resides in the outer reaches of this solar system, where the Dark Legion first broke free in this dimension."

Ragathol felt a sense of relief, but did now show it. So Algeroth would not interfere with him directly—at least, not today. "Then what does Algeroth wish you to say? Speak."

"My lord has sent me with this message: 'The nepharite Ragathol has overstepped the bounds of his authority and threatens the Dark Symmetry by advancing deep into human territory on Luna.' "

Ragathol tensed angrily as he glared at the heretic. Only his status as a messenger from the Dark Apostle protected him here, but it protected him well. Ragathol would not anger the Dark Apostle by destroying his messenger.

"What does he think I am doing here?" Ragathol asked, keeping his voice calm.

"My lord did not say anything further. He sends only that message."

Ragathol drew himself up in his throne. He would not bother to stand in front of a mere human heretic. "Then I will send a message back to him. How did you come here?"

"Algeroth first sent me to Mars on a black technology ship from his palace in the outer planets. On Mars I crossed the front between Dark Legion territory to Bauhaus territory in secret. I traveled to Luna as an ordinary human on a Bauhaus ship from Mars."

"You can return to the Dark Apostle the same way?" Ragathol demanded.

"Yes."

"Then here is your message. Tell the Dark Apostle that I am not mounting an attack on Luna. My supply line would be stretched too far for that, and I have very few followers here. I am present to gather information through my heretics about human life, organizations, and technology on Luna for the future. I will not endanger the Dark Symmetry. Everything we do here is in alignment with the Dark Symmetry."

Kyno bowed in acknowledgment.

Ragathol turned to Boroth. "Tell me, has our guest been here long?"

"No," said Boroth. "I brought him here as soon as he arrived."

"Kyno, you are dismissed. Wait in the outer chamber for Boroth."

Kyno bowed and hurried out of the chamber.

Ragathol gestured imperiously for Boroth to approach his throne.

The heretic moved forward slowly, quivering with fear. "Have I offended my lord?"

"No," Ragathol said serenely, in a voice too low to reach Kyno outside the chamber. "I have orders for you. Do not allow Kyno to leave yet. Give him food and rest. Speak with him. Ask him about the Dark Apostle. If he will speak more of Algeroth, report to me what he says. Then send him on his way."

"Yes, my lord."

"Do not allow harm to come to him. He must carry my message back to Algeroth."

"Yes, my lord."

"Leave me."

Boroth bowed deeply and hurried out.

Ragathol watched him go, thinking over the message from Algeroth. The Dark Apostle ruled the Dark Legion; his every opinion had to be considered carefully. At the same time, Ragathol expected to learn much from his visit here on Luna. This visit would help him serve.

Originally, Ragathol had come to seek information about the humans' cutting-edge military technology, military positions, and plans for expansion on Mars and Venus, and the identity of humans who might respond cooperatively for bribes, alliances, or intimidation. He had gathered some of this information already. However, word of a renegade mystic wandering the streets of Luna City had reached him through his heretics. This human could be worth more than everything else he had learned combined.

Ragathol leaned back in his throne, considering what his heretics had reported. A mystic had escaped the Brotherhood, and the Brotherhood had assigned only a couple of special agents to find him so as not to attract attention in the population as a whole. Ragathol believed this mystic had special powers, perhaps of great psychic ability. Ordinary mystics did not leave the Brotherhood that created them.

Heavy footsteps approaching the chamber told Ragathol that one of his five necromutants was approaching.

"Enter," said Ragathol.

The one named Gorong entered the chamber. He stood only a little taller than a normal human, though like Ragathol, he had huge muscles that provided immense bulk. Unlike the nepharite, he had no spikes growing from his head and shoulders, but his body was an integrated conglomeration of flesh and metal, a leathery mass of tissue. All the necromutants had bodies like this.

"Speak, Gorong," ordered Ragathol.

"The female has been connected to the black technology computer in her chamber," said Gorong, his gravelly voice rumbling in the cavern.

"I will come." Ragathol stood and marched down the steps of the pedestal to the floor.

Ragathol had received a human female from Azurwraith, the nepharite leading the Dark Legion on Venus. He had been alerted by a heretic from Venus several hours in advance to send his necromutants to the docking ports, but had not been told why. The woman had been delivered by a rogue Capitol ship to his necromutants and brought here. Then the ship had left, leaving no message or explanation. However, Ragathol had understood her purpose. She brought him information.

Ever since she had arrived, Ragathol's necromutants had struggled to hook up to her head sensors that led to a black technology computer and hologram system. Now she was finally ready. Ragathol would learn exactly why she had been sent to him.

Gorong stood aside and allowed Ragathol to lead the way through the network of old mine passageways. The nepharite bent low to avoid the rough-hewn ceiling as he entered a smaller chamber, also lit with the yellow and purple glow of his lamps. His four other necromutants stood waiting for him.

A short, slender human female lay on the hard, uneven stone floor. Her brown hair was shoulder-length and straight, falling limply across her face. She wore a badly torn long-sleeved khaki shirt and matching pants, covered with dirt stains, dried blood, and smoke. A cap of iron bands had been fitted over her head, with many wires leading from it.

The wires ran to a wall of black technology computer equipment. Gorong moved to it and put his hand on a switch, waiting. Dark blue and orange lights blinked on various monitors.

"You have tested her already?" Ragathol asked.

"Yes," said Gorong.

The other necromutants nodded.

"Proceed."

Gorong pressed the switch.

A beam of light shot out of the computer, throwing a hologram into the center of the chamber. Suddenly Ragathol and his necromutants were looking at a miniature image of small village in a clearing surrounded by jungle. Ragathol had been to Venus on his way here, so he recognized the sight. The village was inhabited by human families, with many small children running and playing in the foreground. Several men squatted under a nearby tree, eating; they wore Capitol logos on their uniforms. Ragathol understood that he was seeing the woman's memory, from her viewpoint.

Ragathol watched in silence as the humans looked up and saw a black technology ship descending fast out of the sky. As Dark Legion troopers charged out of the ship and massacred all the humans in the village except this woman, he realized the reason she had been sent to him. She was a Receptacle of Visions, bringing this record of an attack on Venus that conveyed several messages to him.

First, the woman's memories told him how easily the Dark Legion could handle remote Capitol outposts on Venus. Apparently, Capitol was not prepared to intercept fast-moving atmospheric craft in all of its territory. Also, the memories constituted an offer. Azurwraith was showing off his efficiency and thereby telling Ragathol that he would like to aid Ragathol in a future attack on Luna, whenever that time might come. Last, it was an invitation for Ragathol to join him on Venus at some point for a future attack against the humans.

Suddenly, the hologram shut off, leaving the chamber much darker.

"That is the end?" Ragathol asked.

"Yes," said Gorong. "She has earlier memories, but none that follow."

"Very well."

"What shall we do with her?"

"I have no particular future need for the woman," said Ragathol. "Keep her alive for now. She may yet be of use in some way."

"Do you have further instructions?" Gorong asked.

Ragathol glanced around the chamber. All his necromutants watched him with a restless eagerness. They wanted more action than he had given them.

"Yes," said Ragathol. "We have already discussed the

renegade mystic. Go out into the tunnels with the heretics and help them find him. Bring him here. But remember that stealth is more important than force. Do not expose yourselves on street level; that is the job of the heretics. Our numbers are limited and reinforcements will be difficult. I repeat my standing instructions to you: Do not fight to the death as you normally would. Instead, save yourselves when you can and return to serve me again."

As the necromutants smiled with satisfaction and bowed to him, Ragathol turned and strode serenely out of his chamber.

Lane eagerly got up to leave when Yojimbo dismissed the team for the night. Everyone else rose, too, but Yojimbo chose to stay with the Whiz Kid in the command center. Fay and Klaus left together, glancing around carefully before slipping into the crowd on the street. Lane and Pam waited a few seconds for them to go; with their experience as urban free-lancers, keeping their group dispersed was second nature.

"You hungry, Chung?" Pam asked casually.

"Yeah."

"Let's have dinner. I'll buy."

"Sure. Where shall we go?"

"Somewhere secure. I'm tired of being on guard every minute. There's a cellar Cantonese restaurant near my place. It's expensive, but they keep good security."

"Let's go."

Lane followed Pam out to the street, but she moved to back alleys as soon as she could. They moved as though they were on recon patrol out of habit, warily examining their surroundings constantly. However, they reached a small well of steps leading down to a small restaurant without incident.

The Canton Ivory Flower seated only about sixteen people. The atmosphere was cozy, and armed private security guards stood by the main entrance. When the kitchen door swung open, Lane saw armed guards in the kitchen, as well. This was as safe a place as they would find at their income level.

"We should order the daily specials," said Pam. "They're always the best."

"What are they today?" Lane glanced around for a menu and saw none.

"Today . . . fish with black beans."

"Whatever you say."

Pam ordered, then leaned back in her seat. "I've wanted to ask you something, Chung. What do you think of our team so far?"

"Oh . . . I don't know." Lane shrugged. "It's all right, I guess. Why?"

"I'm still getting used to the idea of working with so many people. I don't think I've been part of a team this big since we were in the Banshees together."

"Yeah, I know. I've gotten used to working alone most of the time, myself."

"So what do you think of our new boss?"

"Yojimbo? Well, he's about stiff as anyone I've seen in a long time. More rigid than any officer I had with the Banshees."

"He's got that Mishima efficiency, don't you think?" Pam asked.

"Yeah." Lane grinned. "He really took to his training, all right."

"I'm comfortable following him, though."

"Is that what you're asking me? What I think of him as a leader?"

"I guess so."

"I think he's all right. Not the kind of guy I'd make friends with, but I trust him as a commander."

"I don't feel that way about Klaus."

Lane grinned, shrugging. "He's not commanding anybody. Not even Fay. She's the boss in that pair."

"How is he on the street?"

"I don't really know. All we've done together is walk around and talk a little. Back when Fay first introduced me to him, she told me he was a good fighter, but not a great thinker." Lane shrugged again.

"What do you think of Fay? Do you know her well?" Pam cocked her head, making her blond hair sway. "I've hardly had a chance to speak to her at all."

"No, not really." Lane hesitated. "I've never known what to think about any cyborg, really."

"I've never been friends with one. They usually stay in Cybertronic, and they really hang together. I always had the impression that they don't like opening up to other people. But Fay left Cybertronic and took up with Klaus, so she isn't like the others."

"I thought about that a little," said Lane. "But I don't know if she's completely different, either. She seems to be all business in her own way."

Pam smiled. "And what kind of weirdo would take up with Klaus?"

Lane laughed. "Good question."

They continued their good-natured gossip about their teammates as they ate. Lane realized it was a way of working off the stress of the day, as well as comparing opinions. They were still talking when they had finished dinner.

"Look, Chung, I'm too keyed up to sleep. Want to talk some more?"

"Sure, why not? Where shall we go?"

"I don't want to stay out too late. Let's go back and visit at my place."

"All right."

CHAPTER 12

Lane had never visited her home before; they had always met at the Midnight Star. He found that Pam lived in a very secure but very expensive apartment building on the same level as the Midnight Star. Her apartment was small and cozy, with soft, well-padded furniture. The couch was bright yellow, the two easy chairs bright red, the carpet lavender. None had patterns or prints, just solid colors.

"Sure is cheerful." Lane chuckled lightly, looking around in surprise. "But it's a little hard on my eyes. I never imagined you'd decorate a place like this. You don't dress this way."

Pam glanced down at her gray jumpsuit and laughed. "No. Out on the street I want to fade into the shadows. But this is home, you know?"

"Yeah. I guess I do. But . . . it's so, uh . . . strong. You know what I mean?"

Pam nodded, still smiling. "Sit down, if you're not too uncomfortable." She sat down on one end of the couch and loosened the tight neck of her jumpsuit.

Lane sat down on the couch. "Doesn't it keep you awake, or something?"

"Naw. I'm too tired for that." Pam's manner turned serious. "It's my haven from the rest of Luna City. I'm so tired of dirt, pavement, stone, the darkness in the underground levels where the lights are broken out. I just wanted a place that was bright and clear and happy."

"Yeah." Lane nodded soberly. "I know. My place is a dump, but it's *my* dump."

"Out on the street I live for the adrenaline rush. Here, I just want a personal haven from a nasty world." Pam turned her blue eyes to look at him. "We're awfully driven to pursue our unstable occupation, aren't we?"

"We have to be. You can't be in our business without being driven—if you want to live long."

"But we touched on this before," said Pam. "Why do we bother? Why not just work construction or drive a tubelink train?"

"Well . . . all life here is dangerous. Innocent bystanders get killed all the time. At least we're not sitting targets. We're in on the hunt, too."

"I know I'm hooked on the excitement," Pam said quietly. "But it's a survival trait. Sometimes I think I'd be happy to drop the adrenaline surges altogether if I thought I wouldn't get killed as soon as I let down my guard."

"Yeah, I have some of that, too. But the challenge also means we get to think and use some skills. Driving a tubelink is dangerous, with all the bandits and terrorists shooting them up, but the engineers can't do anything but keep going."

Pam smiled faintly. "You think I'm just going on about nothing?"

"Of course not. What we do isn't nothing. If we're going up against a nepharite on Luna, it's more than just corporate sabotage."

"Maybe we're too late. A major Dark Legion assault could come here any time. For all we know, it could come tomorrow, or any other moment. We don't know if the nepharite is establishing a beachhead or just a spy cell for sabotage—and that's serious enough."

"You make it sound like there's no point going on," said Lane. "You really feel that way?"

"I don't know. But you're the one who asked that question in the Midnight Star, just before we met Yojimbo."

"What did I say?" Lane grinned. "I guess I forgot."

"You asked if I could think of a reason that made this kind of life worth living."

"Oh, yeah. Well, have you?"

"Over the long haul, maybe not, unless it's fighting the Dark Legion."

"In the short term?"

"That depends on you."

"Me? What are you talking about?"

Pam got up and moved over to him, to straddle his lap. She leaned down, brushing his face with her blond hair, and kissed him. Then she drew away slightly, her blue eyes piercing. "Well?"

"Is that what you meant?" Lane put his arms around her. "Why didn't you say so?" He pulled her close again.

The next morning Yojimbo presided in the command center over Team Yojimbo again, crowded once more into the Whiz Kid's little apartment. He had passed out head lamps on straps for everyone to wear if their business took them down into the tunnels again. To his disappointment, however, no new leads had come through the Whiz Kid's cyberspace gang during the night. Now they had to decide exactly how to proceed.

"I think we need more firepower," said Klaus, sitting with his arms folded. "First we have to find this nepharite, then we have to go after him. He won't be here alone. We don't know what kind of unit he's brought with him, but he'll have some serious protection."

"I think that's true," said Fay. "Klaus and I talked about it last night. Our search is almost impossible to conduct as it is. A few more people would increase our chances."

Yojimbo nodded. He did not want to commit himself yet. "Lane?"

"Mm, well, I can't argue with the need for more firepower. A nepharite alone is pretty tough in a fight—I hear they're gigantic. I suppose he's brought a strong unit with him since he's in enemy territory."

"Pam?"

"It makes sense to me. We need help finding him, and then we'll need help fighting him. No question about those two facts over the long haul."

"I see." Yojimbo looked around at all of them. "My fear is that as our team gets larger, the danger of a security breach grows, as well."

"Among us, we know lots of free-lancers," said Pam. "I'm sure we can come up with a few more trustworthy people. We know the ones to avoid."

"It is not just a matter of trust," said Yojimbo. "Accidents occur—inadvertant slips, a gesture or comment made in the presence of the wrong individual."

"That's true, too," said Lane.

"What's the point of finding this nepharite if we don't have the power to kill him?" Klaus demanded. "And worrying about a security leak when we can't even find him hardly matters; if he learns about us, maybe he'll come looking for us. It'll be easier to find him."

Yojimbo saw that everyone laughed except him. Apparently this was funny in a way he could not see. He hesitated, wondering if he had misunderstood something.

"That's a joke, Yojimbo," Fay said gently, smiling at him. "Nobody wants the nepharite to come hunting us. But it would make finding him easier, wouldn't it?"

"We would be very vulnerable," said Yojimbo, still puzzled.

"Never mind," said Lane, grinning. "Look, how many people can we add comfortably for you?"

"I prefer none."

"Oh, perfect," Klaus muttered.

Fay put a hand on his arm. "We should be able to compromise. Say Klaus and I want to start by adding four more team members. Would you accept two?"

"Not at this time," said Yojimbo. "Security is more important than expansion, at least for now."

"I have no interest in a suicide mission," Klaus growled. "If you're not going to listen to the rest of us—"

"This is not a group decision," Yojimbo said formally, stopping Klaus with a hard stare. "I am the leader of Team Yojimbo and your employer. You may resign if you wish, but I am not obligated to accept requirements or conditions from any of you. I ask you opinions for my own information. As former military veterans, you understand lines of authority. Klaus, do you wish to resign at this time?"

Klaus drew in a deep breath and looked away, shaking his head.

"Anyone else?" Yojimbo asked.

No one spoke.

"Today I will accompany Fay and Klaus. We will stake

out the Brotherhood's Tower and try to pick up a sign of activity concerned with the mystic, or some word about him on the street. Lane and Pam, I recommend that you return to the site of Fay and Klaus's fight with the heretic. Do any of you have any questions?"

"Why don't *we* go back to the scene of our fight?" Fay asked carefully.

"You may have been seen by other heretics or some other Dark Legion member," said Yojimbo. "If they recognize you, they may either ambush you or tail you back here. Lane and Pam will not be associated with your fight by any witnesses."

"Logical," said Fay. "It's all right with me."

"Let's hit the streets," said Pam.

The Tower of the Brotherhood rose thousands of meters from the terraformed surface of Luna, a monument of black stone and glass festooned with scowling, frowning, and laughing gargoyles of every shape and size. Luna City in fact had first grown outward from the tower in circles and ripples, leaving it the heart of Luna City forever after. Yojimbo, Fay, and Klaus first walked past it several times on the crowded street, conducting recon of the crowd and nearby towers of the megacorporations such as the Reading Palace of Imperial.

As usual, most of the people in the immediate area wore Brotherhood tunics or armor of one sort or another as they pursued their daily routines. However, Yojimbo saw that they were not particularly excited or determined; if anything, they looked bored. No one in the crowd seemed to be conducting their own surveillance, either, which meant that Yojimbo's squad could settle in one spot for a while. He chose a location near the Reading Palace, where they could see the main doors of the Brotherhood tower easily.

"I'm not convinced we're going to learn anything this way," said Fay. "If the Brotherhood is conducting a search for the missing mystic on Luna, they've probably kept it a highly secure secret."

"I agree," said Klaus. "They will have assigned their best undercover agents to find him."

"What type of Brotherhood follower would that be?" Yojimbo asked.

"Mortificators, their professional assassins, would be best," said Klaus.

"No, I disagree," said Yojimbo. "The Brotherhood would not want to kill a mystic who had mastered his art. They would want to retrieve him."

"Maybe you're thinking too much in the mold of Mishima," said Fay.

"What do you mean?"

"The Brotherhood will have its own reasons for its actions," said Fay. "You're used to Mishima policies, the same way I'm accustomed to Cybertronic values. But when I was with Cybertronic, I had to deal with some Brotherhood liaison, too. So did Klaus."

Yojimbo nodded thoughtfully. "What do you think of the situation, then?"

"If the Brotherhood knows that a nepharite has arrived on Luna, the mortificators would certainly be after him," said Klaus. "Not necessarily to kill him, but because mortificators are the Brotherhood's specialists in hunting specific humans. I wonder if they know about the nepharite."

"If so, I think the Brotherhood would have mobilized heavily and might have announced this alarm publicly," said Fay. "That seems like Brotherhood policy to me."

"We have no evidence that the Brotherhood has learned of the nepharite," said Yojimbo. "If they do know, they must have chosen to keep it quiet. However, we must return to the job at hand."

"Meaning what?" Klaus asked.

"Tracking the mystic."

"Finding the mystic calls for stealth and search," said Fay. "I think some mortificators are probably already on the job, because that's their specialty. Maybe they have orders to bring him back alive. I know they're normally assassins, but the main issue for them is results."

"I will accept this possibility," said Yojimbo. "However, mortificators are very difficult to locate since their business is secrecy. We cannot find them on our own. Who would be able to find them?"

"Their superior," said Klaus. "Whoever gave them their orders."

"That would be an Inquisitor majoris," said Fay. "A Senior Inquisitor."

"How can we get access to someone like that?" Yojimbo asked. "Can we locate the exact Inquisitor majoris we want?"

"I doubt it," said Fay, shaking her head. "Dealing with someone of that rank will be difficult and getting information almost impossible. They're completely committed to the Brotherhood."

"I wonder if we could kidnap one to get some information," said Klaus.

"I don't think we'd gain anything," said Fay. "A Senior Inquisitor would die before revealing important information. But maybe we can use a ruse of some kind."

"What do you have in mind?" Yojimbo asked.

"I don't know yet. But we might think of a way to draw an Inquisitor to us."

"Maybe I have an idea," said Yojimbo suddenly. "I want to call the Whiz Kid to give him some instructions. Then I'll brief you."

CHAPTER 13

Lane and Pam located the spot in the back alleys where Fay and Klaus had fought the heretic. They wore their head lamps strapped to their heads, illuminating the dimly lit area. The heretic's body was gone, but that meant nothing; one of the corporate crews working nearby had probably disposed of it.

The air here was humid from leaking steam. Pedestrians had returned to the main streets in the neighborhood, but it remained more sparsely populated than most of Luna City. No one had come near them since they had arrived.

"I watched the people around us carefully on the main street," said Pam, looking at Lane in the shadows. "I don't think anybody has taken any special notice of us."

"I haven't taken notice of anyone else, either," said Lane. "I'm not sure this is much of a lead—what are we going to do now?"

"We can either patrol the neighborhood and ask questions or lie low and try to spot something," said Pam. "Which one do you prefer?"

Lane glanced around the alley, throwing the beam from his head lamp forward jerkily. Up ahead, in the direction Fay reported the heretic had been fleeing, the alley opened on another street, a dark narrow one. Some refuse had been dumped there, old machine parts and rags.

"Let's check that street."

Pam walked point up the alley. They found the next street deserted. Only a few lights illuminated the blocks in each direction, giving a pale glow to columns of steam leaking from vents in the streets and at the base of abandoned warehouses and factories.

"The heretic was running in this direction. Let's stake out this spot."

Pam grinned wryly, nodding at the heap of filthy rags around the discarded machine parts. "Hide in the garbage, you mean? I can hardly wait."

"That's just a suggestion."

"I'm kidding. Let's do it."

They both switched off their head lamps to avoid attracting attention with the lights. Then, with the familiarity of long experience, they arranged a camouflaged site. They moved the machine parts in a way that gave them a place to sit among them, then piled rags in a formation that allowed them to see out without being spotted easily. After that, they settled into their positions and waited.

"This was boring duty on Mars," said Pam. She sighed, looking up the street. "I have a feeling it's going to be boring duty here, too."

"It's all a matter of luck," said Lane. "But we usually saw what we needed to see on Mars."

"On Mars we knew where the front was. And we had some idea of the enemy's goals. Here, we don't even know what *we're* doing, let alone the other side."

Lane laughed. "Yeah, that's true. But I don't think we should go around asking questions. Word is more likely to reach the heretics about us than the reverse."

"So are we going to track everybody we see going up and down this street?"

"Maybe so."

Pam shrugged, with a wry smile. "All right."

Lane glanced up and down the street also. No one was in sight. He turned back to Pam. "Should we talk about last night?"

"If you want."

"We don't have to."

"Do you mean, has our partnership changed?" Pam looked at him calmly.

"I guess that's the question."

"In the Banshees this happened to people from time to time. We were used to it."

"We aren't in the military anymore. Now we actually

live here, and no one will transfer us. We'll be here in Luna City long after this job's over."

"Whatever works for both of us is fine with me," said Pam. "We can call it a temporary interlude, or . . ." She shrugged. "Anything. The question was, what makes living this life worth it?"

"My answer is, last night does." Lane looked at her soberly. "Not much else has, I'll tell you that."

She laughed lightly. "That's good enough for me."

A dark shape crossed a white plume of steam up the street, drawing Lane's attention. He motioned to Pam, who turned to look. Now the figure was lost in darkness again.

Neither of them moved or spoke. After several moments the silhouette of a single human passed another plume of steam. Then they lost sight of the stranger again.

Lane and Pam waited patiently. Soon they had seen the solitary figure move into the light of a single lamp, then pass them down the street, away from the tubelink station. No one else had appeared.

"Follow him?" Pam whispered.

"Might as well."

"He might just be some scavenger, minding his own business. Maybe he likes it down here."

"Maybe. But he's moving into an area where no one else wants to go. Let's check it out."

"Adrenaline rush," Pam muttered, with a wry smile. "Here we go."

This time Lane led Pam, moving slowly and quietly through the shadows. He stayed behind the stranger, on the opposite side of the street. Then Lane heard a squeak of rusty hinges and the distinctive clank of heavy steel against pavement.

"Access hatch," Pam whispered. "He's going down into a maintenance tunnel under the street."

Lane waited patiently until he heard the loud clank of the hatch cover being swung back into place over the stranger's head. Now that their quarry was out of sight, they walked quickly toward the source of the sound in the shadows, their CAR-24s held forward in ready position.

They reached it without incident and saw in the dim light that it was fully closed.

"We can't go down there without being heard," said Pam. "That cover will make too much noise, even if we're careful. If he's dangerous—heretic or not—he'll be lying in wait for us."

Lane nodded. "Come on." He jogged on down the street, looking around for another hatch. About fifty meters away, he reached another one.

"We'll have to be careful with this one, too," said Pam. "The sound will carry very well underground. Once we're below, we'll hiss to signal each other."

Lane nodded. Routinely used by free-lancers, a quiet hissing sound usually passed as leaking steam. Together, they lifted the cover silently. They set it aside with a quiet clank. Pam shifted her CAR-24 into position and started down the rusting metal ladder.

When Lane heard a quick hiss from below, he followed her. He left the hatch open, knowing he could not risk closing it quietly. At the bottom of the ladder Pam pointed silently up one of the tunnels. He nodded and let her lead. They might not be able to find the stranger now that they had given up sight of him to enter the maze of tunnels at this location.

Pam moved quickly but quietly, even on the hard paved floor of the tunnel. Lane followed her, moving at first by the dim light from the open hatch behind them. When the light grew fainter, Pam trailed one hand on the wall as she advanced. Lane did the same.

Now Pam turned a couple of corners, still working her way back toward the hatch their quarry had used. After the second turn Lane heard quiet voices speaking somewhere through the zigzags up ahead. They both slowed down.

Soon they were moving forward in complete darkness. Lane held one hand lightly on the center of Pam's back and kept the other on his CAR-24. Finally, she stopped, just before turning one more corner. Faint light came around it, and the voices were clear enough to hear now.

"Jaxel, you've known mystics in the past," a woman

said sternly. "Why can't you find Honorius? Or at least find a clue to where he is?"

"Well, *I* don't have mystic powers," a man whined in a high voice.

"None of us has done very well," said another man. "Where is Montez? Maybe he has learned something."

"Maybe he's disappeared, too, Carlo," said the woman. "Yesterday Pilus vanished from this neighborhood. No one can tell me what happened to him. We should stop meeting here. I think people are on to us."

"Pilus brought it on himself," said Carlo. "He kept using his powers on people down on this level without killing them. Word got out pretty fast. I imagine some free-lancer finally got him."

"How can anybody find a crazy mystic?" Jaxel whined again. "A crazy guy can't be predicted. Ragathol ought to know that. What can we do?"

"Watch your mouth," said the woman. "We are rewarded for our service."

"Well, where is Montez?" Jaxel pouted. "Should we wait all day?"

Lane stepped back from Pam slightly. If the enemy was about to disperse, then he and Pam would need to maneuver. He gripped his CAR-24 in both hands.

Suddenly, a wave of terror swept over him and the blackness surrounded him.

"Fire!" Lane screamed in a panic. "They know we're here!" He could not fire forward without hitting Pam, but he heard her CAR-24 chatter in front of him.

"They know now," Pam muttered angrily, as she continued to fire.

Lane felt a flash of pain consume his entire body, causing him to double up and turn, falling into a crouch. Yet he realized, even as he fell, that the heretics in front of Pam had shown no sign in their speech that they knew they were being scouted. The heretic hitting him with psychic Dark Gifts was probably the missing one named Montez, coming from another direction.

Gritting his teeth against the pain, he squeezed the trigger of his CAR-24 and swept the narrow tunnel behind him widely with fire. Instantly, the pain and fear left him.

In the shadows, he could not see what he had hit, but now he could detect the faint light coming from the tunnel in front of Pam.

However, Pam had stopped firing. Instead, she had spun back toward Lane, staring in mystification at the walls, toward him, in all directions, without seeming to see anything. She stumbled against the wall, banged her head on it.

"What's wrong?" Lane asked urgently, pushing the barrel of her CAR-24 away.

"I . . . Can't you see? Hold still!"

"Don't fire, whatever you do." Lane figured her vision had been distorted in some way. Pushing past her, he swung his CAR-24 around the corner without exposing himself and sprayed the tunnel ahead.

Another wave of fear struck him. He continued to fire, aware that he would have to reload in a moment. Pam was in no shape to give covering fire. He flailed behind him with one hand, hoping to grab her CAR-24.

Instead, he felt nothing. When he turned to look, the walls seemed to melt in the dim light and run like liquid. The tunnel down which they had come began to ripple and grow narrow. Even the floor began to pulse wildly, developing into waves. He lost his balance and fell.

Even on his back, he managed to clutch his CAR-24 again and feel for the trigger. However, it was empty. Around him the walls bulged and flattened again. He could only watch, unable to get his feet under him.

Finally Lane realized that this was what Pam saw, too, and that it was not really happening. He clamped his eyes shut, blocking out the visions, and felt more carefully for his CAR-24 to reload. A single pair of footsteps came running up the tunnel behind them, however, and he doubted he would have time to reload before the heretic was on top of him.

He slammed the magazine into place just as the footsteps rounded the corner. Opening his eyes, he saw only a blurry human figure standing over him, rippling and shifting in front of him. Lane fumbled the CAR-24 into position, but before he could fire, another weapon chattered, also from the direction Pam and Lane had taken to get here, firing high.

The figure standing over him staggered back and fell. Lane's vision cleared instantly. He looked back down the tunnel, keeping his CAR-24 down.

A man and a woman advanced quickly out of the shadows, holding weapons forward. The man was tall and burly, running clumsily. He held a CAR-24, which he had apparently just fired; a big Gehenna Puker, the incinerator of the Doomtroopers, bounced on a strap on his back.

A lithe, slender woman jogged after him, carrying a Bauhaus MP-105 handgun. They both wore light armor and helmets of Capitol design, though he saw they wore no logos. Obviously, they were a Doomtrooper unit.

In years past, the megacorporations had formed the Cartel in order to work out their differences and resist the Dark Legion. Corruption and incompetence had prevented it from serving the former purpose, but the Cartel had created Doomtroopers specifically to fight the Dark Legion in the field. They customarily fought in pairs, one a support combat trooper carrying heavy weapons and the other a close combat specialist, trained in light weapons, stealth, and personal combat. Now the two strangers moved past Pam and Lane, policing the tunnel forward of them.

Even recovering from his disorientation, Lane recognized the fine, delicate features of the woman. She was Skippa Hull, a former lover of his. Their romance had been brief, during his first tour with the Martian Banshees, and had ended angrily when her tour with them was up.

Lane switched on his head lamp. He pushed himself to his feet and took Pam's hand, pulling her up. Then they followed the other two.

"All clear," said the man up ahead. He looked down at the body of a male heretic. "Three dead, altogether. You got two, I got one. All male."

"We owe you," said Pam. "Pam Afton and Lane Chung. The enemy were all heretics."

"Thought so. I'm Vic Baer. My partner is Skippa Hull." He smiled grimly, his features large and fleshy.

Pam nodded politely. Skippa nodded in turn to both of them. Lane saw that she gave no indication of having known him in the past. He decided to follow her lead.

"One got away," said Lane. "The first two guys were talking to a woman when we came up. Then another man surprised us from behind."

"The woman's gone," Skippa confirmed.

"Glad you came along," Lane said casually. "What brought you down here?"

"We were following the heretic who came up behind you," said Vic.

"The one he shot down almost right on top of you," said Skippa.

"You were following him? Why?" Pam looked back and forth at them.

"We heard rumors yesterday that a heretic was down here," said Vic. "Then we got here this morning, and someone told us a heretic was killed here yesterday. One of the work crews down here burned the body."

Lane was puzzled. He had always known the Doomtroopers to fight as regular military troops, not as urban assassins. "The Doomtroopers assigned you down here?"

CHAPTER 14

"Not hardly." Vic shook his head. "We're free-lance now, and desperate for some work."

"We're hoping to attract some attention," said Skippa, still acting as though she had never met Lane before. "If we can get a reputation for eliminating some heretics, maybe we'll get a job somehow."

"But you used to be Doomtroopers, didn't you?" Pam asked, nodding toward the Gehenna Puker on Vic's back. "That's an incinerator."

"Yes, we were," said Vic bitterly. "We just got drummed out by the Cartel a few weeks ago for insubordination."

"We used to be Martian Banshees," said Lane. "And I have an independent streak myself. Want to tell us about it?"

Vic and Skippa glanced at each other uncertainly.

"We won't press you," said Pam. "But if you're looking for work, people will want to know your background."

"I say we tell them," said Vic. "I'm proud of what we did, not ashamed of it."

"All right," said Skippa. "We were advancing on a reputed Dark Legion outpost on Mars. Then it turned out our superiors had been ordered—or bought off—to hold back. We were ordered to withdraw."

"Why?" Pam asked in surprise.

"Turns out somebody wanted to let the Dark Legion run all over an adjacent outfit in order to observe the enemy's tactics," Vic said grimly. "We disobeyed orders to withdraw. When we led some of our other units in a flank attack against the Dark Legion, we destroyed them—and the Cartel ran us out of the service for it." He unstrapped his helmet and pulled it off, revealing a bristling brown buzz cut. "That's what you find in the Doomtroopers nowadays. The troops can fight, but the Cartel is corrupt from top to bottom. They don't care about us."

Lane glanced at Skippa, who looked away. When her tour with the Banshees had ended, she had signed up with the Doomtroopers, instead, saying that she wanted to fight the Dark Legion, not other humans. Lane had tried to tell her that the Cartel was corrupt, but she had called him a liar and a sellout to Capitol. They had not seen each other since then.

"So you followed the last heretic down here?" Pam asked. "Did he come down a hatch that was already open?"

"That's right," said Vic. "We thought that was odd, until we saw that others had come down just ahead of us. But we've answered your questions. How about telling us what you're doing down here?"

"We owe you that," said Lane.

"I know we do," said Pam. "But we have orders to maintain privacy, too."

"Orders?" Vic asked.

"Yeah." Lane grinned. "We're free-lancers working for a small team, checking out rumors of the Dark Legion here in Luna City. And we have orders to keep it quiet so we don't make the rumors any worse. But you already know heretics are here, so I don't see how telling you that much makes any difference."

"What was your military record like before that last incident?" Pam asked.

"Good," said Vic. "Solid, not flashy."

Pam turned to Lane. "What do you think?"

Lane knew she was asking about convincing Yojimbo to hire them. "Well, I repeat, we owe them. And they're already doing the kind of work we need." He turned to Vic and Skippa. "You two want to meet our employer?"

"Sure," said Vic. "Sounds like our kind of job. Like I say, we need the work. And we know how to keep quiet, if that's the big question. We don't take any chances where the Dark Legion is concerned."

"Our boss was reluctant to expand the team," said Pam. "But we really need more people."

Skippa shrugged. "Whatever."

"We'll take them back to the Midnight Star and have Yojimbo meet us there," said Lane. "We can put in a good word for you, but it's not our call in the end."

"Understood," said Vic.

"Let's search the bodies for a clue to their identities," said Pam. "Then we'll contact Yojimbo."

As they checked the bodies of the heretics, Lane glanced several times at Skippa. However, he still said nothing to her directly. After all the time that had passed, he was no more than curious about her.

They found nothing of any use. By this time the heretic who had escaped was long gone through the maze of tunnels. Pam led the group back up to the street.

By the time Yojimbo got a message from Pam to meet her squad at the Midnight Star, he was discouraged after a long, fruitless day. That morning, Yojimbo had asked the Whiz Kid to have his cyberspace gang plant false reports of sightings of the missing mystic throughout cyberspace. All of them suggested that the mystic was moving toward the docking ports, down in the tunnels.

Yojimbo had then taken Fay and Klaus to the tunnels below docks in the hope of spotting mortificators drawn to the area by the rumors. They had remained on stakeout the rest of the day and well into the evening, with no success. Finally, Yojimbo had taken them back to the command center, where the message from Pam was waiting with the Whiz Kid. She had not been able to transmit to him directly while he was down in the tunnels.

In the Midnight Star Lane turned on the sonic disruptor in a corner and Pam eagerly introduced their new companions. As Yojimbo listened to their credentials and background, he noticed a certain aloofness between Lane and Skippa, but they did not express any outright objections to working together. Fay and Klaus said nothing, listening patiently. Finally Pam completed her pitch, asking him to hire them.

"I wish to clarify something," said Yojimbo. "Pam says

your superiors in the Doomtroopers ordered you to let some of your comrades in arms be sacrificed to the enemy?"

"That's right," said Skippa. She unfastened her helmet and took it off, shaking out thick, rich brown hair fashioned in a blunt cut similar to Pam's.

"And you willfully disobeyed your direct orders?"

"We did, and we're proud of it," said Vic. "I know it isn't military, but we fought for a corrupt outfit."

Yojimbo suppressed a smile. Normally, he would not want to hire veterans who had deliberately violated direct orders, but their story appealed to him. It reminded him of his own experience with the Mishima Elite. Like Lane and Pam they answered to an inner code of their own, instead of just following orders.

"All right," said Yojimbo. "Lane and Pam want to work with you, so I will accept their judgment. I will pay you equally with everyone else."

"Good enough," said Vic.

"Yeah," said Klaus. "We need the help."

"You need a full briefing," said Yojimbo. "First we'll have dinner and get acquainted. Then we'll return to the command center to bring you up to date. Welcome to Team Yojimbo."

Penyon Cerna crept quietly through the tunnels below Luna City. The narrow, yellowish beam of the lamp he wore on a chain around his neck bounced against his chest, illuminating the filthy tunnels as he moved and sent rats, bugs, and other unrecognizable vermin scurrying away from him. He hoped anxiously to find some sign of Honorius, the mystic whom he sought. Penyon's master, Ragathol, might then reward him with greater powers than he now possessed. Penyon was a heretic, newly initiated and eager to please.

However, Penyon had no idea how to find a mystic. In fact, he was not entirely sure what a mystic was, though he knew they usually belonged to the Brotherhood.

"Penyon Cerna, this is your new life," he muttered to himself.

At his initiation, he had been given a single psychic

Dark Gift, of invoking paralyzing pain in others. He had been ordered to use it at his initiation against another heretic to demonstrate his ability, but he had used it only once against a real enemy. It was all so new.

Until recently, Penyon had toiled in the Capitol warehouses, working for very little pay. On the side, he had stolen stuff on the black market for his supervisor. His only friend had been a young man called Snazzer, who used no last name. He had handled their computer records and sometimes spent many hours in cyberspace.

When Penyon's boss had found out he had held out some cash on a sale, his boss had threatened him. Snazzer, already a heretic, had offered to bring Penyon to Ragathol. In fear, Penyon had turned into a heretic. Then, together, he and Snazzer had killed their boss. Snazzer now ran that warehouse and the black market operation, still reporting to Ragathol as he always had.

Penyon was satisfied, however. He hated the warehouse and the black market. Now that he served Ragathol, he cared nothing about his old life. His master wanted him to serve all the time, and let Penyon live in the caverns that composed Ragathol's home on Luna.

Discouraged, Penyon worked his way back toward the caverns of his master through the tunnels. He had reached the general vicinity when he heard footsteps running toward him. Then he saw a narrow, yellow light bouncing and bobbing from around a corner as someone approached. Cautiously, he stopped and prepared to use his Dark Gift.

When the figure turned the corner, however, he recognized her.

"Halala," Penyon called. "What's wrong?"

The woman, dressed in a loose, flowing robe with a hood thrown back, stopped and stared at him. When she recognized him, she looked behind her, instead. In the beam of Penyon's own light, her straight brown hair was lank and dirty, her profile outlining a heavy brow ridge and a sharp, slightly hooked nose. Then, finally, she relaxed and walked toward him.

"We have lost some of our number," she said quietly.

"Jaxel, Carlo, and Montez. We were to meet and discuss what we had learned, but someone ambushed us."

Penyon looked at her in shock. "What of the Dark Gifts? With so many of you, the enemy should have been blinded, struck with terror, disoriented—"

"They were," she said coldly. "But only Montez saw them at first. When the shooting began, the rest of us were caught off guard. I was lucky to get away."

Penyon nodded. "Did they know who you were? I mean, that we follow a Dark master?"

"I don't see how. As I think back, we were only talking about why Montez was late, and how Pilus vanished yesterday. They were probably bandits looking for an easy score and happened to hear us talking."

"That's good."

"Yes. But tell me now. Have you learned anything about Honorius?"

"No."

"No? Nothing at *all*?" Her eyebrows rose, and her eyes widened.

"Uh . . . no." Penyon felt his heart pounding. Halala was the senior heretic in Ragathol's service. She had many more Dark Gifts than Penyon and could punish him with any of them if she wished.

"You are fortunate, Penyon. Your incompetence will not harm us today because I learned something useful. In future, however, I suggest you apply more effort."

Penyon said nothing.

"Before we were ambushed, if Montez had shown up on time, I was going to report a street rumor I heard. Some people on the tubelink were talking about a crazy man levitating in a back alley in the Mishima warehouse district."

"Really?" Penyon was excited. "That must be a mystic—you've done it! You found him!"

"Easy, Penyon. It may be a false rumor, or a con artist pulling a hoax. Even a different mystic, though I doubt it. We will see."

"Yeah! I bet that's him!"

Halala showed no such excitement. "Keep quiet, then, and follow me."

* * *

After dinner Lane sat through Yojimbo's meeting at the command center impatiently. The main task, of course, was to brief their new team members, and Lane learned nothing important. When the briefing ended, however, he saw a chance to speak to Skippa, if he could first prevent her from leaving.

As everyone stood up, Lane leaned toward Pam and whispered. "Would you distract Vic for a few minutes? I want to ask Skippa something. I'm afraid she'll leave for the night unless Vic's too involved to leave."

"Sure." Pam smiled and patted Lane's arm. "Glad to help. Just fill me in later, okay?"

"Sure."

Pam moved over to Vic and nodded toward his Gehenna Puker. "Would you show me how this incinerator works? I've always wondered about them."

"I'd be glad to. You mean now?"

"If you wouldn't mind."

"All right."

Lane moved next to Skippa, who was putting her helmet on. "Step outside with me a minute."

She glanced at him in surprise, but said nothing.

"Just for a second."

Skippa turned and walked to the door. Lane followed. The other team members were all talking to each other and paid no attention.

Just outside the door, Skippa stopped and folded her arms. "What is it, Lane? Let's get this over with."

"Look, I don't want a hassle. I just wondered why you never acknowledged that we know each other."

Skippa shrugged and said nothing.

"Come on." Lane smiled gently. "That's not much of an answer."

She just glared at him.

"Look, is Vic jealous or something? Are you personally involved as well as partners? I just want to know what you want."

Skippa sighed. "No, it's not Vic. We're involved, but he's all right with this kind of thing. I just ... didn't know what to say to you, so I didn't say anything."

"You could have just said hello."

She started to smile, but fought it. "All right, I messed that up."

"Is something wrong? We don't have to be more than colleagues on this team, but I still want to know how you want to handle this."

"Well." Skippa looked out toward the street. "All right. I should never have joined the Doomtroopers, except that Vic is real decent. You were right about the corruption at the command level—and sometimes even lower. But I still think that fighting the Dark Legion is a lot more important than fighting Mishima on Mars."

"I agree with you. And I'm sure you agree it's more than ironic that we're working for a former Mishima Elite veteran who fought against us on Mars."

"Yeah." She finally grinned. "I thought of that. It is kind of funny."

"The important part of all this is, we agree that fighting the Dark Legion is our top priority."

"Yeah." She nodded. "That's right."

"So we can work together comfortably?"

"Yes, we can."

"Good."

"So now it's your turn. Are you and Pam just partners, or more than that?"

Lane smiled and shook his head. "That's not entirely clear at the moment. That is, we've been just partners, but maybe . . ."

"I get the idea. Come on, let's go back inside." She grinned crookedly. "Pam ought to know how to fire a Gehenna Puker by now."

CHAPTER 15

Titus Gallicus, Senior Inquisitor of the Brotherhood, rode a moving skywalk through the evening shadows with Vitus Marius, a mortificator. They were both tall and slender, but Titus wore a long, white tunic with the Brotherhood logo proclaiming his loyalty and his station. Vitus, of course, wore the plain black outfit, with a cloak, of the professional assassin. On his torso he wore a combat harness with a grappling hook, cable, and several grenades. He also wore his mortificator helmet with its targeting systems. At his belt he carried his Punisher heavy-caliber handgun and his mortis sword.

They watched the pedestrians push and shove their way up and down the street four stories below them, by the light of dim and uneven streetlights. Above them the tall, narrow shapes of darkened office buildings shadowed them. Titus heard unseen vermin scuttling around in the darkness.

Below, to their left, several people were brawling; around a corner Titus heard the snapping of handgun fire. Nowhere, however, did they see any sign of a renegade mystic. Titus had also assigned a few other mortificators to spread throughout Luna City with strict orders to capture him, not kill him.

"This is hopeless, sir," said Vitus. He adjusted the mortis sword at his belt. "Luna City simply has too many people in it. We'll never find one crazy man without some kind of lead to follow."

"We know exactly what he looks like," said Titus coldly. He gazed with approval at a statue of an angry, avenging angel hanging from the seventh-story ledge of a tower across the street. "I met him many times person-

ally. Everyone assigned to find him has seen his like-
ness."

"He could hide out of sight anywhere. A mystic who
has developed his art will be very clever."

"Intelligent, yes, but unfocused."

"Sir?"

"The few accounts we have of Honorius's behavior just
before he left his normal duties report that he is crazy. He
showed no sign of wishing to flee or hide." Titus frowned
sternly at his assistant. "You were briefed on this matter.
Have you forgotten it so soon?"

"No, sir." The mortificator looked back at Titus, re-
spectful but unafraid. "I'm simply not convinced."

"Hm." Titus glanced down at the street below again.
He did not like working with someone who did not fear
him. However, mortificators were often that way. Their
work as assassins required it.

"So you think the accounts are wrong?"

"I believe he may have fooled those around him in order to facilitate his escape."

"I see."

"In that case he may well have a deliberate plan of
flight, and even accomplices to help him hide."

"Honorius was always eccentric," said Titus. "That,
too, was in your briefing, mortificator."

"I am aware of this," Vitus said stiffly.

"It doesn't show." Titus held his head high, glancing
arrogantly at Vitus. "I will continue; pay attention this
time. Honorius also showed an interest in the mystics
long before he began the study. I believe he is, even
among mystics, one of a kind."

"The safest move for the Brotherhood is to assassinate
Honorius as soon as we locate him. Whatever he is planning, he may attempt it soon. Do not risk letting him escape a second time."

"You have your orders—to apprehend him. Do not fail
your orders." Titus turned and glared straight into Vitus's
eyes. "Do not violate your orders."

Vitus finally glanced away.

They reached the end of the skywalk and stepped off
onto a narrow balcony that ran around the edge of a large

building. Titus kept walking at a fast pace to remind Vitus who was in charge, even though they were no longer looking below. The mortificator worked to keep up.

A large rat with glowing red eyes tensed, watching them uncertainly as they passed.

"You may not kill Honorius before I have questioned him," said Titus. "I must know what he learned about the art of mysticism first."

"Why are you so certain that he has learned something of value? Perhaps he is simply a crazy man who has lost all ability to understand his surroundings."

"And now, Vitus, you contradict yourself. If that is all he has become, then surely you have no need to assassinate him on sight, eh?" Titus stopped and smiled triumphantly at his assistant.

Vitus smiled in return, knowing he had been caught. "I only raise possibilities, Inquisitor."

Titus rested his hands on the cold, rusted steel railing of the balcony. Again he looked down four stories to the street below, which was little different from the view offered by the skywalk. Drab, gray buildings lined it on both sides and violent, corrupt people jammed the thoroughfare. Still, all he and his mortificators needed was a single sighting of Honorius to get this search moving quickly.

"So, Vitus, do you have any suggestions about how to find this missing mystic?"

"I only serve, sir."

"Yes, that's what I thought. You have nothing." Titus gazed with distaste at the people below him. "I admit, some Inquisitors actually agree with you that he may not be insane, after all. Some suspect that he either wants to sell his information to the highest bidder among the megacorporations or even change sides and join the Dark Legion."

"A mystic . . . becoming that corrupt?" Vitus sounded genuinely startled for the first time.

"Merely another possibility that has been raised. Other Inquisitors think Honorius is too insane to have any plan. That's my own belief."

"If the others are right, he could have left Luna by

now. He could be on Mars, Venus, in space—anywhere. Even back on Earth, if he's crazy enough to want to go."

"If he planned that well, he's not that crazy. However, I did take the precaution of sending mortificators to screen everyone going in and out of the docks. I am sure that Honorius remains on Luna."

"You think he's too insane to have anywhere to go?" Vitus asked.

"Yes."

Lane accepted Pam's invitation to spend the night again. He decided that as long as their new relationship did not interfere with their work, he was comfortable with it. Then, early in the morning, they ate breakfast at a small diner. Yojimbo had instructed the team to meet at the command center again at seven o'clock.

He poked some scrambled eggs with his fork. "This stuff is almost as bad as what the Banshees served."

"Yeah." Pam grinned wryly. "You think the eggs are bad, wait till you try the bacon."

"It's that bad?"

"Well . . . form your own opinion."

"Why did you suggest coming here?"

"It's fairly safe—too poor and uninteresting to attract much trouble. I can put up with the food. Anyhow, you ate Banshee food for two tours; I only ate it for one. So don't try to tell me you're too good for this."

"Naw." Lane laughed. "But, look, I'm not looking forward to another briefing in Yojimbo's so-called command center. Want to strike out on our own today, blue eyes?"

Pam smiled impishly. "Not enough adrenaline for you in Team Yojimbo meetings?"

He laughed again. "You could put it that way."

"Well, Chung, what do you have in mind?"

"I just think we're wasting time with all this rigid organization. Suppose we call Yojimbo and tell him we're pursuing our own plan of action today to scare up leads. All he can do is say no, and *his* instructions haven't shown much solid progress."

"It's all right with me. But I have to admit, we blew

our firefight with the heretics. If we had captured one alive, we might have learned something."

"Too late now." Lane tasted the bacon and made a face. "Yuck."

"You think Yojimbo will agree? And what do we do if he refuses? I don't think he'll accept a frivolous rejection of his instructions."

"Yeah, I know. I think we should follow his orders—after all, he's paying us, and we don't have anything specific to follow. But we can still make our suggestion."

"Sounds good to me." Pam hesitated, finishing her own eggs. "How much is Yojimbo's structured arrangement a problem for you? You never were much for spit and polish in the Banshees."

"You know, I respect Yojimbo's dedication to his ideals. He really believes in what he does, and that's more than most Banshee officers did. And the Whiz Kid's cyberspace sources have been almost our entire intelligence system. I just feel the team isn't getting anywhere. I could accept even more rigidity if it got us results."

"I guess if we had his Mishima background, we'd be used to his system."

"Well, somewhat. But part of his mind-set is deeply cultural. I'm sure it comes from his respect for Bushido and the traditions behind it."

"Whatever it is, it seems to run deep." Pam leaned back in her chair. "I'm finished. You ready?"

"Here goes." Lane unfastened his belt computer and turned on his sonic disruptor for privacy from the other tables. "Lane calling Yojimbo of Team Yojimbo. You read?"

"Yojimbo here."

"Pam and I want to explore some ideas of our own today. We'd like to get right on it."

"Without attending the morning briefing?" Yojimbo sounded surprised.

"Yes, we'd prefer to move right out. We'll save time that way."

"You have a new lead?"

"No, nothing like that. But we have a lot of contacts in

this city, and we want to see if some of them can help. That's one of the reasons you hired us, isn't it?"

"Yes, that is true."

"So it's okay?"

"Yes, I accept this. Please maintain contact if you obtain pertinent intelligence."

"Agreed." Lane shut off and looked at Pam. "All clear, blue eyes. Let's go." He turned off the sonic disruptor and stood up.

They walked out of the little diner into the crowded street. Lane started toward the nearest tubelink station. It was not far.

"Where to?" Pam asked.

"A very swank office in a Capitol tower." Lane grinned. "Better digs than I'll ever work out of."

"Me, too, it sounds like. But who works in this wonderful palace?"

"I've mentioned Royce Calaveri to you, haven't I?"

"I think so. A Banshee who rotated out before I arrived?"

"That's him."

"You never said much else about him. Were you friends?"

"We weren't real close, but we were in the Banshees together through some nasty stuff at the very beginning of my first tour. His time was up long before you joined. A clearheaded, direct guy—no indecision, no hesitation. I was sorry to see him go when he did."

"Have you kept in contact with him?"

"Well, no, not really. I just picked up word on the street. I heard he's a security executive with Capitol now."

"And he's well-positioned to keep tabs on rumors."

"Exactly."

They took the tubelink up to the surface. Royce worked in one of the lesser Capitol towers there, but it was still a magnificent, shiny black edifice, festooned with gaunt, angry gargoyles on the ledges outside every floor. The gleaming tower rose through the terraformed artificial atmosphere toward the shining globe of Earth in the sky.

As Lane and Pam approached the main doors, armed

guards in clean, crisply pressed dark blue Capitol uniforms leveled their CAR-24s at them. In response, Lane moved both his hands away from his weapons. Pam did the same.

"Good day, sir," said one of the guards, a tall, slender man with bristling dark hair. His tone was polite, but he did not move his weapon aside. He resembled some of the gargoyles crouching vulturelike over his head. "You have business here?" His tone betrayed doubt as he looked over their casual clothes.

"Call Royce Calaveri and tell him Lane Chung has come with a friend."

"Is he expecting you?"

"Sooner or later, he was." Lane grinned crookedly, looking the man in the eye. He knew he would get better results if he sounded confident. Royce was the security chief, and these guards reported directly to him. They would not risk insulting people he expected to see.

"By your clothes and your weapons, I'd say you're free-lancers."

"That's right," said Pam. "Former Martian Banshees."

"Like your boss," Lane added.

"Better check, like he says," the guard said to his partner.

The second guard turned to a speaker set into the wall by the door and spoke into it. The first guard glanced at Lane's hands again and then looked at Pam, his gaze moving from her face slowly down the front of her skin-tight gray jumpsuit. She glared back at him, but said nothing.

"The boss said to send them up," the second guard reported. "But to hold their weapons."

Pam glanced at Lane in alarm.

Lane hesitated, but saw no way out of this. They could either walk away or accept Royce's terms. "All right," he said finally, unslinging his CAR-24. "If Royce is this careful with everybody, the building must be very secure." He handed over his Bolter handgun, as well.

When Pam had also surrendered her CAR-24 and Bolter, the guards stood aside.

"Floor fifteen," said the first guard pleasantly. "The elevators are straight ahead."

Lane and Pam walked in silence across the polished lobby floor. A few other very wealthy, well-dressed men in traditional gray and blue suits glanced at them with distaste as they passed. Two women close to Pam's age left one of the elevators; one wore a glittering gold dress slit on one side up to her waist; the other was dressed in a black suit with a ruffled blouse. Both saw Pam and quickly looked away.

As soon as the elevator doors had closed, however, leaving them alone inside, Pam folded her arms uncomfortably and looked at Lane.

"I feel vulnerable without any weapons," she said irritably. "Are you sure this is smart? We don't really need to see this guy."

With a clunking sound and then a hum, the elevator carried them rapidly upward.

"I feel odd, too," said Lane. "But we live on the street. You know that the kind of people who live and work in these megacorporation towers don't have to defend themselves every minute. We've entered a new world. Look at the clothes these people wear."

"Yeah, I know." She sighed. "Maybe I just feel like we don't belong here. But I'd feel better if we had our weapons."

The elevator doors opened on a small foyer encased entirely in thick steel walls. They were spotted with openings for cameras, machine-gun fire, and two incinerators that shot flames in a crossing pattern. Obviously, Royce did not rely only on the guards at the main doors for his own security. A closed door on the left, under one of the incinerators, probably led to a stairwell.

Lane stepped into the foyer first. After a moment a door in the opposite wall opened, and Royce waved them inside. He was a short, stocky man with tousled, dirty blond hair and a big smile. Royce wore a conservative dark blue suit, white shirt, and a red-and-white striped tie.

"Welcome, Lane. And this is?"

"Pam Afton, my partner," said Lane. "She's also a former Banshee."

"Ah! One of the gang, then. Come inside. Drink?"

"Nothing for me," said Lane.

"No, thank you." Pam shook her head politely, looking around.

"All right, then. Come and sit."

Lane followed him into the living area. It was small and comfortable, designed entirely in white. Long curtains covered floor-to-ceiling windows in one wall. The soft, deep carpet gave gently under his feet as he walked to one of the two well-padded white chairs in front of Royce's desk and sat down. Pam settled into the other, and Royce sat in a straight-backed chair behind his desk across from them.

"Well, my hardworking friend," Royce said pleasantly, toying with a small stone globe of Luna on a metal pedestal. The intricately carved gray stone was about the size of a soccer ball. "What's on your mind? Other than a very small reunion of Banshee veterans?"

"Heretics. Maybe necromutants."

"Really?" Royce raised his eyebrows. "The Dark Legion. You two thinking of signing up again? Going back to Mars? Or will it be Venus this time, or the outer planets?"

Lane grinned. "Not hardly."

"No? Where, then?"

"Right here," said Pam, grimly. "Heretics right here on Luna."

Royce stared at her closely, saying nothing.

CHAPTER 16

Lane and Pam quickly brought Royce up to date on the subject. "I seem to violate my orders to keep this quiet every time I meet someone," Lane said wryly. "But you understand the need to avoid panic."

"Of course," said Royce slowly. "It won't be in my interest to send everyone stampeding aimlessly through the streets, running from every suspicious person. I'm a security chief, after all. But I'm not sure I can help you, either."

"I thought everyone heard of heretics and necromutants in Luna City from time to time," said Pam.

"Yes, of course." Royce frowned, sitting forward earnestly. A lock of his tousled hair fell forward. "But I've discounted all of them. So has everyone else I know. None of them ever proved out." He looked back and forth between them, watching their reactions closely.

"That you know of," Lane added.

Royce nodded slowly. "All right, yes. Since you've actually met heretics here recently, I've give you that. Some of the rumors I heard may have been true. But they were just rumors to me."

Lane nodded.

"And I have to remind you that these rumors were floating around long before any of your experiences proved out a few of them. Most of the rumors probably don't have anything behind them."

"Yeah." Lane sighed. "I know. That's what makes our job tough. But some of them will prove out."

"Aw, Lane." Royce pushed himself up and began to pace around the small room. He stopped suddenly and pulled on a cord, drawing open the white curtains to reveal the floor-to-ceiling windows. With a deep sigh he turned and gazed outside.

Startled by Royce's sudden shift in behavior, Lane said nothing. Past Royce, Lane saw Imperial's tall, gleaming Reading Palace and the huge, baroque Brotherhood Cathedral dominating the skyline. All the towers rose in sharp, narrow angles and blocks, black or gray, many topped with spires. Statues of pious, winged angels ringed the upper ledges of the Cathedral, while snarling, angry gargoyles perched on the roof.

"The Brotherhood resists the Dark Legion in every way it can," said Royce. "Its Inquisitors prod and poke into the lives of ordinary people, seeking signs of corruption and weakness. They think that if they can make everyone holy, then the violence and decadence of our society will stop."

Pam glanced at Lane, puzzled. He shook his head for her to remain silent. Like her, he did not understand what Royce was trying to say, but he wanted to let Royce speak.

Without turning, Royce went on. "Lane, why were we fighting in the Martian Banshees for Capitol?"

"For a living," said Lane.

"That's right," Pam added.

"Wrong," said Royce, finally turning to face them. "We were fighting for Capitol so they could sell their products to everyone within the territory we maintained for them. Luna City is the only neutral zone where everyone lives together."

"Well, of course," said Lane. "Capitol pays troops to fight for territory. That's how all the megacorporations work; we know that. But *we* fought to make a living."

"Too many people, Lane. We have too many people. They—we—will accept pay to become cannon fodder because on the street, we're all desperate. Only those who make it in the upper crust here in these towers live the good life. In the meantime Luna City is bareful livable for the masses. You two know; you're on the street yourselves."

"I don't get your point," said Pam. "What does this have to do with looking for heretics and necromutants?"

Royce looked at her for a moment, then turned back to Lane, ignoring her question. "You've never seen me dressed this way before, have you?" He fingered the lapels of his suit.

"No, I never have," said Lane. He decided to go along with Royce to find out where all this was leading. "We spent most of our time together wearing those red and black Martian Banshee camouflage fatigues."

"Consider the change symbolic," said Royce. "Lane, my job will be much easier with fewer free-lancers around, especially good ones like you two who know about a Dark Legion presence. I really do want to keep the city from panicking."

"I don't want to work for you, if that's what you mean," said Lane.

"That's not what I mean."

"Then I don't get it," said Pam.

"Lane, I just want you to know it's all business. It's not personal. You were a great Banshee and a reliable comrade."

Lane still did not follow what he meant. However, he recognized the move Royce made next. Still standing by the window, Royce's right hand reached behind his back, under his suit jacket. That was where a man wearing a suit carried a handgun.

"Move!" As Lane shouted, he kicked both feet against the front of the desk, shoving his chair over backward.

In the same moment Royce pulled out a Bolter handgun from behind his back and fired right over Lane's head.

Lane rolled on the carpet in front of the desk as Royce fired over him again and again; at the same time, Lane heard Pam hit the floor and roll on the other side of him.

Without weapons they both would have to make do with what they could find or be sitting targets. As Royce moved around the far end of the desk to get a better shot, Lane got his hands under the near end and gathered his legs under him. He rose suddenly, lifting his end of the desk to distract Royce. By this time he had lost track of Pam's movements completely.

As Lane stood up, he could hear the various office

items on the desk sliding away. The desk was too heavy
for Lane to flip over on its end on top of Royce, but he
grabbed the right leg and turned the desk on its front, instead, forcing Royce to dodge out of the way. As the desk
crashed to the floor, Lane saw Pam chop the edge of her
hand down on Royce's wrist, forcing his hand to loosen.

The Bolter fell to the floor.

As Pam and Royce grappled, Lane saw the main door
behind them opening. The desk blocked him from reaching the Bolter. Royce's shots had obviously brought
someone coming to help, probably his own security staff.

"Behind you!" Lane shouted. He glanced around for
something to use as a weapon and saw the stone globe of
Luna rolling on the carpet.

Lane bent down and snatched up the globe in both
hands. He knew that he had a very brief advantage over
whoever was coming through the doorway; the newcomer
would have to glance over the room carefully before firing, because Royce was here. Lane raised the heavy globe
over his head.

As a blue-uniformed Capitol security guard kicked
the door open with his CAR-24 forward, Lane heaved the
round stone across the room. Without waiting to see the
result, Lane threw himself across the desk and flung himself on the Bolter lying at his feet of Royce and Pam, who
were wrestling each other to a stalemate in an awkward
shuffle.

The stone globe smashed the forehead of the man in
the doorway with a crunching sound, dropping him
limply. In the same moment two more security guards appeared behind him. Lane snatched up the Bolter and fired
twice, hitting both new guards in the chest before they
could fire.

Above Lane Pam finally yanked herself free of Royce
and swung the edge of one hand hard against his wind-
pipe, crushing it. Royce's eyes bulged and he fell to his
knees, wheezing. Pam grabbed the Bolter out of Lane's
hand and blew out Royce's brains with it, point-blank.

"Nothing personal," she muttered. "Just business. You
were a great Banshee, I'm sure."

Lane leaped to the doorway, alert for more security

guards. None appeared, and he picked up two CAR-24s. He tossed one to Pam, who caught it in her free hand. Then he drew a Bolter out of the holster of the one of the guards and looked at the elevator doors.

They were just closing. Someone on another floor had called the elevator. The noise could not have gone unnoticed on other floors.

"See any stairs?" Pam asked.

Lane stepped into the foyer and yanked open the steel door under one of the incinerators. He saw stairs, but he also heard the pounding of many feet hurrying up toward them. Grimacing, he closed it again. The lock required a key, and they did not have time to search for one.

"Guards are coming up that way, too. We can hold them off in this steel foyer for a while, but that won't help us get out of here. Sooner or later they'll get us." He came back in the apartment and slammed the steel door, then shot a heavy bolt. "This door will stall them, too, but I don't know for how long. Depends on what weapons they bring."

Pam and Lane both glanced around the small office for a way out.

"We're fifteen floors up," said Pam, looking at the tall, vertical windows. "I didn't bring my wire and belt pack this time, we're too high to use it, anyway."

Ceon Reese plodded among the pedestrians on the sidewalk in a Mishima warehouse district. A short, chubby man with unkempt black hair, he normally survived by picking pockets, selling rumors, and lifting small items wherever he found them, to resell on the street. The big money, of course, lay in con games, but Ceon did not have the imagination or acting skills to develop one. Now he was just checking out crowds in different neighborhoods, looking for a way to make a few more Cardinal's crowns somehow.

This warehouse district did not look promising. Too many people were walking too fast, probably on important business of some sort. Ceon picked the most pockets when people got jammed up in crowds, delaying their motion and distracting their attention.

"No go," Ceon muttered to himself. "Might as well find somewhere else to go."

As Ceon headed for the nearest tubelink station, however, he noticed a distinctive white tunic in the crowd ahead of him. The man wearing it was wandering up the sidewalk lazily, gazing around as though he might be lost. Spotting a possible mark, Ceon moved up through the crowd to get closer.

Soon he saw that the man wore a smudged white tunic with the Brotherhood logo on the back. Ceon hurried up alongside him, pretending not to take special notice of his mark. A quick glance showed him that the man was in his midthirties, clean-shaven with medium-length brown hair. The front of his tunic also featured the Brotherhood logo and was somewhat dirtier than the back. He was muttering to himself, too quietly for Ceon to understand.

"What's that you say, sir?" Ceon asked politely, pretending he thought the stranger was speaking to him.

"Let the lamb return to her flock and accept the ram in her stead."

"Uh, yeah? What lamb would that be?"

"The meek must inherit," the other man said calmly.

Ceon knew instantly that he had a sure mark; the guy was crazy. He took the man's arm gently and steered him into an alley between two Mishima warehouses. The alley was narrow and dirty, but deserted.

"I think you're the lamb in this stew," Ceon said cheerfully, patting the man's tunic for valuables. "What have you got on you, pal?"

"To everything, there is a season."

"And this is your season for plucking." Ceon patted the man's other side, but felt nothing.

Calmly unresisting, his mark sank to the broken pavement of the alley, sitting down cross-legged.

Ceon stiffened, alert for a hassle of some sort, but the mark just sat where he landed and closed his eyes. Instead of wasting time on more conversation, Ceon bent down and continued to search him. It was more awkward, now that the man was sitting.

"Come on," Ceon muttered. "You must have something worth taking. I mean, you're certainly some kind of Brotherhood hotshot, right?"

As Ceon shuffled through the mark's clothes, he straightened slowly from his stooped posture. At first he hardly noticed. Then he realized that he was almost standing straight again, even though the mark had not made any obvious effort to stand.

"Hey, how did you get up so high—" Ceon stopped, staring at his mark.

The man in the Brotherhood tunic remained in a cross-legged sitting position, but he had risen off the ground. He now floated over a meter high with absolutely nothing under him. Ceon took a couple of steps backward, terrified.

"Uh . . . hey, pal, I didn't mean any harm, know what I mean?" Ceon felt his heart pounding.

"Judge not that you not be judged," the man said calmly, gazing in the distance somewhere over Ceon's head.

Ceon was ready to run, but the man's placid tone and continuing lack of interest in Ceon made him hesitate. If Ceon could spot anything, it was a chance for a couple of quick Cardinal's crowns to be made on the street. Still watching the Brotherhood man carefully, he moved to the opening of the alley and waved at the closest pedestrians.

"Step right up!" Ceon shouted. "Come and see the miracle! Five Cardinal's crowns each to see the religious, uh, expert! See the man from the Brotherhood perform a miracle! Only five Cardinal's crowns!"

Lane looked around Royce's office one more time. If it had any more exits besides the elevator and the stairwell off the steel foyer, they were hidden. He and Pam did not have time to conduct a search.

"Window," said Pam. "It's all we have."

"Go."

Pam raised the Bolter he had thrown her and shot out one of the tall windows, starting at the top; each snap of the pistol was followed by a crash of shattered glass. She ran to the windowsill, holstering the Bolter. Lane slung his CAR-24 out of his way and followed her.

On the ledge just below the window a huge stone gargoyle crouched with folded wings as it laughed wickedly at the street fifteen stories below. Pam climbed awkwardly through the sharp shards of broken glass and over the carved wings. Carefully, she made her way along the ledge, which was almost a meter wide.

As Lane waited for her to move along the ledge, he heard the elevator doors open into the foyer. He thought about defending the foyer with the incinerators and machine guns Royce had built into it, but he decided against it. The security guards were only doing their jobs. Royce had betrayed Lane's trust, but no one else had. He would fire at them only if he and Pam could escape no other way.

Pam had moved along the ledge to their right. Lane stepped out, climbing over the winged gargoyle as she had, and heard voices shouting for Royce in the foyer. Taking care not to look down, Lane moved along the ledge after Pam, wondering where they were going. At any moment he expected to hear the security guards smash down the steel door from the foyer.

Pam was now passing a section of stone wall that had no windows. She came to another gargoyle, one that lay lazily along the ledge. It had a long, hooked beak and dangled one long foreleg that ended in a lion's paw down over the edge of the ledge. Still moving with great care, Pam put her arms around the neck of the gargoyle and lowered herself down next to the dangling foreleg. Then she hooked one arm around the foreleg and moved to hang from it.

Lane watched in terror as she calmly slid down the foreleg until her toes touched the ledge one floor below. She let go of the gargoyle's foreleg and looked up, waving to him once that she had landed safely. Lane moved toward the reclining gargoyle, knowing that he had to follow her, but not at all pleased.

Behind him Lane heard another sound from Royce's apartment: a key sliding into the lock of the main door. The guards did not have to blast through it at all. They would see the smashed window immediately.

As Lane reached the gargoyle, he heard the security

guards shouting inside Royce's apartment. Some came running to the window; others would be securing the entire apartment. Lane slowly lowered himself from the gargoyle's neck, in a completely defenseless position, and glanced up at an angle to the shattered window.

Four security guards had leaned out through the opening, but they were all peering straight down to the street. None had seen Lane yet. With agonizing slowness, he reached out to grab the dangling foreleg. The stone felt cold in his hands.

Lane looked up at the window as he slowly lowered himself, reaching down with toes to feel the ledge under him. As he moved lower, the ledge above gradually hid him from the sight of the guards still talking in puzzled tones at the open window.

He felt Pam ease his legs forward to the ledge; she also grabbed his belt. When he finally let his weight down, he found that she had braced herself behind another snarling gargoyle, this one in the shape of a goat with wings, in order to help him down.

"They didn't see me," Lane whispered. "But now what? We can't chance going down another fourteen floors that way."

"No." Pam moved out from behind the gargoyle along this ledge. "Come on."

When she reached another tall, vertical window, she peered inside for a moment. "Good! Nobody home." She drew her Bolter and fired through the glass, shattering it in a great crash.

As the broken glass fell around her, bits of it clinging to her hair and shoulders, Lane glanced up again, but the ledge from which they had just come completely blocked his view of Royce's window. Still, the guards certainly had heard the shots. They would be coming down a floor inside, probably using the elevator again as well as the stairs.

Pam slipped through the window, going back inside the building. Lane moved after her as quickly as he could. Ahead of him, she held her Bolter ready; he brought his CAR-24 up.

They had entered a deserted conference room. Lane

heard nothing as they moved to the main door. Unlike Royce's apartment, this conference room had an ordinary door that simply opened on a foyer leading to both a stairwell door and an elevator door.

Pounding footsteps echoed from above them in the stairwell. The elevator doors one floor up also slid open. Lane tensed and looked back through the conference room at the shattered window.

"Back outside?" Lane asked. "Or into the stairwell? They'll hear us, but maybe we can outrun them."

"Quiet," Pam whispered sharply. She pried the elevator doors apart, forcing them open to reveal the empty shaft. Above her, footsteps moved into the elevator itself.

On the wall to Pam's right, Lane saw a deep groove inset into the wall of the shaft. A rusted metal ladder ran up and down the groove set into the wall. Over her head the elevator doors closed.

"I've used these before," Pam said quietly. "Capitol builds these in all its towers. Move fast." With that she jumped through the doorway and grabbed the rungs of the ladder. "Hurry!" She climbed down out of his way. "Jump!"

Lane drew in a deep breath. Pam liked the adrenaline surges; he did not like this much at all. However, he knew she had found an escape that should work. He came up to the open doorway and leaped.

His hands hit the hard metal rungs of the ladder and slipped, but his feet caught on lower rungs and supported his weight. Pam reached up and pressed his lower back forward so that he was shoved against the ladder instead of falling back; he finally caught handholds on the ladder, his heart pounding.

The elevator descended. Safe in the deep groove in the wall, Lane and Pam waited quietly as the car stopped right next to them. However, Pam slowly began to climb down the ladder, and Lane followed as he heard the footsteps leave the elevator.

In only a moment Lane developed a rhythm as he descended the ladder. Pam moved quickly below him and, one rung at a time, they passed down floor after floor. They did not make any significant noise.

Lane counted the stories. As they approached the ninth floor, the elevator descended again. It passed them and stopped on the main floor. He heard the guards inside leave the elevator, but it remained where it was.

When Pam reached the top of the elevator, she stepped quietly onto its roof and pulled up an access door. She glanced down and then waved for Lane to follow. He joined her and looked down into the elevator. The doors stood open to the lobby.

"The guards at the main door know we went to see Royce," Lane whispered. "We can't go out that way."

"Another window," said Pam. "Outside, look for the nearest access hatch down into the tunnels."

"Got it. My turn with point."

"Go."

Lane dropped down to the floor of the elevator and leveled his CAR-24. Only a few people were walking past in the lobby, but the sound caused the two security guards at the main doors to turn and look. They recognized him instantly. Then Lane saw that a squad of ten more security guards stood out there with them; most likely they were the ones who had ridden the elevator down a moment earlier.

"Come on!" Lane fired his CAR-24 toward them as he ran out of the elevator, sending them ducking flat on the pavement just outside. As he moved to his left, looking for a window on the side wall of the lobby, he fired at them again, keeping them down for Pam. When she had dropped to the elevator floor, she fired, too, now providing cover for them both.

Lane spotted the window he wanted and ran toward it, glancing around for more security guards. He saw none. As he neared the window, he blasted it out and leaped up on a couch to jump onto the windowsill.

He jumped outside and turned, sliding his CAR-24 back through one corner of the window. Before Pam entered his line of fire, he shot one more burst at the main doors to keep the security guards pinned; then he swung out of the way as Pam followed him through the window.

As Pam landed on her feet next to him, they turned and found themselves in some decorative bushes growing next to the building. Now, however, the security guards would not be chasing them through the lobby, but hurrying around the outside of the building to cut them off. Lane pushed his way out of the bushes and ran down the crowded sidewalk, looking for an access hatch.

Voices shouted angrily behind them on the street, but the dense crowd of pedestrians blocked the security guards from view. Lane spotted an access hatch only twenty meters away through the crowd. Pushing and shoving other people out of the way, he reached it and flipped it open with a clang. Turning, he saw their pursuit just coming into view as other people saw their weapons and hurried out of their way.

While Pam hurried down the hatch, Lane crouched by the lid and fired into the sidewalk just ahead of the guards. As before, they flung themselves out of the way, rolling. Before they could bring up their weapons to fire, Lane swung his legs into the hatch over Pam and let himself down.

Light machine-gun fire chattered overhead as he swung the hatch lit shut with another clang.

The tunnel was dark, but Lane did not need to see. He descended the ladder and joined Pam. They held both their CAR-24s aimed at the lid, ready to fire if anyone opened it.

No one did. The security guards were not that reckless. After a few moments Lane moved to one side, sliding his feet cautiously on the tunnel floor to get away from this hatch. Pam followed.

Lane remained tense, listening for that hatch lid or any other nearby to open. However, none did. After he had turned several corners and left the immediate danger behind, he stopped and lowered his CAR-24.

"I guess they gave up. They must know how easy it would be for us to ambush them down here." He began to relax, finally.

Pam let out a long breath. "What now, Chung?"

"Royce was my best idea—or so I thought. I know some other street people. You have any suggestions?"

"Yes, I think so. I remembered something when we

were climbing down the elevator shaft. Did I ever tell you about Cela Malle?"

"Mm—is she the con artist?"

"That's right. But she's a white-collar crook who deals strictly in high-level schemes. Like your friend Royce she tends to have networks in place; at the very least, she knows a lot of people in her own profession."

"You think she can help?"

"One way to find out. Last I heard, she had talked her way into a public-relations position with Capitol." Pam pointed up toward one of the other Capitol towers. "She worked up there. As long as we're here, we might as well see if she's in, don't you think?"

"She must have a certain taste for adrenaline, herself. Will she cooperate?"

"She'd better." Pam grinned. "I've saved her in the past from irate customers when her scams fell through. She always said she owes me."

"Sounds good to me. Let's go."

Lane followed Pam this time. Cela Malle worked in a Capitol business tower, with armed guards at the main doors, but Pam called Cela Malle and received clearance. In a few minutes they had ridden the lift to a middle-level floor, where it opened on a quiet, well-lit corridor.

A tall, slender brunette with rich, shoulder-length hair strode down the hall to meet them. She had the pretty, angular features of a megacorporate fashion model and wore a bright blue skirted suit with a ruffled white blouse. After Pam introduced Cela to Lane, they went into her office.

Lane looked around in surprise. The office was almost as large as Royce's. Decorated in a blue carpet and wallpaper that matched her blue suit, it looked out over the street with a view of the Capitol headquarters tower a few blocks away.

Cela walked to a wet bar set into one wall. "What will you have?"

"Nothing for me," said Pam.

"Oh, I forgot. You're working, I suppose." Cela smiled at both of them. "All right. It's been a long time, Pam. What can I do for you?"

"Can we . . . talk plainly here?" Pam asked, with a knowing smirk.

Cela laughed lightly and walked over to her desk, which was larger than the Whiz Kid's entire computer station. She switched on a sonic disruptor and sat on a corner of the desk. "If someone suspected me, they could record and unscramble that, but I've been careful. What's on your mind?"

"So I'm right that you always have some scam going." Pam moved to a large chair in front of Cela and sat down. "Not that I want to interfere."

"Well, I usually do. I guess you know that. But this one is long-term. It won't develop for quite some time." She hesitated. "You know I can't talk about it in detail, of course."

"Of course," said Pam. "That's not really what I came about. You have a lot of connections in Luna City."

"Yes, that's true."

Pam glanced at Lane, who said nothing. Just as she had let him decide how much to reveal to Royce, he would let her judge how to handle Cela. She frowned thoughtfully, looking back at Cela.

"Can you find out about a rogue Capitol Ship that made a brief stop at the Luna City docks recently? I'll write down the exact date and time for you."

"A *rogue* Capitol ship?" Cela cocked her head to one side. "What do you mean?"

Pam looked at Lane again, who nodded. "We . . . don't think a Capitol crew brought it in."

"Who did?"

"We don't know for sure. But we found evidence that a firefight occurred at the dock where it landed. Capitol security guards must have been involved. That means someone at Capitol got some kind of report."

"That's true." Cela played idly with a small wooden statuette of a running horse on her desk. "I might be able to get into the computer banks about that, but it will take some time. It's far outside my own authority in the public-relations area."

"Whatever you can do will be appreciated," said Pam.

"If you can manage it, see if Capitol knows anything about a Brotherhood search for a missing mystic."

"A mystic? Aren't they really high up in the Brotherhood?" Cela looked up in surprise.

"That's right," said Pam. "We don't know exactly what the story is, but we can use a tip about him, too. His name's Honorius."

"I'll do what I can," said Cela. "I owe you. We both know that."

"This will mean a lot," said Pam. "If you can help with these two problems, we're square."

Penyon stood behind Halala in the shadowed entrance to an alley in a Mishima warehouse district. A small crowd of pedestrians had gathered in the alley around a single, composed man, after paying a few coins to a barker on the street. Wearing a white tunic with the Brotherhood logo on the front, the ordinary-looking man in the alley sat cross-legged on the filthy sidewalk, muttering to himself.

"Come on, father!" One man yelled from the back of the crowd. "Can you throw lightning? Or levitate again?"

People in the crowd laughed.

The barker at the end of the alley turned with a confident, reassuring smile. "Of course he can, of course he can! I, Ceon Reese, saw him only a few minutes ago! Rise, my friend! Show them!" Then he turned his attention back to the street. "See the miracle! Step right up and see the miracle man!"

"Float up in the sky," suggested a young woman, giggling. "Or conjure up coins for me!"

"Everyone else here knows he is a mystic," Halala said quietly.

"I wonder how they know," said Penyon. "Do you think he has done something only a mystic could do?"

"No, fool," Halala said wearily. "The cut of his tunic tells them. Someone in the crowd knew the design."

Penyon moved up next to her, straining to get a better look. The man's tunic looked ordinary to him. Penyon reminded himself that Halala knew much more than he did.

The mystic, if he was one, showed no sign that he heard anyone around him.

"He's not levitating now," said Penyon. "You said that was the rumor you heard."

"He may just be a crazy mystic who can't do anything," said Halala. "However, we have no need of these others. Stand back." She flattened herself against a wall and pushed him next to her, leaving the alley open to the street.

Penyon watched. From the hard, angry look on her face, he knew she was using her pyschic power to throw out one of her Dark Gifts. Suddenly squeals of shock rose up from a young woman in the crowd.

"I can't see! Help me!"

"He's blinded her!" Halala shouted. "Run! Run before he blinds us all!"

A roar of surprise and fear swept through the crowd. Everyone began screaming and bumping into each other in panic in their hurry to flee from the alley. The barker turned in shock and was carried away from the end of the alley by the rush of frightened spectators.

"See another miracle!" Ceon Reese yelled, even as he was pushed around the corner.

"Come on, you fool. Hurry." Halala hurried forward, shoving people out of her way, either knocking them down or sending them stumbling into each other.

Penyon also pushed them out of his way, hurrying after Halala.

Ahead of them, the stranger had noticed nothing. He still sat in the same place, muttering too low for Penyon to hear him. Halala squatted down in front of him.

"Speak," she commanded. "Who are you?"

Penyon stopped behind Halala, looking down at the other man. He now heard that the stranger was speaking in some language Penyon did not recognize. He speech had a rhythmic sound and sometimes seemed to rhyme.

"What is that?" Penyon asked. "Do you know?"

"Latin, I think," said Halala. "I don't understand it, but the Brotherhood often uses it. I've heard it before," Her tone hardened as she addressed the stranger again. "Listen to me. What is your name?"

The man did not respond. He continued to speak in Latin for another moment, then suddenly switched to English. "Field of daisies," he said clearly, looking up suddenly. He faced Halala, but seemed to be looking right through her to another sight. "Washed by the sun, but with clouds gathering. Sweet aroma, don't you think?"

"I am Halala. Who are you?"

"I don't recommend it," said the stranger.

"He's weird enough to be a mystic, isn't he?" Penyon asked. "He might be Honorius."

Halala glanced toward the end of the alley, where the crowd was still shouting and screaming as they hurried away. "Whatever we do, we must hurry. Using the Dark Gifts in public like this always increases the rumors of our presence."

"Maybe we should take him home with us." Penyon looked toward the end of the alley. "Mishima security comes fast. I know that from my black market days."

"That's exactly what we'll do," said Halala, getting to her feet. She firmly grasped one of the stranger's arms. "You get his other arm. Let's see if he'll stand."

"Maybe he'll levitate," said Penyon cheerfully, taking the man's other arm.

Penyon and Halala pulled, and the man stood normally. He did not acknowledge their presence or help, however. Instead, he continued to talk as though he was conversing with someone who was not present.

"The daisies will need the rain," said their companion. "We must seek shelter, however."

"Let's see if he'll walk with us."

Penyon followed Halala's lead in turning him and walking him out of the alley. The strangers had scattered, except for a few people consoling the young woman who had gone blind. Their companion stumbled slightly, but did not resist or protest. At the end of the alley Halala jerked her head to the right.

"How long will she stay blind?" Penyon asked. "We don't want them coming back this way for another look at us."

"Only another minute or two."

"Let's go. Where to?"

"We can't take him on the tubelink like this. Sooner or later, some Brotherhood type will demand an explanation. We have to get him down into the tunnels."

"We still might run into people down there," Penyon said anxiously.

"They will pose no danger to us." Halala grinned ferally. "Down there we can use our Dark Gifts with little fear of detection. Anyone who crosses us . . ."

Penyon smiled, filled with sudden confidence.

CHAPTER 17

Yojimbo led the rest of the team through the crowded streets. He had kept them together in case they got a lead sometime today. At that point he intended to split his companions into two squads, one to check the new lead and one to keep searching for more leads.

"Are we going to spend all day at this?" Klaus demanded,

"We have checked this area of Luna City," said Yojimbo, halting to speak to him.

"Like hell," said Klaus, stopping next to a concrete kiosk. He leaned against it with feigned weariness. "Anybody could have walked right in behind us."

Yojimbo, using his Mishima training, had led everyone on a systematic search pattern through the city in an effort either to spot heretics and necromutants or to buy information about such sightings. Even by late afternoon, however, they had found nothing. Yojimbo knew that his subordinates were becoming bored and restless.

"Klaus has a point," said Vic, but his tone was much more relaxed. "We don't have any way to seal off a perimeter, so more people with rumors to share—or even heretics themselves—can enter the same area we just left."

"Rumors move like ripples," said Yojimbo. "Some eventually reach the far end of the pond, but some never do. Many are limited to a certain radius from their point of origin. That doesn't change just because people move around. Human movement is part of this system."

"This still feels like a waste of time," said Skippa, toying with a lock of her rich brown hair. "We don't have anything to show for a day's work, do we?"

"No." Yojimbo could not argue with that.

"Most of the day is shot now, anyway," said Fay. "Why don't we take a break and talk about a new approach? Or Klaus and I can take a walk on our own."

"I will call the Whiz Kid." Yojimbo pulled out his belt computer. This was a critical time for him; he knew that his subordinates were forming their opinions of him as team leader. He would earn or lose their respect quickly, no matter how much he was paying them. As he called, he switched on his sonic disruptor to shield his voice from passersby.

"Sai," said the Whiz Kid, as Yojimbo had ordered him to do when responding.

"Sai. Yojimbo here."

"Hi ya, boss. Zowee! Listen, I just got something through cyberspace a minute ago."

"Proceed."

"A woman was temporarily blinded in a Mishima warehouse district. Supposedly, she was part of a group that had been teasing some crazy guy in a Brotherhood tunic."

"Temporary blindness is reportedly a Dark Gift," said Yojimbo. "Are they saying that the Brotherhood man is a heretic?"

"Zowee, no. But some other witnesses saw a man and a woman drag the guy out of the alley after the blindness scared the crowd away."

"Where did they go?"

"Down an access hatch into the tunnels."

"Sounds good," said Yojimbo. "When did this happen? How long?"

"Several hours ago, but word of it just came in, like I said."

"I understand. Do you have anything else? Which direction they took or more sightings?"

"I have contradictory information. Some people picked up sightings of this trio a half hour later, down in the area where Fay and Klaus first wiped out that heretic."

"What else?"

"Just a few minutes ago a big convoy of strangers on foot were sighted heading for the docks down in the tunnels. One woman fit the description of the woman who dragged away the guy in the Brotherhood outfit."

"Yeah? Do you have any other description? For instance, how many of the enemy are present?"

"No, I don't have anything else. The only witness got scared when he saw them and ran off, pronto."

"I do not blame anyone for that." Yojimbo thought a moment. "All right. I see the sequence of events, I think. A couple of heretics found Honorius a few hours ago and reported with him to their superior. The nepharite then ordered an escort to take the mystic off Luna, and they are moving toward the docks now, down in the tunnels. The timing matches, and the motivation is reasonable. But we're a long way from the docks."

The Whiz Kid waited patiently, through a faint crackle of static.

"Can you get their route to me?" Yojimbo asked. "Maybe a map of the tunnels?"

"Zowee! Of course I can. I got it all ready and waiting. A full map of the city tunnels marked with the sightings and apparent direction of the enemy. Stand by, and I'll transmit it right to your computer."

"Begin." Yojimbo watched the small screen on his hand-held computer as it registered reception of the transmission. When it had finished, he spoke again. "Received. We'll be going into the tunnels quickly, so we'll be out of touch by radio. Stand by for communication whenever we can arrange it."

"You got it," said the Whiz Kid.

Then Yojimbo called Lane and Pam. They both responded, and he reported the information from the Whiz Kid. After he had transmitted the tunnel map to them, he asked for their current position.

"We're even farther from the docks than you are," said Lane, with static distorting his voice. "Not too much, but we'll have some catching up to do. Look, can we realistically stop them?"

"They're closer to the docks than either of our squads," Pam added. "And we don't have time to arm more heavily, either."

"Yojimbo," said Lane. "Does this mean they have a

ship and a crew coming in to meet them? Or waiting for them? They may have allies at the docks."

"We have no reason to believe so," said Yojimbo. "I believe it would be more in character for them to hijack a ship they find spontaneously."

"That's right," said Pam.

"Refer to your maps with me," said Yojimbo. "Please locate the part of the maze of tunnels that leads to the docking area."

"Done," said Pam.

"The maze narrows to a relative bottleneck of eight access tunnels that feed into a main trunk serving the docking area," said Yojimbo. "Remember? We used them when we went to the damaged docking port together. Just over three kilometers from my location, according to the legend on my screen."

"Got it," said Lane. "What about it?"

"If all of us reach the area before the enemy, we can deliver fire into five of the eight tunnels at once. We might be able to move fast among them to make the enemy believe that all are blocked."

"That means getting in front of them," said Lane. "I repeat, can we do this?"

"I suggest that you two move directly across town on one of the street levels as fast as you can: take any transportation that looks good at the time. Go straight to the docks and try to beat the enemy there."

"They still have a big head start," said Pam. "We're about four kilometers away. But we can take a shot at it."

"Down in the maze the enemy cannot move in a straight line," said Yojimbo. "Their indirect route will slow them down. Also, we'll try to get close enough to begin delaying action somehow. If we are successful, you may still reach the bottleneck before they do."

"The two of us can't block all eight access tunnels," said Lane.

"Do not worry about that," said Yojimbo. "Without you two we cannot block them, either. But we will still have them in a cross fire. Ready?"

"We're moving out," said Lane.

Yojimbo stashed his belt computer and turned off the sonic disruptor.

"We've been watching your facial expressions," said Fay. "Something's up. What is it?"

"Our big break has arrived," said Yojimbo, looking around for the nearest access hatch into the tunnels. "I will brief you as we go—as soon as we're in the tunnels, safely out of hearing. Where's the closest hatch?"

"Over there!" Vic pointed about a block forward, through the normal press of pedestrians. "Come on!"

Easily the biggest member of the team, he pushed his way forward, leading the others in single file. He yanked open the access hatch and started down the ladder, reaching back with one hand to keep the big Gehenna Puker on his back from catching on the edge of the opening. As his partner, Skippa followed next. Yojimbo took the rear, waiting for Fay and Klaus to precede him.

As the team descended below him, Yojimbo clanged the cover shut over his head. They all switched on their helmet lamps, throwing angled beams jerkily in every direction at the stained, filthy walls of the tunnels by the motion of climbing down the ladder. When Yojimbo reached the bottom, he glanced at his belt computer to choose a route. He transmitted the tunnel maze to each of their belt computers, then pushed past them to take the lead at a jog. As he picked his way through the maze, he briefed them on their current maneuver.

"We don't have the best weaponry with us," Vic warned, first in the file behind Yojimbo. "My Gehenna Puker is the biggest weapon we have. Otherwise, we're using light machine guns and side arms, right?"

"That's true," said Fay from farther back.

"Figures," Klaus muttered. "We finally get our break, and we don't have time to arm properly. And Team Yojimbo just isn't big enough."

"We'll do the job we're being paid for," Fay said sharply, more to Klaus than to anyone else.

"I accept the fault," Yojimbo said as he hurried forward. "I did not expect to enter action with a significant number of the enemy so soon, without warning."

"Sound really echoes in these tunnels," said Skippa. "We gotta be careful."

"Agreed," said Yojimbo. "Essential talk only from this point. As we draw closer, we will have to slow down, as well, and shut off all lamps."

Yojimbo could not maintain the pace without a break, anyway; repeatedly, he had to stop and refer to his computer screen, then study the intersections of tunnels to find his way. Some of the tunnels were too narrow for a normal forward position; they had to turn sideways and slide between the walls. Other tunnels were crooked or curved; Yojimbo slowed down to advance carefully in these.

Finally, halting to study his computer at another juncture, he estimated that they had zigzagged approximately three kilometers through the maze in order to advance less than two, as measured in a straight line from their starting point toward the docks. However, the docks were now less than three quarters of a kilometer away. If the enemy had not yet reached the docks and ascended from the maze, then they were very close up ahead.

He turned and motioned for silence to the team behind him. Then he switched off his helmet lamp. They turned off theirs, as well. Now in total darkness, Yojimbo swung his Windrider into ready position and advanced carefully. He felt gently for each forward step before putting his weight down and trailed his left hand on the wall as a reference point.

Behind Yojimbo his team also moved fairly quietly. On the hard surface of the tunnel floor, however, they could not move quickly in complete silence, and the skittering of unseen vermin could also reveal their presence. Yojimbo had to accept that as a calculated risk.

Ahead, Yojimbo heard nothing. He carefully turned a corner, and a sudden feeling of overwhelming fear suddenly swept over him. Momentarily disoriented by the fear, he stumbled forward, surprised and unable to act or speak. He fell to his knees, his Windrider clattering against the floor of the tunnel as it dangled from his shoulder strap.

Over his head the massive flame of Vic's Gehenna

Puker shot forward down the tunnel, suddenly illuminating the passageway. Yojimbo glimpsed three human figures about fifteen meters ahead before two darted around corners. The third flashed up helplessly, then fell, burning, to the floor of the tunnel.

Yojimbo's terror disappeared at once. Embarrassed, he felt for his Windrider.

"Stay down," Vic ordered, stepping over Yojimbo. He let the flame shut off for a moment. Then he shot it forward again, but no one became visible in its light this time.

More team members advanced after Vic. Yojimbo understood that the fear had been artificially induced by the psychic power of a heretic, paralyzing almost as much from surprise as from fear itself. Now at the end of the file, he got up and moved forward.

Walking point, Vic shot his flame forward again, then suddenly staggered, colliding with one wall. By the light of the flame Yojimbo saw Skippa come up behind Vic and hold the Gehenna Puker steady. Then she took it from him and swung it around a corner. Someone gave a high-pitched scream that shut off abruptly.

Klaus and Fay moved past Vic and Skippa. Yojimbo came up behind Vic, who was just getting to his feet. Skippa returned the Gehenna Puker; its strap had never actually left Vic's shoulder.

"Disoriented," Vic muttered breathlessly. "Another Dark Gift."

Now in front, Klaus and Fay fired their Destroyer and AR3000 machine-gun fire into the darkness ahead.

Yojimbo heard footsteps and muffled voices in several of the tunnels in front of them. The numbers worried him, but their position was good; it implied that Yojimbo's team was not outflanked, though quieter forces might be laying a trap. Also, the large group ahead of them might mean that Honorius was still close by—that the main enemy group had not moved on to the docks already.

"Keep up the pressure," Yojimbo ordered loudly, unconcerned with being overheard now. "Force them to engage."

For the first time, now, return fire came from the enemy out of the tunnels. Yojimbo identified it only as heavy machine-gun fire from a single weapon. Then he also heard single shots fired, probably from side arms.

Yojimbo judged that the heretics were probably using pistols. Since they masqueraded as ordinary citizens, they would not want to draw undue attention to themselves. With their ability to blind and disorient their enemies, and maybe with other abilities he did not know about, they would not require heavy armament to protect themselves from most citizens on Luna, who would not expect to face Dark Gifts. Yojimbo's team was different in that they knew they were stalking heretics.

Vic, once again moving with determination, pushed his way back to the front. Yojimbo saw the reflected flash of the flame as Vic shot it forward again. Still following the team in the rear, Yojimbo readied his Windrider and moved up.

About ten meters forward, the team turned a corner, then found four narrow openings to other tunnels. Vic, Skippa, Fay, and Klaus each had stopped to one side of the openings and were firing up the tunnels, Vic with his incinerator and the others with their light machine guns. Scattered, single-shot return fire told them that at least some of the enemy remained close. Yojimbo worried that this was a delaying action now, allowing others to take Honorius away.

"Skippa," Vic said loudly. As she moved behind him, working as a Doomtrooper pair normally would, he advanced up his tunnel, shooting the flame out ahead of them. That left Skippa's tunnel untended, so Yojimbo moved up to cover it.

Suddenly, hard, heavy footsteps sounded on the tunnel floor behind Yojimbo. He whirled, and switching on his helmet lamp, saw a very large, silent figure run toward him out of the shadows.

CHAPTER 18

"Rear assault!" Yojimbo shouted, throwing himself to the floor of the tunnel.

A strangely deep rumbling of machine-gun fire thundered from the shadows, firing where he had just stood.

Yojimbo fired his Windrider forward, at the same time getting a good look at the assailant just entering the beam from his head lamp.

The figure was huge, bulky with muscle as well as tall, but crouching low in the tunnel and nearly filling it from side to side. The rumbling fire came from a massive, misshapen heavy weapon held in both the attacker's huge hands. His skull was misshapen, and his face a flat black color, like soot. As Yojimbo continued to scatter fire down the tunnel, he realized that this was a necromutant.

He also saw that his Windrider fire was striking the charging necromutant. Rounds ripped into the sootlike flesh and streaked the being's face. The necromutant flinched and momentarily halted, but did not fall, grimacing to show long, large teeth.

Yojimbo knew he was trapped. He began scooting backward, staying low, but he had no cover. All he could do was continue to fire.

The necromutant staggered forward, spraying fire erratically. He was injured, but not falling. If he regained full control of his weapon, Yojimbo would die.

Suddenly a stream of flame rushed out directly over Yojimbo, flaring down the tunnel. Under its protection, Yojimbo scrambled back, then around the safety of a corner. He took the moment to reload his Windrider.

When Vic released the flame, the necromutant had become a blazing heap on the floor of the tunnel. He reached down to grab Yojimbo's arm and lift him to his feet. Then Vic turned and motioned up the four tunnels.

"These tunnels are clear. The others have secured them to the next intersection. Come on."

"What happened?" Yojimbo followed Vic up one of them, still catching his breath.

Vic said nothing as they ran. In a moment they reached a perpendicular tunnel that joined all four of the tunnels they had just taken. The squad was reunited.

"Report," said Yojimbo.

"We apparently forced them to change direction," said Fay. "I'm not sure exactly why, though. Our own position didn't divert them."

Yojimbo consulted his computer map of the maze. "Yes, I see. They heard us coming up behind them and drew us into an area that was good for an ambush, especially from the rear. But if they had headed straight for the docking ports from here, they would have hit dead ends. In order to reach them, they have to backtrack from this location."

"It's a maze, all right," said Klaus, frowning at his own computer.

"Good," said Skippa. "We really did cause a delay. Maybe Lane and Pam have a chance to beat them to the bottleneck now, eh?"

"We're near an access hatch to the level above us," said Yojimbo, still studying his map. "Vic and Skippa, come up with me. We will try to beat the enemy to the docks on the street, as Lane and Pam are doing. The way will be crowded, of course, but we can move in a straight line. Fay and Klaus, keep up the pursuit down here and try to delay them as much as you can. Any questions?"

No one spoke.

"Good," said Yojimbo grimly, hitching the strap of his Windrider. "Move out."

Near the docking ports Lane found an access hatch and quickly led Pam down into the tunnels. She closed it carefully, with only a quiet clank over their heads, leaving them in darkness. Lane stopped at the bottom of the ladder, his CAR-24 ready, listening.

Pam came down next to him and halted, also. They switched on their head lamps, looking and listening in opposite directions. The tunnels were silent.

Lane could not see anyone or any sign of recent passage in the dirty, damp tunnels. He consulted his map of the maze and switched off his lamp. They would have to move without giving away their position in advance. Pam turned off her lamp again, too.

Now Lane advanced carefully, holding his CAR-24 ready with his right hand. He felt for each step tentatively in the blackness, brushing the left wall with his elbow to keep it as a reference point. Each time his elbow led him around a curve or a corner, he halted and listened again.

Finally, he stopped and checked his map again. "We're close to the bottleneck of eight access tunnels. This tunnel we're in runs along the back of them, feeding into each individual docking port."

"What if the enemy has already entered one of the ports?" Pam whispered.

"We got here fast. I don't think—"

A faint chattering of light machine-gun fire echoed through the tunnels.

"There's our answer," said Lane. "Let's find those eight access tunnels fast." He switched on his head lamp and jogged forward.

By the light of his lamp, they located the access tunnels easily. Lane judged their width to be two meters, their height three. He turned his lamp on inside each one just long enough to see that they ran twenty meters up before reaching another intersection.

Pam jogged up the perpendicular tunnel into which they fed, beneath the docking ports, for reconnaissance. Then she hurried back.

"What did you see?" Lane asked.

"They're a consistent ten meters apart," Pam whispered. "No way we can move from one to another quickly when the action starts."

"Even if we could, you and I alone could only cover two each, at most." Lane turned off his lamp again. The intermittent fire echoing toward them was drawing closer.

"Got any ideas, Chung?"

"No. Not really." Lane looked at his computer map. "If we move up to establish a different ambush, we get into a more complex part of the maze. The enemy could bypass us entirely, even by pure chance if not design. As Yojimbo said, this is the smallest bottleneck we have."

"All right." Pam shrugged. "We can still move up and see if we can anticipate which access tunnels they will use. Then we can fall back and take our positions."

"Yeah. But unless the rest of the team slows them down from behind, I don't see how we can stop the convoy. They may secure all eight access tunnels just to be on the safe side. If so, we can't do much alone." Lane hoisted his CAR-24, then heard a faint metallic clank behind and above them, in the area from which they had just come.

Instantly, Lane and Pam both moved around corners, waiting. Depending on who had followed them, they could now be the ones caught in a cross fire. Neither of them made a sound as quiet footsteps scraped on the metal ladder leading down from the access hatch. Then Lane heard three pairs of footsteps moving toward them on the hard pavement.

After several long moments yellowish light jerkily leaked around a corner. "Sai," said a familiar voice quietly on Lane and Pam's belt computers. "Yojimbo here. Pam, Lane, report if you hear me."

Lane relaxed slightly and spoke without bothering to use the belt computer. "Sai, Yojimbo. Straight ahead. Keep your voice down. Who's with you?"

"Vic and Skippa." Yojimbo came around the last corner, his Windrider forward.

"Klaus and Fay are still in the tunnels behind the enemy?" Lane asked.

"Yes. We are in time to cut them off?"

"We're in time," Lane said grimly. "But we have eight tunnels, ten meters apart."

"And five of us to block them," said Skippa. "I think we have a good chance."

"Fay and Klaus should keep some of the pressure off us," said Vic. "The enemy can't mass its entire attack on us while defending its own rear."

"Did you find out how many of the enemy there are?" Pam asked. "If they have enough to rush all the tunnels at once and still hold Fay and Klaus back, that's all they need."

"We do not have an exact number," said Yojimbo. "But we did not hear a lot of footsteps."

"I would guess we face fewer than ten, now," said Vic. "We've taken out three."

"I agree," said Skippa. "More than ten would make more noise than they've made."

The chattering of light machine-gun fire, answered by single shots, sounded closer than before.

"From what I saw, our light machine guns may not stop a necromutant," said Yojimbo. "Vic's incinerator may be our only effective weapon against them."

"Are there some necromutants?" Lane asked.

"I killed one back there," said Vic. "We don't know if there are more."

"That one carried a weapon with a very distinctive sound," said Yojimbo. "I haven't heard it again."

"What about hitting the mystic?" Klaus asked. "When we ambush the enemy, we won't be able to pick and choose our targets."

"We will have to hope the enemy keeps him safe," said Yojimbo. "He means something to them. That is really our only hope of avoiding him."

"We better take positions and shut up," said Pam quietly. "They're coming closer every minute."

Penyon crept slowly through a dark tunnel, holding the arm of Honorius. He had shared the praise from Ragathol with Halala for apprehending the mystic. Now, as the most junior heretic in Ragathol's cell, he escorted Honorius through the tunnels in the very center of the squad convoying the mystic toward the docking ports.

Ahead of them, Halala and another more powerful heretic picked their route forward into the darkness. A necromutant followed them; a second necromutant followed immediately behind Penyon and Honorius. Another powerful heretic, Lebec, brought up the rear, shooting sometimes into the tunnels behind them.

Honorius did not resist exactly, but neither did he co-operate. Penyon had to pull on his arm, sometimes jerking him, to make him move. Sometimes when they passed an intersecting tunnel, the mystic would try to turn and wander into it; other times, when the convoy turned a corner, Honorius would try to walk straight.

Then, for no apparent reason, the mystic would do exactly what Penyon wanted for a while. Penyon was convinced that Honorius did not know where he was or what was happening around him. The mystic was much too calm and placid to have realized that he had been kidnapped.

Yojimbo stood at one of the middle access tunnels, looking up and down the perpendicular tunnel into which they fed. In the darkness he could not see any of his team members, but he had ordered each of them to a position. Of the eight tunnels, Yojimbo had assigned the middle two tunnels to himself as team leader.

Then he had ordered Vic to take the next two to the right, with Skippa on the end. As Doomtroopers, they were almost inseparable, and their sense of teamwork, combined with Vic's Gehenna Puker, anchored that side well. Yojimbo had ordered Lane and Pam to guard the three remaining tunnels on the left in their own way; he trusted them to work out their own teamwork. As Pam had said, the real question was whether the enemy would simply rush every tunnel at once while holding off Klaus and Fay in the rear. In that event, these positions would not matter much to anybody.

Yojimbo stood at the two middle tunnels because he had felt obligated to take the most challenging assignment for himself. In the darkness, punctuated only by the intermittent fire from the tunnels in front of them, his anxiety mounted. It was not only because of the coming fight, however.

This would be his first opportunity to prove his leadership to his own team and earn their respect. In addition, the chance to get Honorius and somehow find the nepharite on Luna would be their first real accomplishment. That would lead to their ultimate success and, eventually, the further respect of Lord Mishima.

Up ahead in the darkness the sounds of gunfire became muffled. Yojimbo hesitated, wondering if Fay and Klaus had diverted the enemy's direction. Then, once again, the shooting sounded even closer.

Lane stood at the tunnel on the far left. He and Pam had chosen to leave the tunnel to his immediate right unguarded; she had taken a position at the next tunnel up, adjacent to the two middle tunnels Yojimbo had assigned himself. Lane and Pam had agreed that they could cover their three tunnels best by sharing the empty one between them.

Still, Lane was worried. Since the team members were positioned in a single line, they could not help one another by firing laterally if the enemy reached this far; doing so would just endanger all of them. If one of them left a tunnel to support someone else, that tunnel became completely unguarded. As Lane saw the situation, their only chance was to pour fire up the tunnels and fall back up the access hatch if necessary—leaving the enemy to use other access hatches and possibly outflank them that way.

Suddenly, the sound of footsteps became much clearer. Lane knew the enemy had just turned the final corner before entering the access tunnels. The echoes came down the tunnel in front of him, but of course that did not mean the enemy would choose this one. He tensed, waiting.

Scuffling footsteps on the tunnel floor suddenly entered the tunnel Pam was guarding. Like the experienced veteran she was, she waited while the footsteps came well into the tunnel before revealing herself; otherwise, the enemy would simply withdraw from the far end safely again.

Abruptly, Pam fired her CAR-24 up the tunnel; as the chattering of her weapon announced her presence, the repeating flashes from the end of her barrel illuminated her face, her bouncing, short blond hair, and the walls around her. Shouts of surprise echoed through the tunnels from the enemy. Then, before the enemy could return fire, she swung back around the corner again.

However, only side-arm fire snapped down her tunnel.

None of the other Team Yojimbo members revealed themselves, Lane noted with satisfaction. They were all seasoned veterans who understood that the ambush depended on maintaining as much secrecy and surprise as possible. Lane prepared for an enemy advance down his own tunnel.

Now enemy fire roared back in tunnels on the far left—not just side-arm fire as before, but a thundering heavy machine gun. At this distance Lane could not tell exactly which tunnel was being attacked. He supposed he was now hearing the distinctive sound Yojimbo had mentioned earlier.

Meanwhile, Pam crouched, leaned her CAR-24 around the corner, and fired back without exposing herself to return fire.

Lane realized that no one had come down his tunnel yet. He had no idea if they were going to use it. If so, he should remain where he was. If not, he could rush the tunnel and catch the enemy in either the rear or the flank.

He remembered that the tunnel ran twenty meters before reaching a corner he could use for cover. If he began his rush and the enemy turned the corner ahead of him, he would be trapped with no cover and no backup. It was a very high-reward, high-risk move.

If fighting the Dark Legion made life worth living, then this was the moment it all came together.

CHAPTER 19

Lane heard a whooshing roar that lit up the service tunnel on the far side of Yojimbo. When Lane looked, he saw Vic standing just around the first corner past Yojimbo, firing his incinerator up the tunnel he guarded, his big body lit up by the glow of the massive flame. That meant the enemy had advanced up at least two tunnels, Pam's and one of Vic's, leaving Yojimbo's two tunnels between them.

On impulse, Lane suddenly raised his CAR-24 and charged up his access tunnel.

He ran with intense determination, hot with adrenaline, his eyes wide and staring for danger ahead. Ahead of him, a faint flicker of reflected light from Vic's long flame illuminated the corner he had to reach to be safe.

The twenty meters seemed to get longer as Lane ran. He kept his eyes on the corner as his feet pounded up the tunnel. Even running as hard as he could, he felt horribly slow.

Suddenly, a shadow darkened the glow of reflected light ahead of him. Lane had only covered about half the distance; he still had ten meters to the corner and no chance of getting there before someone came around it first. At this point he could not possibly get back to the service tunnel behind him, either. He was trapped.

In panic, Lane threw himself facedown on the tunnel, striking the floor hard. He brought up his CAR-24 and waited for a target. The mixed rattle and roar of various weapons reached him from the other tunnels.

A huge, dark shape came around the corner, blocking the light from ahead completely. Lane could see only that the silhouette was roughly humanoid, yet much too tall and bulky to be normal. Beyond that, he could see no details. He squeezed the trigger of his CAR-24 and sprayed his fire in a tight circle at the black silhouette.

A thunderous roar of heavy machine-gun fire filled the tunnel over Lane's head, with red and yellow flame spitting from the center of the silhouette.

Lane fired again, focusing on the spot in the black shape where the weapon had to be.

First his enemy's spitting flame suddenly jerked upward; then it halted entirely, and Lane heard chunks of hardware strike the floor. The big silhouette had staggered backward, but not fallen. Now, with an almost human growl of rage, the figure charged toward Lane.

He finally realized that he was facing a necromutant; to this point everything had happened too fast for him to think about it. Firing again, he struggled up to a kneeling position, concentrating his fire in the center of the hulking shape. Once again the necromutant slowed, but this time it did not stop; it still staggered forward.

Lane quickly got to his feet, still firing, and skipped backward.

Instead of slowing more, the necromutant growled wordlessly and charged again, backlit once more by flickering, indirect light.

Lane ran backward, afraid of stumbling, and fired again. This time, instead of wasting his fire on the huge body, he aimed for the necromutant's head. When he found his target, he tightened his grip and kept firing, halting his retreat to steady his CAR-24.

At last the shape finally crashed to the floor at Lane's feet. To make sure the necromutant was dead, Lane quickly turned on his head lamp. The massive body showed hundreds, maybe thousands, of wounds from the CAR-24, but they had not brought him down. However, most of the creature's head had been blasted away; hunks of it lay scattered on the tunnel floor. Lane shut off his lamp.

As before, Lane looked up the length of the access tunnel. Shouts, the staccato of machine-gun fire, and the whoosh of Vic's Gehenna Puker reached him from the other tunnels. By the reflected light at the far end of the tunnel still reaching him from Vic's flame through the other tunnels, he saw that the tunnel seemed clear again.

Now Lane knew that if he faced another necromutant, his CAR-24 was only effective at the monster's head. The knowledge gave him a better chance this time. He stepped past the body of the dead one and slammed another magazine home; then he charged up the tunnel once more.

Lane watched the corner even more carefully than before, but no shadows blocked the light this time. Maybe the enemy believed that only the incinerator would stop a necromutant, and that this tunnel was now secure. In any case, he covered the twenty meters without incident and stopped safely at the far corner, where an intersecting tunnel opened on the far ends of the eight access tunnels.

Lane swung around the corner sharply, his CAR-24 forward, but he held his fire. Vic's incinerator did not throw its bright flame right then, but small, stabbing flashes of light accompanied machine-gun fire in several of the tunnels. No one was in his line of sight.

He heard nothing from Pam's tunnel, either.

The enemy did not know, then, that Lane had circled behind them. However, he did not know where the mystic was—in one of the access tunnels or behind the firefight in some other tunnel. He had no idea where Fay and Klaus were, either.

Lane did not want to get into his own teammates' lines of fire, but he could not announce his location to them without alerting the enemy. He would just have to make whatever moves he could. First he ran forward to the end of the next access tunnel, the one he and Pam had left empty between them. He found it still empty and darted into it, to crouch just inside its corner and look carefully forward again.

The firefight had shifted farther away. By the sound and the flashing of gunfire, he guessed that the action was now in the farthest three tunnels. In the near-darkness, however, he could not be sure.

Suddenly side-arm fire snapped from another direction, back up the maze.

That told Lane what he needed to know; part of the enemy remained to the rear, and Fay and Klaus were still in contact with them.

"Sai! Pam, you there?" Lane shouted over the sound of all the weapons.

She did not respond, at least that he could hear. He ran to the end of her tunnel. "Sai! It's Lane; I'm at the far end."

She did not answer. He swung around suddenly, ready to fire if necessary or withhold fire if Pam was coming up the tunnel. However, this one was empty, too.

He left his crouch and ran forward, now ignoring the other access tunnels. Honorius was almost certainly farther to the rear. Instead, Lane looked for a tunnel leading back to the rear-guard action.

Before he found it, brilliant light surrounded him, and he turned to see the incinerator's huge flame shooting out the end of a tunnel. A flaming figure, the size of an ordinary human, staggered backward and collapsed on the tunnel floor. Lane grimaced involuntarily and hurried on his way, finding a tunnel back up the maze by the flash of the flame.

Within a few steps, Lane had gone past the point where the flame behind him lit his way. If he turned on his head lamp, however, he would reveal his position far in advance. Instead, he moved forward slowly, sliding his left foot along the tunnel floor and holding his CAR-24 ready to fire.

Yojimbo pushed himself up to his hands and knees, feeling for his Windrider. When the enemy had chosen to move to his right and enter the three access tunnels guarded by Vic and Skippa, he had moved up to block one of those tunnels. However, he had been struck by blindness, numbing fear, and a whirling disorientation that had thrown him on the floor.

In his confusion he had seen Vic fall, too. Now, however, in reflected light from the third tunnel, Yojimbo saw the big man also pushing himself to his feet. He no longer held the Gehenna Puker, but a whoosh from the third tunnel told Yojimbo where it was.

The tunnel Yojimbo guarded was dark and empty.

Yojimbo staggered to Vic and glanced up the next tunnel. It, too, was empty, dimly lit by indirect light from the far end. They rushed to the end of the third tunnel.

Skippa, supporting the big incinerator clumsily with her light frame, had reached the far end of the tunnel. A big, hulking, smoldering mass halfway up the tunnel had been a necromutant. A smaller, burning figure just past the far end must have been a heretic. She released the flame for a moment and glanced back at them.

"Come on! Lane just moved up ahead of me!"

Yojimbo led Vic up the tunnel. Skippa waited for them. Then she gave the incinerator back to Vic.

"Report," said Yojimbo, moving to take point. Carefully, he led them up the next tunnel. He could hear side-arm fire ahead in the darkness.

"We only faced three, two heretics and one necromutant," said Skippa. "One of the heretics disoriented you so that you were firing wildly up your tunnel at nothing."

Yojimbo nodded. "It was all I could manage. I got hit with more than disorientation."

"The same happened to me," said Vic. "I kept firing the flame in case something was coming."

"Nothing was," said Skippa. "A necromutant came down my tunnel. I kept shooting and hitting him, but he kept forcing himself forward."

"So you came back and got the Puker," said Vic.

"Yeah. I pulled it away from you just in time to get the necromutant. Then I moved up and got one of the heretics, but the other ran off."

"No sign of the mystic?" Vic asked.

"No."

Yojimbo held up a hand for silence. "We have to be careful, now. We don't want friendly fire with Lane, Klaus, and Fay. We're all out of contact now."

"Hey," said Skippa. "Where's Pam?"

Pam crept forward carefully in a dark tunnel, feeling her way through the blackness. When the firefight had begun, Pam had heard footsteps start down her tunnel.

She had fired blindly around the corner, hoping to avoid the psychic powers of the heretics.

Then she had pulled back around the corner while side-arm fire came down in return. When it had stopped, she had cautiously looked around the corner in time to see a shadow darting back to the far end. The figure moved to her right, toward Yojimbo's tunnel or even farther.

A moment later, Pam had seen the massive shadow of a necromutant move across the far end of her tunnel toward Lane. In a very risky move she had charged silently up her tunnel. By the time had she reached the end, however, she had heard Lane firing at the necromutant.

When she had found her path to the rear open and had heard more action farther up the maze, she had gone looking for Honorius. It was too good a chance to ignore. She trusted Lane to handle the necromutant himself.

Now she advanced as quickly as she could into the darkness, following only the chattering of Fay and Klaus's light machine guns and the side-arm fire answering them. Honorius had to be up ahead somewhere. Whoever guarded him probably did not expect her to have slipped past the enemy point this way.

Pam wanted to be very careful about engaging the enemy. Fay and Klaus had no reason to expect her to come up so close, so she carried the burden of avoiding friendly fire with them. She also did not want to kill Honorius by accident. Yet, she could not allow that concern to paralyze her actions completely.

She would have to take some risks with Honorius, even while she tried to rescue him. After all, if the team did not save him, he would certainly be killed by the Dark Legion at some point anyway. From all she had heard about the Dark Legion, necromutants would not negotiate for him or surrender to save themselves. By all accounts, they would fight either to the death or to victory.

Pam moved up to another intersection, listened to the gunfire, and turned left. However, at the next corner, she realized that the sound was fainter than before. Her map of the maze could not help since she had no idea where the fighting was located.

She finally decided that she was taking too much time.

Keeping her CAR-24 firmly in place with her right arm and her finger on the trigger, she used her left to switch her head lamp on quickly. Then she turned it off immediately, but she had seen that the tunnel was clear, level, and led about fifteen meters straight ahead.

Pam knew that the momentary flash of light might have reached the enemy indirectly, around corners she could not see from here. However, she now ran up the tunnel in front of her, secured the far corners, and flashed her head lamp again in both directions. Then she waited to locate the sound of the firefight again. When she had chosen another tunnel, she ran toward the sound once more.

Flashing the light briefly again, then advancing at a run, she turned three more corners. The sound of gunfire grew louder, and she wondered how the group with Honorius had become separated so far from their advance group. Maybe Fay and Klaus had found a way to move between them.

Hesitating at another corner, she switched on her head lamp and swung around the corner, her CAR-24 ready. In the sudden light she saw two figures at the far end of the tunnel. One man was dragging another, stumbling, toward her. Suddenly realizing that the second man was probably Honorius, she held her fire and tried to duck back around the corner. Before she could, white-hot pain shot through her body, totally disorienting her, consuming all her attention.

Through the sensation of total pain, she felt herself fall on the cold, paved floor of the tunnel, banging the back of her head.

Two sets of footsteps ran toward her, but she did not move. She could not focus her attention on anything. All she could do was writhe helplessly.

Pam feared, even in her pain, that she would die. However, the footsteps passed her and hurried on down the tunnel she had just come up. She felt a gradual lessening of the pain in her feet and remembered that the blindness and disorientation created by heretics was not permanent.

A deep, thundering heavy machine gun fired somewhere up ahead. That, according to Yojimbo, was probably another necromutant. The weapon roared again, closer this time. Light machine-gun fire responded.

As the pain in her body receded, she remained motionless, playing dead. She felt the vibrations in the hard, cold floor beneath her as a very heavy individual ran down the tunnel toward her. He stopped again to fire a heavy machine gun to his rear, and then ran past her after his two companions.

Pam finally opened her eyes.

CHAPTER 20

As Lane cautiously advanced up the maze into darkness, he knew that Pam was apparently ahead of him somewhere. However, each time he came to an intersecting tunnel, he had to guess which way she might have gone. He moved toward the sound of gunfire ahead, now a necromutant's heavy machine gun against two light machine guns from Fay and Klaus, but he could only hope that he was following a route that would lead him either to Pam or else to the enemy.

He turned a corner to his left, hoping to reach the edge of the action. After walking slowly, blindly sliding his left foot forward with each step, he heard two sets of footsteps running behind him. He whirled, his CAR-24 ready, but could see nothing. However, he heard them go farther down the maze toward the access tunnels. It would not be Yojimbo or the Doomtroopers. They were either Fay and Klaus or the enemy.

Lane worked his way back to the corner in the darkness. He heard two more sets of footsteps similarly working their way behind the last set. In all likelihood that was Fay and Klaus. Deciding to take a chance, he tightened his grip on his CAR-24 and remained around the corner.

"Sai," Lane whispered, revealing his position to the new arrivals.

"Sai," said Fay, quietly. "Who's there?"

"Lane. Two people and a necromutant just passed me, ahead of you. Have you seen Pam?"

"I'm here, too," Pam said huskily. "I played dead when a heretic hit me with pain, and the necromutant didn't bother with me."

In the darkness Lane could not see them, but he heard Pam, Fay, and Klaus come up and join him.

"We've had them engaged, but we don't know who they are," said Klaus. "Are we too late? To stop the mystic, I mean. And how did you come so far forward?"

"It's the maze. I came up too far and decided to look for Honorius."

"So did I," said Pam. "What happened behind us in the access tunnels?"

"You got me," Lane said quickly. "I shot down a necromutant in my tunnel and then followed you up here pretty closely, I think. Except maybe for taking some different turns in the maze."

"We better go," said Fay.

"That's right." Lane moved to the front. "Let's go. Be alert. We're likely to meet Yojimbo and group. No friendly fire."

Lane walked through the darkness as fast as he dared, back down the way he had come. The route was somewhat familiar. He heard heavy machine-gun fire ahead again and rounded a corner, anxious to join the action.

Before Lane could get his bearings, he heard the scuffle of human footsteps right in front of him. Afraid to fire blindly, and unwilling to reveal himself first by turning on his head lamp, he launched himself forward in a tackle. If his targets were friendly, no damage would be done.

In the blackness Lane felt his arms go around someone's waist. Lane's momentum carried them both to the hard floor of the tunnel. Ahead of them, a man gasped in surprise, and a moment later Lane heard the thump of someone behind him on the tunnel floor.

From the light sound, it was probably Fay's petite body falling with disorientation or pain.

Lane gambled that he was holding onto the mystic and tightened his grip, expecting to be hit with a Dark Gift of some sort.

"Head lamps on!" Lane shouted frantically. "I've got somebody!"

A second later, three beams of light shot down the tunnel. Lane looked up and saw a strange man slip around a corner. Light machine-gun fire chattered after him, over Lane, but missed. Lane looked to see who was in his grasp.

The man was in his mid-thirties, clean-shaven with brown hair, of medium build. Nothing about his appearance was distinctive, except his white tunic. It was long, emblazoned with the Brotherhood logo on the front.

Farther down the tunnels, the necromutant's heavy machine gun roared again. In response, a whooshing roar lit up the tunnel with indirect light. The heavy machine-gun fire stopped, leaving only silence.

"Sai!" Klaus shouted down the tunnel, as he jogged forward to Lane.

"Sai!" Yojimbo called back.

"Beware one more heretic," Pam yelled.

"I'm ready for him," Vic said firmly. "But Skippa needs help."

Lane looked behind him and saw Pam helping Fay sit up in the tunnel, lit by Pam's head lamp.

"You must be Honorius." Lane spoke politely, but kept a firm grip on the man's arm.

"Valley of darkness," said the stranger, lying where he was. "Many shadows."

Lane pulled him up to a sitting position. "Are you all right?"

"We shall have fish and loaves for dinner." The man did not seem to see or hear Lane.

"He sure sounds like a mystic," muttered Klaus. "That must be him."

"Well, he's no necromutant," Lane said dryly, standing. He gently drew the man up after him. "And he doesn't seem to have any Dark Gifts."

"So that makes him Honorius, the mystic," said Pam. "Nobody else would be here."

"Sai," Yojimbo said again, just before appearing around a corner. "You got him?"

"We got him," said Lane. "And we have a chance to get a heretic alive, if we move fast."

"Skippa's hurt," said Yojimbo. "By a necromutant's heavy machine-gun fire, before the incinerator got him.

Vic's back around the last corner with her. We'll get her to a Mishima trauma center."

"Fay and Klaus, will you hold Honorius?" Lane asked, looking at them both.

"Can do," said Klaus, shrugging.

Lane released the mystic and turned to Pam. "Ready, blue eyes?"

"Ready."

Lane moved up to the corner around which the last enemy had fled. He turned on his head lamp and swung around it with his CAR-24 ready, but the tunnel was empty. Pam came up right behind him.

"What do you think, Lane—lights on or off?" Pam asked, nodding toward his head lamp.

Lane knew that with their lamps on, their quarry could see them coming. In darkness, however, he could more easily lay a trap for them. It was a question of which problem they preferred to face.

"Lights on," said Lane. "From the sounds I heard earlier, his only weapons are his Dark Gifts and a handgun. For a change, we have him outgunned. If one of us goes down with a Dark Gift, the other sprays fire fast."

"Got it. Let's go."

Lane jogged up the tunnel, holding his CAR-24 ready. Pam kept pace just behind him, and a little to his right. The man they pursued had a good head start, but using their head lamps could also help them gain ground by showing them which tunnels were dead ends, and which ones narrowed to a size too small for him to have passed.

Yojimbo turned to Fay and Klaus, who were each gripping one of the mystic's arms firmly. "Bring him." Then Yojimbo moved down the tunnel back toward Vic and Skippa, glancing back over his shoulder to see how Honorius responded.

"Come on," Klaus ordered. As he pulled, Honorius cooperated, but did not acknowledge the instruction.

"I don't think he knows where he is," said Fay. "We'll have to steer him every step of the way."

Yojimbo turned a corner and found Vic helping Skippa sit up. She grimaced with pain. One of her thighs had a rough bandage tied around it; blood splattered her clothes and had smeared Vic's, as well.

"I gave her a painkiller we carry," said Vic. "But it's not strong enough to do more than take the edge off the pain. I'll have to help her walk."

"I'm not hurt too bad," said Skippa, through her teeth. "I just need a little tissue regeneration."

"You took an unnecessary risk," said Vic, chiding her in a concerned tone. "I saw you step out in front of that necromutant to fire when you could have just fired around the corner. What were you doing?"

"Had to make up something to Lane," said Skippa. "I should never have left the Banshees to join the Doomtroopers; you know what kind of corruption we got into. I just wanted to make sure I got that necromutant." She smiled weakly. "But you got him for me."

"Can you help her through the tunnels?" Yojimbo asked. "We can't risk staying here too long. One heretic got away. If Lane and Pam don't stop him, he could bring reinforcements back to us here."

"It's going to be tough, moving through the tunnels while supporting her," said Vic. "But we're ready."

"We'll go up the same access hatch we used to come down here from the surface," said Yojimbo. "It isn't far. As soon as we're on the streets again, we'll prioritize getting her to some help."

"Well, she needs it." Vic slung one of Skippa's arms over his shoulders. Then he stood slowly, helping her rise. She winced, but managed to stand, relying on Vic and her good leg.

"What about our friend, here?" Klaus asked, jerking his head toward Honorius.

Yojimbo turned and looked Honorius directly in the eye. "Can you understand me?"

Honorius looked back, but did not seem to see him. His eyes seemed focused somewhere in the distance beyond the tunnel walls. He said nothing.

"Just in case you can understand but not respond, I want you to know that we are friends," said Yojimbo. "We will take you to safety."

Honorius merely looked past him down the tunnel, but remained silent.

"Where to?" Fay asked.

"After we arrange help for Skippa, we'll take him back to the command center," said Yojimbo. "On the way, we will pick up a set of handcuffs."

"You really think it's necessary?" Fay asked doubtfully. "He's hardly moved at all."

"I do not think he will deliberately try to escape, but he might wander off. I have to keep him with me during the night, while I sleep. Then tomorrow we will decide what to do next. Now we must get up to the surface."

As Lane and Fay hurried through the tunnels, they turned the beams of their head lamps down every turn and around every corner. At first, they found nothing but empty pavement, often with streams of hissing steam or small animal skeletons picked clean. Lane kept choosing tunnels arbitrarily, hoping that he was thinking like a fleeing heretic.

After several minutes they both heard a sound of footsteps scraping on rough pavement up ahead. It was very brief, but gave Lane a direction to follow. Several more minutes passed, however, without another clue to their quarry's whereabouts. Finally he stopped.

"I think we've lost him," said Lane as Pam halted behind him. "I took too much time making sure Honorius was held and Yojimbo okayed our pursuit."

"Yeah. We should have moved out on our own as soon as we saw him escape us."

"We'll have to talk to Yojimbo about that," said Lane. "We don't have clear enough standing orders for different contingencies."

"You know, Chung, I'm no expert, but something's bothering me. Every rumor I ever heard about the Dark Legion said they don't run away."

Lane looked at her. "Yeah. I remember that now, too. But what about it?"

"We're *chasing* a heretic—and he's running away. I heard that Dark Legion forces come on in suicidal waves, without retreating until orders are given."

"Well, he's just a heretic. They function mainly as spies. The necromutants fought us to the death."

"Yeah." She shrugged. "Maybe that's all it is. But it doesn't feel right."

"The nepharite is still hidden away somewhere," said Lane. "The heretic is probably reporting back."

"If we've lost the heretic, then we might as well do the same."

"Yeah. Back to the command center."

Ragathol sat on his throne with every muscle tense as the pathetic, quivering heretic reported to him. The man lay facedown on the floor, with the heavy, booted foot of Gorong the necromutant on his neck. Gorong watched Ragathol. At the slightest nod from his master, he would snap Penyon's neck with the merest shift of weight.

The yellowish light in the cavern flickered over Gorong and Penyon as the high, thin, terrified voice recounted the fate of the escort. Three necromutants had been lost, leaving Ragathol with only three; the advanced heretics Halala and Lebec had been destroyed, meaning the effort placed in corrupting them was a waste; Honorius, the renegade mystic, had been taken. Worst of all, some organized group of humans now knew for certain that Ragathol's cell existed here on Luna.

As Ragathol's rage increased, he could not stand the tension anymore; he reared back on his throne and let out a long, thunderous scream of rage, pounding his fists on the arms of his throne. The stone of his throne vibrated beneath him; the roar of his own voice echoed back to him throughout the chamber. Even Gorong stared up at him in fear.

When the echoes finally faded, Ragathol glared down at Penyon. He gestured casually with his left hand for Gorong to step back. The necromutant did so, and Penyon let out a long breath.

"Stand," ordered Ragathol.

Penyon struggled to get to his feet.

Ragathol wanted to destroy the worthless human as an example to his other followers, but that would have to wait. Now Ragathol had to reclaim the mystic with a

much smaller cell. Boroth and Penyon were his only surviving heretics on this project. Penyon would have to be
impressed with the need to perform better than his recent
predecessors.

"Why should I not destroy you?" Ragathol demanded.
"For your failure to deliver the mystic to the docking
ports as I commanded?"

The heretic could only stare up at him, shaking. He
said nothing. His face was covered with sweat.

"Do I understand from your report that no one in your
escort actually reached the docking ports? I command
you to answer!" Ragathol's voice rumbled through the
cavern again.

Penyon nodded. "Yes," he said weakly.

Ragathol nodded. He had ordered Halala and the
necromutants to pirate a human ship and fly Honorius to
Azurwraith, the nepharite on Venus. Given their failure,
he was privately glad they had not reached the ports. At
least no one other than the mysterious group in the tunnels knew of their presence.

"And I ask you again," Ragathol thundered. "I ask you,
why should I allow you to live? Answer!"

"It wasn't my fault!" Penyon screamed, his voice
cracking. "I didn't do it!"

Ragathol laughed suddenly, amused by the sheer mind-
less terror in the creature before him.

Penyon's eyes grew even wider at the sight of his master laughing. He collapsed to his knees, unable to stand.
However, he still looked up at Ragathol anxiously.

"Heed me." Ragathol glanced at Gorong and spoke to
them both. "You must find this mystic again. However,
you must also find and destroy the humans who killed
your colleagues and took away the mystic. Since they are
together now, you have only one simple task." Ragathol
fixed Gorong with a glare. "You, Gorong, will supervise
this attempt in discussion with Boroth and . . . this
Penyon."

"As you wish." Gorong bowed deeply.

"I have ordered previously that our heretics move
through Luna City carefully, and that our necromutants

remain hidden here. My purpose was to avoid the notice of humans. Maintain this priority."

"I only await your orders," said Gorong, his voice eager.

"Waste no time. I expect the authorities here will issue an alert to our presence at any time. That will make our work more difficult. So act quickly!"

CHAPTER 21

Yojimbo convened the team back in the command center, except for Skippa. She remained in a trauma center for regeneration treatment. Honorius sat down cross-legged in the middle of the crowded floor.

Yojimbo, standing by the Whiz Kid's station, looked up as Vic arrived last, falling into a chair heavily.

"How is Skippa?" Yojimbo asked.

Vic leaned his Gehenna Puker against the arm. "She'll be okay," he muttered.

"How serious is it?" Fay asked from a spot on the floor by Honorius.

"They aren't exactly sure," said Vic, shaking his head. "She'll walk again, but she may not have all her movement back. That could mean the end of our partnership."

No one spoke for a moment.

Yojimbo glanced down at Honorius. The mystic was chanting quietly to himself, too low for the words to be heard clearly. He did not seem unhappy.

Lane was sitting on one end of the couch, with Pam perched on the arm next to him. "What do we do next, boss? Now that we have Honorius."

"I welcome any suggestions," said Yojimbo. "Clearly, we cannot learn much from our new guest simply by asking him questions."

"We haven't really tried," said Pam. "Maybe if we really focus on him for a while and keep him talking, he'll say something we can understand."

"Maybe," Klaus said doubtfully. He remained standing over Honorius, glowering down at him suspiciously. "I wouldn't spend a lot of time on it."

"If we're lucky, he might do something that will reveal

why he's so important," said Fay, looking at Honorius. "I mean, the Brotherhood and the Dark Legion both want a crazy man. They must have some reason."

"We can try asking him questions a little later," said Yojimbo. "Right now we have to decide how to proceed. For instance, we could use Honorius as leverage to communicate with the Brotherhood."

"Bad move, I say, Yojimbo." Vic frowned. "I don't want anything to do with them. You can't trust them. They justify anything they want to do in the name of purity as they see it."

"What do you have in mind?" Lane asked Yojimbo. "Communicate with the Brotherhood for what, exactly? Help fighting the Dark Legion?"

"Not precisely," said Yojimbo. "My employer emphasized the need for secrecy. We cannot make a public issue of the Dark Legion presence here. But the Brotherhood might tell us why Honorius is so special. That could help us, in turn, track down the nepharite."

"Forget it," Klaus growled. "The Brotherhood won't tell us anything worth hearing. We're on the outside; they'll consider us impure. Even if they tell us something about him, we can't rely on it."

"I'm afraid that's right," said Fay, looking up at Yojimbo from the floor.

"Yeah, me, too," said Vic. "Let's just keep the Brotherhood out of it."

"All right." Yojimbo was persuaded that this was a dead end. "We still need a plan of action. What else do we have to work with?"

"The Dark Legion is still here," said Pam. "We know the nepharite was not in the convoy, since the only enemy who escaped was a human male."

"Obviously a heretic," said Fay. "But what kind of information does that give us? We already knew heretics were here."

"We know we didn't get them all," said Pam. "And we can rely on the nepharite getting a full report. That's something, anyway."

"From what you have heard, do nepharites have any predictable tendencies?" Yojimbo looked around the entire group. "For instance, how many of his subordinates would he send in the convoy, and how many would he keep with him as protection? We have no idea of his total strength."

"I don't think we can infer anything like that," said Vic. "A nepharite does what he wants."

"That's what I've always heard," Pam said slowly. "But I also heard that the Dark Legion attacks in suicidal waves. Lane and I noticed that the necromutants did that, but the heretic who escaped certainly didn't."

"So you believe that something is different here?" Yojimbo asked. "What do you think?"

"I've been mulling it over," said Lane. "Either the rumors we've heard are wrong, or maybe this nepharite is taking some unusual precautions."

"I don't think the rumors are wrong," said Vic. "I've heard the same thing about suicidal waves, and I saw it for myself on the front line."

"Then the question is why our local enemy is different?" asked Yojimbo.

"I'd say the heretic who fled is following a different set of orders," said Fay.

"But why?" Vic insisted. "There's something suspicious about this."

"Maybe the answer is the most obvious one," said Lane. "The nepharite doesn't have a very large cell here and ordered his followers to escape if possible, especially once we had won the firefight."

"To preserve their numbers." Yojimbo hesitated. "It is plausible."

"We can't go too far with that, either," said Vic. "We can't possibly know how many followers the nepharite considers too few, or enough, or too many."

"That's right," said Klaus. "He may not feel he has enough, but that could still mean that twenty, fifty, even a hundred or more are still with him."

"I wouldn't go that far," said Pam. "Think of it in practical terms. I can't see a hundred necromutants sneaking into Luna without leaving behind more destruction, sightings, rumors. . . . They're too big and aggressive."

"I'll go along with that," said Vic. "Maybe fifteen or

twenty necromutants at the outside. And even that's probably pushing it."

"We killed two," said Pam.

"Fifteen or twenty," Lane repeated. "That's a lot for Team Yojimbo, as we're presently constituted."

"Exactly," said Klaus.

"Well ... I spoke too soon," Vic added slowly. "As I think about it, I'd say the nepharite has even fewer necromutants. Consider their situation here: Wherever they're hiding, they're confined, probably together."

"What about it?" Fay asked.

"As Pam said, they're big, aggressive, and used to action—meaning violence."

"I get it," said Lane, grinning. "You're saying they won't handle claustrophobia well."

"Not at all well. Keep ten of them together in one small place for a week, and I think they'd kill each other."

"We don't know that they're hiding in one spot," said Klaus. "They could be scattered all over Luna."

"What about that?" Yojimbo asked, looking at Vic. "Does that match your knowledge of the Dark Legion?"

"No," Vic said slowly. "It doesn't. Now, I can't say it's impossible, but we're dealing in likelihoods, not absolutes. I think a nepharite hiding in enemy territory would keep his forces together."

"Why do you think so? Are you sure enough for us to gamble on it?"

Vic paused. "I guess I don't really know what they'd do. They just seem to work that way."

"You know them better than any of us," said Pam. "I'd like to hear your thoughts."

"All right. Well, for instance, in battle they don't have great military discipline. They charge in a mob. I can't see the nepharite working out an elaborate spy system of cells with necromutants; spying is what heretics are for. Necromutants provide raw power and calm, cool, unthinking courage in battle. Yeah, I think I'd rely on this, at least till we learn something different."

"Fair enough," said Pam. "For what it's worth, I agree.

And if they're together without destroying each other in a big commotion, their number is probably fairly small."

"How small?" Klaus demanded.

"Under ten, originally, I would guess," said Vic. "Minus two now."

"Maximum of eight, then," said Lane. "If we're right, of course."

"And a nepharite," said Vic. "Bigger and more powerful. Don't forget him."

"Your Gehenna Puker is the most effective weapon against them," said Yojimbo. "I will buy one for each of us. Can you connect me to a black market seller?"

"I sure can," said Vic.

Yojimbo looked at Honorius. "He will be safe here, I believe, but we cannot leave him alone."

"I'm always here," said Whiz Kid from his station. "But maybe you should handcuff him to the furniture or something. If he decides to leave, I don't know if I can wrestle him to the floor and hold him." He fingered the front of his black satin jacket with a grin. "And I don't want to mess up the material."

Lane glanced down at the mystic. "He's not in any hurry that I can see."

"No, he isn't." Pam leaned toward Honorius, who was still chanting. "Can anyone understand him?"

"I can barely hear him," said Klaus.

"You're the closest to him," Pam said to Fay. "Can you tell what he's saying?"

"Sometimes I can catch phrases," said Fay. "It's all religious, I think. But sometimes he seems to think he's somewhere else."

"Yeah?" Lane moved off the couch and sat on the floor in front of Honorius.

"Honorius, can you understand me?" Lane looked right into the mystic's eyes.

"Pillar of salt," muttered Honorius. "Look forward, friends, not back."

"Have you mastered the mystics' art?" Lane asked. "Can you see the future?"

"Blessed are the meek," said Honorius. "But they have not left the Earth."

"I don't think he understands us," said Fay. "Whatever the nepharite wants him for, I doubt he can actually provide it. If he can see the future, maybe he's in it all the time."

"Could be," said Lane with shrug.

"It's been a long day," said Fay. "Yojimbo, suppose we break for the night."

"Yeah," said Klaus. "I want some dinner."

"Agreed," said Yojimbo. "I will cuff Honorius here so the Whiz Kid can watch him more easily. From what I can see, Honorius will not even notice. Vic, we will go out for those incinerators."

"Right."

"Team Yojimbo, we'll meet here in the morning," said Yojimbo.

Lane walked with Pam, Fay, and Klaus to the Midnight Star for dinner. The mystic's failure to respond rationally bothered Lane. Either Honorius was actually worthless to the nepharite, or he possessed some unknown power.

At the Midnight Star the group gathered at a corner table in the rear. The usual evening crowd was just arriving. Lane turned on a sonic disruptor so they could talk freely over their food.

"I want to ask you two something," Pam said to Fay and Klaus. "How do you feel about our progress so far?"

"What progress?" Klaus snickered. "Oh, I know we killed a couple of necromutants and heretics. But I don't see how snatching a crazy mystic has helped us any."

Fay looked up from a dish of lasagna. "What's on your mind, exactly?"

Pam glanced at Lane. He nodded, sure of what she wanted to say. Then he tasted his veal.

"Lane and I wanted to get out on our own today so we could use our own judgment," said Pam. "We feel that Yojimbo is maintaining too tight a rein."

Klaus shrugged.

"He left us alone to harry the rear of the enemy," said Fay. "He trusted our judgment."

"And we did the job," Klaus added.

"I think he trusts all of us," said Lane. "but he has the rigid Mishima training."

"That's right," said Pam. "He's used to a highly organized system. But what I'm really asking is, are you comfortable with it?"

"Sure." Klaus shrugged again. "It's not that different from Bauhaus."

"But I agree we haven't made much real progress," said Fay. "I'm open to suggestions. Do you two have something specific you'd like to do?"

"We don't have a plan, exactly," said Pam. "But how would you feel about loosening the reins a little?"

"You mean separate more and act on our own?" Fay asked. "We still need new leads."

"That's it, exactly," said Pam. "But I think we need to present this to Yojimbo as a group."

"Count me in," said Fay. "Klaus, what do you think?"

"I don't care either way," said Klaus. "But as your partner, I'll back you."

"I knew you would."

"But as soon as we're finished eating, I want to head home," Klaus added. "I'm worn out."

Lane looked up from his veal. "This stuff isn't as bad as usual. Eat up."

CHAPTER 22

After dinner Klaus and Fay hurried away. Lane let out a long, satisfied breath just outside the Midnight Star. Pam stopped next to him.

"It's hard to believe," said Lane, looking at the crowd on the street. "Life seems just the same as always. No one knows except us ... and them."

"I know what you mean."

"Besides, we shouldn't be too discouraged. We did kill two, you know."

Pam laughed. "And we rescued ol' whathisname, even if he's not too communicative."

"Yeah." Lane grinned.

"And our only wounded comrade will be okay. Not a bad day's work for the adrenaline, Chung."

"That's true, blue eyes."

"So. You coming back to visit me again tonight?" She looked at him with a teasing smile.

"I thought you'd never ask." Lane put his arm up around her shoulders. "And you know what else?"

"What?"

"Tonight, even this life seems worth living."

They both laughed.

The next morning Titus Gallicus stood in the service tunnels beneath the docking ports, watching a Brotherhood investigation team examine the site of a recent firefight. Vitus Marius followed everyone around, demanding immediate answers, pestering the technicians and scientists. They all wore plain tunics with the Brotherhood logo and head lamps that threw narrow beams of light.

Titus hated to see them scurrying around down here like this. No one wearing the Brotherhood logo should behave like vermin in these tunnels. The sooner they finished, the sooner they could return to their normal routines.

The night before, the Brotherhood had picked up reports from the docking ports about unusual sounds and vibrations down here. Most people assumed they were just another malfunctioning municipal system, or a routine fight among outlaw gangs or terrorists, but Titus would not leave any puzzle unexamined. Now he was glad.

Vitus walked back to him. "They have a preliminary conclusion."

"What is it?"

"Well, they used scanners to study the damage and the remains. From the marks they know how much heat and ammunition was required—"

"Spare me the details."

"All right. Ten to fifteen individuals fought here. At least one incinerator was used, a number of light machine guns, two heavy machine guns, and a few side arms."

"How many people were on each side?"

"They don't know. Because of the tunnels, they aren't sure which side shot in which direction."

"The location is no accident," Titus said coldly. "Someone wanted to reach the docks, and someone else wanted to stop them. Did they stop them?"

"Apparently. No sign of unusual entry to the docks has been recorded."

"What about those heaps of ash? Two of them were much bigger than the others."

"Apparently, the incinerator hit two or three people together."

"More than once?"

"So it appears, according to the investigators."

"No."

"Sir?"

"The Dark Legion has been here."

"*What?*"

"Two necromutants were killed here," Titus said quietly, eyeing the technicians carefully. He did not want them to overhear.

"They don't know that. The piles of ash contain no identifying residue."

"*They* don't know it. I do. Now, so do you."

Vitus said nothing, but he watched the Inquisitor cautiously in the shadowed tunnel.

"The Dark Legion was represented down here. No evidence of Dark Gifts such as fear or blindness can be detected this way, of course, and that explains the relative lack of destruction visible to us."

"Anyone could have been in a fight like this," Vitus said casually.

"And why did one side bring an incinerator?" Titus asked. "Clearly, they knew they would meet an enemy of unusual size and strength."

"Incinerators are not rare weapons."

"No. But they are large and bulky. Why bring one down into these narrow tunnels without a good reason?"

"Your logic is sound, sir." Vitus spoke politely, but firmly. "We still don't have real proof."

"I have the evidence I need," said Titus. "If you could read corruption and evil as I can, you might be an investigator yourself, mortificator."

Vitus's face tightened. "I prefer the occupation I have chosen."

"I'm sure you do." Titus turned away before the other man could answer. "I do not know specifically why a Dark Legion presence has come here, but of course to corrupt and infiltrate in a general way. However, the evidence of this firefight raises a new lead. We must learn who the other party was."

"I agree."

"We have finished here. Now we will return to the surface. Your work as a mortificator has given you more experience on the street than my work has given me. Make a suggestion. Where shall we begin our new search?"

"In the free-lancers' hangouts," said Vitus. "They keep up on gossip of this kind because it affects their job prospects. For instance, if the mystery group sustained any casualties, they might have openings for new recruits."

"Excellent."

"We'll need disguises, however—at least a change of clothes. They'll respond better if they think they're talking to fellow free-lancers when we ask questions."

"You will prepare them for both of us. Let's get out of this filthy hole."

Yojimbo and Vic bought Gehenna Pukers for everyone on the team except the Whiz Kid. After bringing them back to the command center, Vic went to visit Skippa. Yojimbo spent the night in the command center with Honorius.

While they were gone, Yojimbo had left the mystic's left wrist cuffed to the arm of the Whiz Kid's heaviest chair. Honorius never showed the slightest interest in moving. In fact, Yojimbo decided to uncuff him long enough to show him the rest room. He noted that Honorius recognized his surroundings sufficiently to use the private facilities.

After returning to the living room, Yojimbo made a few more unsuccessful attempts to communicate with the mystic, then gave up. However, this incident bothered him. He did not feel that Honorius was faking his mental condition. The mystic did have more comprehension of his surroundings than anyone had realized. He cuffed Honorius to the chair again and spent the night on the couch next to him.

The next morning Yojimbo jerked awake suddenly, concerned about Honorius. However, he found the mystic sitting in the chair, still cuffed, muttering quietly in Latin. The Whiz Kid was already sitting at his computer station, as always in his black satin jacket, his concentration somewhere in cyberspace.

By the time the team gathered, Yojimbo had showered, dressed, eaten, and placed a bowl of hot cereal in Honorius's hands. At first the mystic simply held it. Then, slowly, he began to eat, his eyes still vacantly unfocused.

Vic showed Fay and Klaus how to use their new Gehenna Pukers. Skippa was still in the trauma center. Lane and Pam came in last.

"Hey! How did you get him to eat?" Lane asked. "Is he talking?"

"Not to me," said Yojimbo. "He still speaks quietly to himself, sometimes in Latin. Not always."

"But he's eating," said Fay, looking up from her incinerator. It was almost as big as she was, though light enough for her to maneuver. "I think it's a breakthrough."

"Not a very practical one," Klaus said disgustedly. "I still wonder if he's faking."

"What's he actually saying now?" Pam asked.

"I have not been listening," said Yojimbo. "Take your incinerator from Vic. I will listen to Honorius."

"Me, too," said Fay, moving out of Pam's way. She sat down on the floor next to Honorius in his chair again.

Pam and Lane accepted their incinerators from Vic. Lane listened to his instructions. Pam, of course, had heard them earlier, when Lane had wanted to talk privately to Skippa.

Honorius held the empty bowl and spoon on his lap. "Power and glory. Darkness falls."

"Are you still hungry?" Fay asked. She took the bowl from his lap and held it up. "Did you like it?"

"Welcome, Inquisitor," said Honorius. "We have no darkness here."

"Maybe he thinks he's in a Brotherhood facility," said Fay. "Honorius, we're friends, but we aren't with the Brotherhood. Can you understand me?"

"You have sought and you have found," Honorius muttered, looking at the wall. "Lead us from the valley of shadow if you can."

"I do not think he is answering you," said Yojimbo. "I believe he hears and sees someone else."

"And someone else's speech," said Fay. "I guess he can sense some of his surroundings, but not all."

"He thinks he's talking to a Brotherhood Inquisitor," said Klaus. "But maybe he can hear your questions. Try something specific again."

Yojimbo spoke in a more authoritative tone. "Answer me, Honorius. Who am I?"

"I seek only the mystic art," said Honorius. "Judge me for my purity if you wish."

"You are right, Klaus," said Yojimbo. "He thinks he is talking to an Inquisitor. But I cannot tell if he hears what I say or something else entirely."

"We need to get our briefing started," said Pam, slinging her Gehenna Puker over one shoulder. "Yojimbo, several of us want to discuss a specific issue with you."

"All right." Yojimbo straightened. "What is it?"

Klaus looked doubtfully at Honorius. "Can we talk in front of him?"

"That's a good question," said Fay. "Maybe he can understand us, but just responds strangely."

"Even if he doesn't understand it, he might remember what we say in the future," said Lane. "He might repeat what he overhears in someone else's hearing."

"I agree," said Yojimbo. He glanced at the Whiz Kid, whose attention was still in cyberspace. "The mystic is cuffed to the chair. Come with me."

The team members glanced at each other in surprise, but they hefted their Gehenna Pukers and followed. Yojimbo led them outside, across the landing that separated the Whiz Kid's apartment from his own, and took the team into his own living room. Inside, he gestured for them to find places to sit in his spare quarters. As in the command center, most of them had to stand or sit on the floor.

"You live right here?" Lane grinned and leaned one shoulder against the wall. "That's handy. You have a real short commute, don't you?"

"Yes. What do you wish to discuss?"

"I guess it falls to me," said Pam, glancing at the others. "We want the freedom to act more spontaneously."

"In what respect?"

"We feel our separation into only two squads with specific assignments confines us," said Lane. "We're all experienced in one way or another, and we know Luna City."

"I respect all your abilities," said Yojimbo. "My instructions have not reflected any doubts about your efficiency."

"I think we realize that," said Fay. "But we aren't making progress fast enough."

"I have to second that," said Klaus.

CHAPTER 23

"I prefer strict organization and a clear line of authority," said Yojimbo. "Since I have hired you all, I must insist that the team reflect my belief in how we must proceed. All of you experienced a systematic approach as veterans yourselves. This cannot be unfamiliar to you."

"No," said Vic slowly. "But we aren't on the front lines here, either."

"That's the heart of it," said Fay. "We're basically urban guerrillas now."

"That's it," Lane said suddenly. "We're urban guerrillas on recon patrol."

Yojimbo smiled at the familiar terminology. He knew they were playing with him, in a sense, but he also recognized their point. Besides, none of them wanted out or to violate the basic principles of secrecy under which he had hired them. This was only an argument over tactics.

"What do you say, Yojimbo?" Pam asked.

"Do all of you feel this way?"

Lane and Pam looked at the others.

"I just want results," said Klaus. "Your way, their way, I don't care."

"Since my partner's out of action, we don't form a squad right now," said Vic. "Otherwise, I think we need a looser structure, too."

"How is Skippa?" Yojimbo asked.

"She's receiving accelerated tissue regeneration today. Then we'll see."

"Good." Yojimbo looked at them all. "Then how do you want to divide up? And do you have particular plans of your own in mind?"

"We haven't worked out details," said Pam. "First we wanted to know if you were flexible about this."

"Yes, I am. Shall we return to the command center, then, before splitting up for the day? Maybe the Whiz Kid will have leads we can use."

"Sure." Lane shrugged.

Yojimbo led them back to the command center. As soon as he opened the door, he saw that the chair was empty and that the handcuffs dangled, empty, from one arm. The Whiz Kid still had his head in the hood of his computer station.

"Check the rest room and remainder of the apartment," Yojimbo ordered quickly. A horrible emptiness swept through his gut. He had failed to do his duty.

As Pam drew in her breath sharply and Klaus swore, Fay hurried into the back. Yojimbo pushed past them to go back outside again. He jogged to the street and looked in all directions, but could not see Honorius in the crowd. For a moment he considered running after him, but that was pointless. The mystic could have wandered in any direction.

By the time Yojimbo got back inside, Pam and Klaus had gotten the Whiz Kid's attention out of cyberspace. Fay hurried up from the back, shaking her head. Lane fingered the empty handcuffs. Yojimbo stiffened, consumed with shame at losing Honorius.

"Zowee," muttered the Whiz Kid, looking around in embarrassment. "I didn't know you'd left, Yojimbo. I'm real sorry."

"Do not be," said Yojimbo grimly. He felt cold inside. "You pursued your responsibilities. I am at fault. This occurred because of my carelessness."

"No sign of him in the back at all," said Fay. "He must have gone right out the front."

"We weren't gone very long," said Lane, lifting the empty cuff. "This was opened, but not damaged that I can see. He must have known something about picking the lock. And he didn't waste any time."

"I knew it," said Klaus. "He knows more than he's letting on."

"He knows something, all right." Lane dropped the empty cuff, letting it swing.

"The question is, what kind of knowledge is it?" Fay pointed out.

"Sleight of hand," Klaus growled. "Are we back where we started with this guy?"

"Maybe it's more than sleight of hand," said Fay. "I mean, he's a mystic, after all."

"I don't see anything mystical about escaping handcuffs," said Klaus.

"Fay, what do you mean?" Yojimbo asked stiffly. He knew the others would see this as his personal failure to secure their prisoner.

"I'm not sure what I mean. Just that . . . well, he does seem genuinely crazy to me, and I think it must come from his study of mysticism."

"I get it," said Lane. "We all agreed earlier that he must have special value to the Brotherhood and the Dark Legion. That means he must have learned something of his art. This escape could be part of it."

Yojimbo nodded, keeping his anger at himself tightly controlled. "Maybe so. But of course, he was only a lead to the Dark Legion. We have no other business with him, or his concerns."

"He might be good for barter," said Klaus. "With either side."

"Let's quit talking and get moving," said Lane. "How about it?"

"As you wish," said Yojimbo. "You have asked for more flexibility. How do you want to proceed?"

"Lane and I want to go back to the site of our firefight under the docks," said Pam.

"I'll stay with Yojimbo," said Vic, "since I don't have my partner."

"I want to follow the mystic," said Yojimbo. He knew that part of this was a matter of personal pride, but he did not want to admit it aloud. He turned to the Whiz Kid. "Have you found any more leads through cyberspace?"

"A quarter zowee—no, I haven't," said the Whiz Kid. "But I can get back on it. In fact, now that we know exactly what Honorius looks like, and which neighborhood he was in up to a few minutes ago, I should send out an alert." He turned back to his computer station.

"Fay," said Pam. "What are you and Klaus going to do? You want to come with us?"

"I'd rather follow Yojimbo," said Klaus. "The mystic can't be too far, and he's still a lead of some kind."

"We'll split up," said Fay. "You go with Yojimbo and Vic. I'll join Lane and Pam. If either squad needs one of us, we can shift."

"All right," said Klaus.

"Let's go," said Pam.

Titus followed Vitus into the Midnight Star at midmorning. They were both dressed casually and also carried different weapons. Vitus had arranged Capitol CAR-24 light machine guns for both of them and Capitol Bolter handguns.

"I wanted to get Bauhaus MP-105 handguns," Vitus said casually as they sat down at a counter along one wall. "But I got word recently that a really bad shipment of them went out a few days ago. Some kind of manufacturing malfunction ruined them all."

Titus nodded, only half listening. He had expected more action here, but the Midnight Star was sparsely patronized at this hour. However, he saw that Vitus had done his job of disguising them well. Everyone else was also casually dressed and armed similarly. The only real variety was in the faded logos of different megacorporations that the free-lancers sometimes still wore on their clothes.

"What shall we do here?" Titus asked. "This is not much of a group to work with."

Vitus nodded toward a heavy-set, white-haired man eating eggs alone. His face had Slavic features. A Capitol M516 shotgun was slung over his shoulder, even as he sat. "I'll see if this man is in a gossiping mood. Come with me, but do not speak if you can avoid it."

Titus nodded. He resented taking orders from a mortificator, but in this case it could not be helped. Later, he would remind the mortificator of the true line of authority in the Brotherhood again, to make sure Vitus did not get too large an opinion of himself.

"Morning, friend," Vitus said pleasantly. He approached the stranger with both hands empty and away from his weapons. "Good eggs, are they?"

"Taste like chalk," said the older man. "But then, I like chalk. I eat this stuff every morning. What's it to you, either way?"

"I wonder if you could help me with a little scuttlebutt," said Vitus.

"It might cost you. Then again, it might not. What's on your mind?"

"I want to buy some handguns, but I heard MP-105s aren't reliable right now."

"I heard that, too. A big shipment went out recently that can't fire. But they aren't the only handguns in town. You must know that."

"Let's just say I need good black market stuff, and I have a taste for Bauhaus products. Who's hot right now?"

"Yeah, all right." The man shrugged. "This isn't even worth charging for; everybody knows this—Cameron Glen in an Imperial warehouse."

"Thanks."

"Sure. Now get lost."

Vitus grinned and motioned for Titus to follow him out. On the street Vitus kept walking, forcing Titus to keep up. Finally, Titus shoved past another pedestrian and came up alongside the mortificator.

"You know where we're going?" Titus demanded. "You didn't ask him."

"I do."

"Yeah? Then why didn't we just go there? Why did you have to ask?"

"Because different black marketeers get hot at different times. Cameron Glen has been in business for years, but he's not always the hot guy to buy from. Now we know that he is, right now."

"So you know him."

"Yeah. He's a pain to talk to, but he's not as crazy as his reputation."

"Crazy?"

"That's just a gimmick."

"What of his spirit? Is he pure of heart?"

The mortificator laughed cynically. "If you mean, has the Dark Legion turned him into a heretic, I doubt it. The free-lancers who buy from him would be spreading the word, if not eliminating him themselves. If you mean, is he eligible for Brotherhood approval, don't count on it. And when we get there, remember, we're free-lancers. He won't help us if he knows our true vocations."

"I'll remember, mortificator."

Vitus took him to a lower level of the city. They entered an industrial area full of factories first, even darker and filthier than most of the city. Then they reached blocks of warehouses, where gaunt, savagely angry gargoyles crouched in attack perches over the dark, virtually deserted streets.

Ahead, Titus saw a large warehouse with the Bauhaus logo over the main door. Instead of approaching it, however, Vitus led him through a dark, narrow alley. They followed it down one side of the warehouse to a small door. With a conspiratorial glance at Titus, Vitus rang a buzzer.

"Anything I should know about this man?" Titus asked quietly.

Vitus shrugged. "He used to be in the Imperial Blood Berets."

"So? What's that to me, one way or another?"

"I hear they fight the Dark Legion in the jungles of Venus," said Vitus. "But I don't know if it's true."

"Most of what people say about the Dark Legion is hearsay," said Titus.

The lock in the heavy door clicked open loudly. Vitus opened the door with his left hand, holding his CAR-24 ready with his right, taut on its shoulder strap. Titus took his own CAR-24 in hand, but let the mortificator enter with a good margin.

Nothing happened as Vitus entered, so Titus followed him. The lock had obviously been controlled from a distance. Inside, giant stacks of huge crates stood off to one side of the main aisle down the center of the warehouse.

A man's voice boomed through a loudspeaker up near

the ceiling. "Welcome, lowland friends. Come into the highlands of Luna where the jungle never grows."

Following Vitus carefully, Titus moved up through the aisle between the stacks of crates. He heard and saw no sign of anyone else. At the far side of the warehouse, they reached a small security station on a raised platform. Consoles full of control panels and screens filled the station. Transparent security screens protected it.

A small man with dark hair and a pointed face stood in the open doorway with his arms folded. His jersey had the Imperial Blood Beret logo on it, but he also wore a Scottish kilt in a green hunting tartan. He glanced at both of them, but eyed Vitus cautiously.

"Good day, Cameron," Vitus said politely, lowering his CAR-24.

Titus reluctantly did the same.

"We two have run about the braes," said Cameron. "You've come to pull the gowans, eh?"

Titus understood none of that. His right hand itched to take up his CAR-24 again, but he knew the movement would cause trouble. He watched Cameron warily.

"I've done business with you before," said Vitus. "Do you remember me?"

"Almost." Cameron studied his face. "Something different about you, John Riley. Your clothing, mayhap. Your name would be . . . Vincent?"

"Close enough. But I'm not here for hardware, shall we call it, today."

"What, then?"

"We're here about a certain firefight in the tunnels that happened lately. I'm looking for some scuttlebutt about those involved."

Titus knew that Vitus was bluffing, hinting that they knew more than they did in case Cameron was also informed about the incident.

"Luna City is full of black marketeers dealing in weapons," said Cameron.

That was the first statement Titus had understood clearly. He looked at Cameron more carefully, suspecting his strange manner of speech was merely a posture. Cameron might be able to help them, after all.

"You're hot right now," said Vitus. "Your job brings you word from the street. If you didn't deal with those in question directly, you may have heard rumors that would serve us." His tone had subtlely shifted to one of menace.

Suddenly, without a word, Cameron's eyes widened as he looked at Vitus's face. He straightened up in the doorway, alert and wary.

CHAPTER 24

"You remember me now." Vitus's voice had taken on a cold authority.

"Yes, mortificator. I finally recognize you. We have done business in the past. How may I help?"

"I want a lead to those who fought in the tunnels. I believe they needed special weapons—they may have bought incinerators, for instance."

"I haven't sold any incinerators recently," said Cameron plainly. "Nor have I heard of any notable sales by anyone else. But a small sale would not cause unusual talk on the street, either." He hesitated. "Incinerators. They're favored by those who expect to meet representatives of the Dark Legion in the near future."

"You have heard of someone with this concern." Vitus's tone made this a statement, not a question.

"An old Bauhaus contact of mine named Klaus Dahlen," said Cameron.

"What about him?"

"He's the only lead I have along this line."

"What did he say about the Dark Legion?"

"Nothing directly," said Cameron. "He asked me if I knew anything."

"So he came in looking for rumors of the Dark Legion." Vitus studied Cameron's face.

Cameron said nothing.

Titus stiffened. The man clearly knew more than he was offering. If anyone could get the rest of his knowledge out of him, an Inquisitor of the Brotherhood could do it.

Vitus glanced at him and shook his head. "Cameron, I

owe you. You can do well someday with a mortificator in your debt."

Cameron nodded. "It is payment enough."

"Let's go," Vitus said to Titus.

Vitus led him at a brisk walk back through the shadowed warehouse. Behind them Cameron said nothing. Their footsteps echoed on the hard floor until they reached the door. Titus was glad to get outside again.

"I could have learned far more from him, mortificator," said Titus, once they were out in the alley.

"I know. But we have enough. And leaving this man in place for the future is wise."

"What is your next suggestion?"

"First we should pick up a couple of incinerators. Since you believe necromutants were crisped below the docking ports, this Klaus Dahlen may lead us to others. Then we will return to the Midnight Star and ask after him."

"Very well."

That night Lane sat with Fay in the Midnight Star. Pam had called Cela, who had information for her. However, Cela had insisted that Pam meet her alone, so Lane and Fay were waiting for her.

As usual, the place was crowded. They took no more than ordinary notice of those around them. Yojimbo and Klaus were in the command center, hoping for more leads from the Whiz Kid; Vic had gone to see Skippa again.

Lane looked over his drink at Fay. "How did you decide to join Cybertronic, originally?"

Fay looked at him cautiously. "Why?"

"Huh? Is it private?"

"Why do you ask?"

"Well ... I've known lots of free-lancers, but you're the first veteran of Cybertronic I've known to leave."

"I was scared to leave, too, just like all the rest who change their minds." She sighed. "I first signed up because I'm so petite, and life is so violent now. When I was young, I wanted the physical advantages of being a cyborg. But I got tired of fighting the megacorporation wars. I wanted out and realized I had made a mistake."

"A mistake?"

"You and Pam could quit the Martian Banshees and still be yourselves. But when a Cyborg leaves Cybertronic, you lose your legal access to mechanical parts. You have to get repair and replacement on the black market, and it's expensive because the black marketeers know you're desperate."

"If only a few of you leave Cybertronic, the demand in the black market for parts must be low. Wouldn't that keep the price down?"

"No. The demand is *so* low that nobody stocks the parts at all. When I need something replaced, I have to make a special order."

"I'd never thought that through before." Lane shook his head. "Life is a mess, isn't it?"

"Why do you ask? Is it just the normal fascination many of you ordinary people have for cyborgs?" She smiled cynically. "Klaus asked the same questions. So do most noncyborgs, if I know them long enough."

"It's more than that. Pam and I were talking recently about . . . well, about how lousy this life is. Whether it's really worth living."

Fay stared at him, her dark eyes hard and pointed. "You serious?"

"Yeah. So was she."

"You're both spoiled."

"What?" Lane was mystified.

"I have a simple answer. All the physical changes Cybertronic made in me proved that my life is all I have. My cyborg parts have reminded me of just how fragile my body is. I don't take anything for granted."

Lane looked at her, slowly understanding what she meant. "You have to work at maintaining your health."

"If you call it health." She smiled slightly. "Maybe I should call it staying in good repair."

"I see what you mean. Pam and I aren't very happy with our lives, but we don't worry about this stuff."

"In fact, this is why I'm involved with Klaus, really." She shrugged self-consciously.

"I don't get the connection."

"That's the right word—I want the feeling of connection, of closeness to other people. The more mechanical your body becomes, the more you feel like an outcast."

Lane nodded slowly. Fay had suddenly become more of a real person to him. Up to now she had been an acquaintance and sometimes a colleague, but he had regarded her cyborg status as a barrier between them. This talk made her seem like a normal person.

"Pam's here." Fay nodded toward the door.

Lane watched as the tall blonde worked her way through the crowd. He could tell by the tight smile on her face that she had learned something useful. By the time she joined them, he had already turned on the sonic disruptor.

"You look smug, Pam." Fay grinned.

"Cela gave me what she had," said Pam. "It isn't everything, but it explains something about Honorius."

"Go ahead, blue eyes."

She got into Capitol's files on the Brotherhood," said Pam excitedly. "Supposedly, Honorius really has achieved some of the mysticism that he was studying. Among his apparent mystic abilities is alleged short-term clairvoyance and minor telekinesis."

"Telekinesis," said Lane. "That may explain his escape. He probably unfastened his handcuffs with his mind. No way we could have predicted that."

"That's right," said Pam. "The file also notes that Honorius is always zoned out to some degree."

"What does that mean, exactly?" Fay asked.

"The Brotherhood believes his mind cannot always tell the difference between his clairvoyant visions and events actually happening around him at the time. So far, he hasn't been useful to them because he communicates so poorly and can't really control his visions."

"He handled those handcuffs just right." Lane hesitated. "That could explain a lot about him, though—almost everything he does."

"That's right," said Pam. "He isn't crazy in the normal sense."

"He's passive because his mind is sometimes living a life independent of his body's location," said Fay slowly.

"He always looked like he saw visions that weren't there. And he really was talking to people who weren't there."

"That's my guess," said Pam.

Lane nodded.

"I have a little more," said Pam. "Just two names from the Brotherhood. Titus Gallicus, Senior Inquisitor of the Brotherhood, and a mortificator named Vitus Marius have been assigned to bring Honorius back to live with the other mystics and be studied. But I don't have descriptions."

"How did Honorius get away from the Brotherhood in the first place?" Lane asked. "Do they know?"

"I don't think they know for sure," said Pam. "But from the vague language in the file, I think he just sort of wandered off."

Lane grinned. "We learned the hard way that he's capable of that."

"I want to get some dinner," said Pam. "Then tomorrow morning I'm going to see Cela again. I already asked her to see if the Capitol files have anything else that might be related to the firefight in the dock or sightings of heretics. Now that she's done it once, she's more willing to help. If we're lucky, she'll have more tomorrow morning."

"Sounds good to me," said Lane. "You had a good day, blue eyes."

Ragathol glared down from his stone throne at yet another heretic. This man was short and heavy, with pale skin and red-rimmed eyes. The nepharite dared not rage at him, however. Like another before him, he had arrived on Luna in secret with another message from Algeroth. Kyno had left shortly after giving the Dark Apostle's message to Ragathol; this new one must have been sent soon after Kyno had reported back.

Gorong, the senior necromutant, stood guard in the chamber doorway.

"Speak, Slumoig," Ragathol ordered. His angry but controlled voice rang against the stone walls.

Slumoig looked up at him, unafraid. "Our master is displeased."

"What is the Dark Apostle's complaint?" Ragathol demanded haughtily.

"You and your cell still remain here, exposed to discovery by the humans who infest this rock."

"Our mission here continues," Ragathol said coldly. "What of it?"

"The Dark Apostle is displeased with the delay in your mission. He wants results, and he wants Ragathol the nepharite to withdraw from Luna soon."

"Oh? And what does our Dark Apostle fear?" Ragathol sneered, but did not dare call Algeroth cowardly in so many words.

"My lord wishes Ragathol to return to the citadels of the Dark Legion before he is captured," Slumoig said calmly. "Valuable information about us must not fall into the hands of the Brotherhood."

"*I* shall decide when this mission has ended," Ragathol growled, his voice rising again. He stopped himself from shouting, however. Emissaries from the Dark Apostle had to be treated carefully.

For a long moment Ragathol stared down at the human before him. The heretic knew he had the protection of the Dark Apostle in this chamber, but of course he was vulnerable to the hostility of his fellow humans in the event that his status as a heretic was discovered. They both knew that Ragathol could arrange for him to lose his cover, given sufficient provocation.

In the meantime, Ragathol had only three necromutants, led by Gorong, and a couple of low-level heretics, of whom Penyon seemed to be the most devoted. Ragathol had a few other heretics placed around Luna City who had not seen the extent of his cell here, such as the one named Snazzer, who had brought Penyon to him. However, Ragathol wanted to leave the others in place for the future. He preferred to keep them away from this cell and his current activities.

"You may help me serve our lord," said Ragathol, looking deep into the pale eyes of the heretic. "We will finish sooner with more help."

"I am ordered to return to our lord the Dark Apostle promptly."

"I will arrange for your departure," said Ragathol. "When I deem it safe."

The heretic drew himself up. "I demand—"

Ragathol straightened angrily in his throne, and the heretic froze, suddenly silent.

Slumoig glanced nervously over his shoulder and saw Gorong standing in the only doorway, blocking the exit with his massive, heavily muscular body.

"I shall arrange for your departure at the proper time," said Ragathol. "Gorong, see that our guest has sufficient food, water, and rest. We know these humans are weak and must have care."

"As you wish." Gorong bowed deeply and stood aside for Slumoig.

"Dismissed," said Ragathol. As he watched the heretic reluctantly bow and leave the chamber, the nepharite considered the state of his mission. The humans who took Honorius had to be found somehow. However, now that he had asserted his authority over Slumoig, he would send him on his way soon. Ragathol did not want him to have the opportunity to spy on this cell for the Dark Apostle.

Penyon began the morning with an idea. He did not have many, but he had one today. For the first time since he had become a heretic, he returned to the site of his former job in a Capitol warehouse, where he asked his old pal Snazzer to pose questions for him in cyberspace. Penyon asked, in the name of their mutual master, Ragathol the nepharite, if anyone had heard rumors about people fighting a mysterious battle in the tunnels beneath the docking ports with an incinerator and light and heavy machine guns.

Snazzer received many responses, but Penyon recognized that only one answer was useful. One rumor reported a very recent black market sale of Gehenna Pukers. Penyon had very clear, terrifying memories of a single incinerator roaring in the tunnels under the docking ports, forward of his own position, and of the fact that Halala, Lebec, and three necromutants never returned.

Whoever the enemy had been, they certainly must have

noticed the same fact. Maybe they had bought more incinerators. Penyon would have, in their position. In any
case, it was the only new information worth considering.

The rumor was not very detailed. The source only provided the area where the sale had apparently taken place.
That was not much, but Penyon thanked Snazzer and
headed there. It was better than nothing.

Shortly, Penyon found himself in a free-lancer's neighborhood. That, too, seemed to mean that this would be a
good place to start. On the crowded streets he began to
ask if anyone had seen some friends of his who often
wore Gehenna Pukers. Most of those he asked were too
busy, or just shook their heads. However, a few passersby
recalled seeing some people in the last day or two wearing them, and they directed Penyon gradually to one specific block.

At midmorning, Penyon saw a tall, very attractive
woman with short blond hair walking down the street
through the crowd. She wore a gray jumpsuit that was
skintight on her lean, athletic body. A headband around
her hair held a lamp that would be very useful down in
the tunnels. Strapped to her back, a Gehenna Puker
bounced slightly as she walked.

CHAPTER 25

Pam left the command center alone, after telling Yojimbo that she planned to meet with Cela again. Yojimbo had no objection. The rest of the team would divide again into squads and try to figure out how to do a better job today than they had done before. Pam was not optimistic that they would think of anything.

In recent days Pam had become accustomed to using the maintenance tunnels routinely. They were never crowded, though she often heard other people moving around elsewhere in the maze. Sometimes she even caught sight of someone, but everyone had wanted to avoid direct contact with her as much as she had wanted to avoid meeting any of them.

This morning she moved to an access hatch near the command center, eager to get off the jammed street. Now the routine was familiar; she swung the cover open on its hinge, started down the ladder, and paused to swing it closed over her head with a clank. Then she switched on her head lamp and descended the ladder, listening for sounds of other people nearby.

At the bottom of the ladder she paused again, but heard nothing. She consulted her belt computer for its map of the maze and picked her direction. Then she quietly moved forward, keeping the beam of her head lamp angled sharply downward to prevent the beam from revealing her position too far forward. She held her belt computer in her left hand, so she could glance at it conveniently as she turned corners and chose branching tunnels. As usual, she kept her right hand on her CAR-24 in case she ran into unexpected trouble.

Pam had just turned a corner to her right, leaving the

ladder out of sight, when she heard a very low, metallic clink in the tunnels behind her. The same access hatch she had used had been closed quietly again, just as she had carefully let it shut a few moments before. She stopped where she was, listening.

If a member of the team had come to get her for some unexpected reason, she would hear the code-phrase "sai" spoken quietly in a few seconds over her belt computer. If the stranger had no interest in her, she would merely avoid him. As she waited, she heard a slight scraping sound of footsteps on the hard floor of the maze, but could not tell at first in the echo chambers of the tunnels if they were coming closer.

Pam did not expect any trouble, but she was too experienced to let down her guard. She waited patiently, figuring the stranger would move past her in a nearby tunnel in a few minutes and be on his way. When she heard more quiet footsteps now clearly approaching her, she turned off her head lamp. Its light had been visible in the tunnels behind her, even indirectly around the corners. The stranger might have followed her simply because it helped illuminate a path.

She held her CAR-24 ready, but still did not anticipate trouble. A single set of footsteps came right up to the corner around which she had come, their sound revealing someone of ordinary weight. Since she had turned off her head lamp, however, the steps were moving more slowly.

That concerned her. The other person might have simply slowed down because it was dark now, but the stranger could also be stalking her. She supposed a mugger or a pickpocket might have seen her on the street and decided to rob her, probably for her weapons.

However, it was also still possible that the stranger was one of her team members who had decided to be as cautious as she was. She heard the footsteps come up just around the corner she had turned. Instead of turning right as she had, though, the stranger moved on straight. Now she was behind him, feeling the familiar adrenaline surge that always preceded action.

Pam readied her CAR-24 with her right hand and reached up with her left, still holding the belt computer, to turn on her head lamp. She did not want to give the code-phrase in the dark and be answered with a burst of gunfire by a stranger. Turning on her light would show her if this was a team member or not. She stepped back around the corner into the first tunnel and switched it on.

An unarmed man whirled in surprise, looking at her in shock with frightened eyes. Before Pam could reassure him that she meant no harm, she suddenly went blind.

With her Martian Banshee's and free-lancer's reflexes still sharp, she squeezed the trigger of her weapon and moved it in a tight circle, hoping to hit him. Now she understood that he was a heretic, but before she could think any further, she felt him tackle her at her knees. She went down, too close to him to train her CAR-24 on him.

While she was fighting blind, he now had the advantage of sight by her own head lamp. As she flailed for a hold on him of some kind, she felt her CAR-24 yanked out of her grasp. In her left hand she flicked on the voice function of the belt computer, hoping to call for help, though she doubted the signal could get out of the tunnels to the surface.

Before she could speak, something hard struck her head, dazing her.

Yojimbo had decided to head out today with Vic and Klaus, while Lane and Fay formed the other squad. Then they waited to see if the Whiz Kid could get any new leads for them in cyberspace. However, he leaned out of the hood with a puzzled expression.

"What is it?" Yojimbo asked.

"I'm not sure," said the Whiz Kid. "I don't have any real leads, but . . . half a zowee. I'm receiving a faint, irregular signal of some kind."

"Yeah?" Lane frowned. "What do you mean, 'some kind'? Is it Pam?"

"It's not a voice," said the Whiz Kid. "In fact, it's not even steady." He turned to his computer. "Display visual graph of radio reception," he ordered. "And put the sound on the speaker."

Yojimbo joined Lane in looking over the Whiz Kid's shoulder at the screen. The speaker began to hiss intermittently and irregularly. At each sound a line on the graph lengthened slightly on the screen.

"You know more about this than anyone," Yojimbo said to the Whiz Kid. "Is it significant? Or are we just picking up random static?"

"Suppose it's Pam," said Lane before the Whiz Kid could respond. "What would make it sound like that?"

"She would have to be in a place where the transmission is blocked, at least partly. Maybe she would be moving, so that her transmission is blocked sometimes and not others. But she's not talking. It's just that her belt computer's voice function is turned on."

"That's all it is," said Klaus, snickering. "She left her communicator on by mistake."

"She's in trouble," said Lane. "Could she be down in a tunnel?"

"Maybe if she's close to the surface and some of the access hatches are open," said the Whiz Kid. "But ... zowee. I don't see how. She must be on the street."

"Let's just call her and tell her," said Klaus, reaching for his own belt computer."

Fay put a hand on his wrist, stopping him. "Wait. I agree with Lane. Something's wrong."

"Computer," said the Whiz Kid, "enhance any background signal against the noise."

The hiss of static shifted subtly. A faint rumble of voices reached them. A vehicle honked.

"Street noises," said Lane. "Something happened to her, but she's giving us a tracking signal. We have to use it, Yojimbo. She must be onto something."

"Agreed," said Yojimbo. "Whiz Kid, bring up a map of Luna on screen and see if you can find her location."

"I can bring up the map," said the Whiz Kid. "But I can't locate the source of the signal using only one locus of reception here. We have to triangulate."

"And the rest of Team Yojimbo has to use a different frequency in our own communication," said Fay. "Otherwise, our signals will be heard through Pam's belt computer and could be overheard by someone else."

"Of course," said Yojimbo. "Whiz Kid, choose a frequency and give it to us. Then both squads will move out.

We'll start with positions one block apart, and each squad will pursue the signal the best we can. Set your belt computers to display automatically when the signal gets stronger and weaker."

"Will do," said Lane.

The blow to Pam's head did not knock her completely unconscious, but she was disoriented by it, and remained blind. She felt herself lifted partly to her feet, then was bent over the man's shoulder. He stood, lifting her, then began to walk, his footsteps unsteady with her weight.

The man carried her through the tunnels for a while, but then had to set her on her feet, with one of her arms across his shoulders for partial support. She began to regain her thoughts, despite a pounding pain where he had struck her head, but her blindness had not gone away, even after she thought it normally would have. He was probably hitting her every so often with his Dark Gift again, to prevent her from recovering her sight.

Her CAR-24 was no longer strapped over her shoulder, and she surreptitiously patted the holster where she wore her Bolter side arm, finding it empty. The Gehenna Puker was no longer bouncing on her back. It must have been left behind, too big for him to wear while he carried her and too dangerous for him to leave on her.

She still clutched her belt computer in her left hand. If the heretic had noticed it, he had not recognized that it might have communication capability. Pam decided that pretending to remain dazed was in her best interest, so that the heretic would not injure her any further. Blind and unarmed, she would not be able to escape, anyway.

After a short time the heretic stopped and manipulated her limp body onto his back. Pam did not resist. She realized that if she could ultimately learn something by remaining with the heretic for a while, she might still be able to transmit it back to the team.

The heretic carried her on his back for a while, then finally began climbing a ladder. She felt the butt of her CAR-24 banging against one leg and realized that the heretic had strapped it over his own shoulder; the knowledge reinforced her decision not to resist. Without sight, she could not possibly grab it away from him.

Then she heard the familiar sound of an access hatch clanking open and then the routine noises of the street. Apparently, he had decided to give up carrying her through the tunnels. Still blind, and now with her injured head throbbing, Pam remained limp, to tire the heretic as much as possible. He reached over and turned off her head lamp.

"Judge not, that you not be judged," said a familiar voice quietly, behind them. Pam recognized Honorius's voice, speaking more clearly and directly than ever.

The heretic turned suddenly, letting Pam's feet slide to the pavement, though he still supported most of her weight. "What are you doing here? Never mind—don't move!"

Pam felt the heretic move jerkily toward Honorius's voice, almost letting her fall. She was sure that the heretic had grabbed hold of the mystic. Now she was partly standing on her own, but her captor had not seemed to notice.

"The meek must inherit," said Honorius.

"Easy, there, easy," said the heretic in a whiny, plaintive voice. "I'll flag down a minicab to take all three of us."

"Cast your bread upon the waters," said Honorius calmly. "Let the lamb return to her flock and accept the ram in her stead."

While the heretic was distracted by Honorius, Pam unzipped the top of her jumpsuit just enough to slip her belt computer inside. It was still transmitting, and now that they were on street level again, the signal would carry back to the command center or any of the team members. She did not dare speak into it directly, however. With it in her jumpsuit, the heretic was even less likely to notice.

"You mean you want me to trade you for her?" The heretic's voice revealed amazement. "Really? You aren't running away? How did you find us?"

"Seek and you shall find," said Honorius.

Pam suddenly realized that Honorius must have had a

clairvoyant vision of where to find the heretic holding her. He had obviously experienced this vision far enough in advance so he could intercept them. She was still confused as to his precise abilities, but this was no time to worry about particulars.

Her vision, though blurry, was suddenly returning. Distracted by Honorius, the heretic had neglected to hit her again with his Dark Gift to maintain her blindness. She closed her eyes and then opened them slightly, carefully, still pretending blindness. Now she did not want to escape. If the heretic was going to take her somewhere, she wanted to go. Locating the nepharite was the team's real goal, not just taking Honorius back.

The mystic, however, was blinking oddly, not focusing his eyes at all. Pam realized that the heretic had just blinded him. Startled, Honorius said nothing.

"Come with me," the heretic said calmly. "All three of us will take a ride."

Lane led Fay through the crowded streets, holding his belt computer in his left hand, up by his ear. The Gehenna Puker bounced on his back as he worked his way among the crush of people. Behind him Fay scanned the street constantly with her cyborg vision.

On Lane's belt computer the screen showed him the direction from which Pam's signal was coming. On the alternate frequency suggested by the Whiz Kid, an automatic tracking signal also came from Yojimbo. Lane's own belt computer was returning a similar signal to Yojimbo, while the Whiz Kid picked up all three signals at the command center. The Whiz Kid sent back a location to Lane and Yojimbo that reflected the apparent source of Pam's transmission as it moved.

"I had some voices for a minute," Lane said urgently to Fay. "I didn't hear Pam, though."

"Who was it, then?" Her tone was all business, but her face revealed a genuine concern for Pam.

"Two men's voices, kind of muffled. I couldn't understand them. And they've quit talking."

"See if your belt computer can enhance the sound," said Fay. "Maybe it can make out the words."

"Don't have time." Lane glanced down at the little screen again. "The signal's getting weaker. They're leaving us behind—moving faster than we are."

"Keep your eye on it as we go," said Fay. "I'll call Yojimbo. Sai! Fay here."

Lane heard Yojimbo's voice come through Fay's belt computer.

"Sai! Go ahead, Fay."

"We're starting to lose the signal. If we do, the team as a whole can't triangulate. Did you hear voices?"

"Yes, we did," said Yojimbo. "I had the Whiz Kid enhance them, run an analysis, and report back. One is Honorius, the other unknown. From the dialogue I believe a heretic is taking both Pam and Honorius in a minicab somewhere."

"You don't know where?"

"I hope it is the lair of the nepharite," said Yojimbo. "Get a minicab if you can. Prioritize staying in range of the signal. Out."

"Flag one down," said Lane, still glancing at his belt computer. "This could be good for us. If the heretic is taking Honorius back to their hiding place, it means the nepharite will either try to get Honorius's knowledge before making another attempt to send him off Luna, or else he wants to set up another escort to send him to the docks. Either way, it buys us some time."

CHAPTER 26

Pam continued to remain limp as she rode with the heretic and Honorius in a minicab. To avoid revealing that she could see, and therefore reminding the heretic to blind her again, she kept her eyes closed. She hoped the team was receiving the signal from her belt computer.

When the minicab halted, she continued to be passive as the heretic helped both his charges get out. Then she walked under her own power, though the heretic held one arm above the elbow to guide her. Since her head was still pounding where he had struck her, she did not have to pretend being hurt.

Honorius remained just as cooperative. The heretic took them down into another access hatch. Once they were in the tunnels, Pam knew that her belt computer was probably not going to transmit back up to the street. However, she could not do anything about it. The heretic turned on her head lamp again for light.

She found that they did not spend much time in the standard tunnels with which she was familiar. Almost immediately, she felt that the floor under her feet was no longer solid pavement, but gravel. It was not level, either, but angled downward. She reached out with her free hand to steady herself and felt a wall that was not flat. The surface was rough, as though this tunnel had been blasted out of solid moon rock, and it curved, suggesting that the shape of this passage arched over their heads.

Finally, Pam felt the gravel floor become more level. A moment later she realized that they had moved onto an uneven floor of solid rock, not gravel. She opened her eyes slightly, for only a second, to glance at her surroundings. The heretic was walking between Pam and

Honorius, pulling them forward into a large cavernous doorway.

Heavy footsteps, like those of the necromutants in the tunnels, approached. Pam closed her eyes again quickly, hoping that remaining passive and apparently blind would make her seem harmless. The heretic pulled her forward until the heavy footsteps halted right in front of them.

"It's him," the heretic said eagerly, his voice whining slightly.

"Excellent. Who is the woman?" A stranger spoke in a low, guttural voice.

"I'm not sure. But she might have been one of the enemy down in the tunnels. The mystic seems to know her. He offered to trade himself for her."

"Very well. I shall tell Ragathol that you await his presence. Take the woman to join the other one, but keep the mystic with you."

"Okay," the heretic said happily.

Pam let herself be taken through a couple of narrow passageways. She heard a heavy door creak open, then felt herself casually shoved forward. When she hit her shoulder against the door, banging it open wider, she lost her balance and fell on the hard, uneven floor. Before she could rise, she heard the door closed and a loud lock snapped into place.

Pam pushed herself up and looked around. A blue and orange glow lit the chamber dimly. The lights came from the far side of the small chamber, which was about four meters in diameter. The air in the chamber was cold. She got to her feet and cautiously moved toward the lights.

A short, slender woman lay on the stone floor. Her shoulder-length, straight brown hair was strewn over her face. She was dressed in a badly torn khaki long-sleeved shirt and pants, which were covered with dirt, bloodstains, and smoke smudges. A cap of iron bands was on her head. Wires led from it to a wall of necrotechnology computer equipment, lit with dark blue and orange lights on its monitors.

Pam knelt down and gently shook the woman by the shoulder. She was in her mid-twenties, Pam guessed. The woman remained completely limp.

"Can you hear me?" Pam asked gently.

She did not respond in any way.

Pam realized this was almost certainly the woman who had arrived from Venus. After a moment Pam unzipped the front of her jumpsuit far enough to check her belt computer. The voice function was still transmitting.

She thought about calling quietly for help, in case someone in the team was close enough to hear, but decided against it. So far, the enemy had not noticed its faint transmission of static and background noise; she did not want to risk her voice being picked up by an enemy receiver. Instead, she repositioned the belt computer more comfortably in her jumpsuit and zipped it up again.

Then she sat down and idly scratched and tapped the bulge it made in her jumpsuit. The added sounds would create a stronger signal, but might not attract the attention of her captors the way her voice would. If she was lucky, no one among the enemy would be monitoring frequencies down here, anyway; they could not pick up anything from the street levels.

Lane and Fay stopped on the street at an access hatch, ignoring the crowds of people around them. They had taken a minicab through the streets to this area, where they had finally lost Pam's signal completely. Yojimbo reported that he had lost the signal at the same time.

"What do you think?" Lane asked. "Should we look for her on the streets or try the tunnels?"

"We lost the signal abruptly," said Fay. "If she was still on the street, it would have faded out slowly."

"Unless the heretic found the belt computer and just turned it off."

"A smart one would have left it on, but discarded it someplace to throw us off the track."

Lane grinned despite his worry about Pam. "Maybe he's not that smart."

"We're taking a risk either way," said Fay. "I say we go down into the tunnels. We know the enemy was using them before to take Honorius to the docks."

"Good enough." Lane opened the hatch with a clang. "Let's go."

While he descended, Fay took a moment to report their location and plan to Yojimbo.

At the bottom of the ladder Lane turned on his head lamp and looked around, holding his CAR-24 ready. Above him Fay closed the hatch and joined him. Lane saw nothing of interest near them in the tunnel.

"Yojimbo said he would also find a hatch and come down to the tunnels," said Fay. "He'll use the map in his belt computer to come in our direction. After that we'll have to hope we link up somehow."

"Where is Yojimbo now?"

"Here." Fay pointed to a spot on the screen.

"Good. He's not far, even working through the maze. Since we aren't getting Pam's signal anymore, we might as well join up."

"Yeah."

"Hey!" Lane looked again at his belt computer.

"What is it?"

"She's down here, all right. I can't get the Whiz Kid's signal anymore, but I'm getting a faint signal directly from Pam again."

"Enough to follow it?"

Lane turned slowly. "Yeah. It's coming from that way." He pointed.

Fay shifted her AR3000 light machine gun off her shoulder and swung her Gehenna Puker into firing position, still strapped to her. She moved the AR3000 to her back, out of the way. "Just in case we find necromutants along the way."

"All right, but be careful not to fire too fast," said Lane, starting to move up. "I'll keep my CAR-24 ready. That incinerator won't distinguish between Pam, Honorius, and anyone else."

"Copy." Fay left her own belt computer on her belt. "What do we do if we lose her signal? It can't travel well in these tunnels."

Lane studied the maze on his screen as he walked forward, his head lamp lighting the way. "I'm guessing that the heretic is going to continue in the same direction he was going on the surface, at least for a while."

"Why? This could simply be the nearest hatch to his

destination, even if he has to change directions down here. Once he got into the maze, he might have gone anywhere."

Lane held the screen toward her so she could see the maze. "We're close to a section of tunnels that are basically a dead end."

Fay looked without speaking for a moment, then nodded. "I see. When the nepharite chose a site for his secret cell, he probably looked for a spot where humans would not chance across it."

"That's my guess. You have the map. I'll bring up the rear."

Lane walked point, keeping the beam of his head lamp aimed sharply downward. He did not want the light shining too far up the forward tunnel, where it would betray their advance to anyone who saw it, but he did not want to lose time by moving slowly in darkness. They both walked quietly, but he could not hear any sounds ahead of them.

As Lane advanced, he checked his map again for the location where Yojimbo had stood at their last contact. If Yojimbo was also picking up the weak, intermittent signal from Pam, both squads would be led together eventually if the signal continued. In any case, Lane had to be careful not to shoot at anyone too quickly.

Lane led Fay slowly but steadily through the tunnels, following the signal when he could. At times it faded out, but he continued, and was able to pick it up again. He was getting a tapping sound now, and a rough, scratching noise. Exactly what caused them did not matter. As the signal gradually became stronger, he realized that Pam—or at least her belt computer—had stopped moving.

When the signal suddenly became very clear, Lane slowed down. Now he was worried about coming up on the enemy unexpectedly, possibly into a trap. He turned very slowly around a corner, his CAR-24 ready to fire.

Down the next tunnel he saw no people, but a gaping, arched hole in the left wall caught his attention.

Keeping his CAR-24 trained on the opening, Lane studied the hole in the direct beam of his head lamp. The opening had not been cut into the wall of tunnel, but blasted, in a rough oval shape. He could see a portion of the wall of passage behind the opening, leading into darkness.

Past the thickness of the tunnel wall, the rock and dust of the moon had been fused into a hard, rough surface by extreme heat. The passage angled downward, with a rough, uneven gravel floor. Lane checked his belt computer and turned slowly from side to side. Pam's signal came from the mysterious passage.

Lane instantly shut off his head lamp and listened for sounds of movement. He had no way of knowing if anyone was close enough to have seen his light shining down the passage. When he heard nothing, he turned and leaned close to Fay.

"Fall back quietly," he whispered. "No lights, no sound. Stealth over speed."

They turned. Now Fay walked first. They moved back up the tunnel slowly by feeling their way. Around the first corner Lane stopped.

"Halt," he whispered. "Did you see it?"

"The passage?" Fay whispered back. "Yes. I looked over your shoulder."

"Pam's signal came from it. I think it leads to the place we're looking for, but we don't know how far it goes. See if you can raise Yojimbo. If he's in a tunnel close enough, we might reach him. But keep your voice down."

While Fay called Yojimbo in a whisper, Lane studied the maze again on his belt computer. From a military standpoint, the biggest problem they now faced was that a single, narrow passage of unknown size could be an impregnable position. It was ideal for either an ambush, a trap, or direct defense. Lane could not possibly recommend entering it blindly, so he wanted to plan with Yojimbo.

They had already entered the section of the maze that represented a dead end in the standard tunnels. However, depending on the exact shape and direction of the enemy passage, the passage might run very close to several of the tunnels in the area. That could mean that only a narrow wall of concrete and lunar rock separated some sections of the enemy passage from the regular tunnels.

Fay was whispering into her unit; obviously, she had a response.

"Yojimbo?" Lane asked.

"Yes. We're exchanging locations the best we can, but even the computers can't nail down distance or direction with the signal bouncing around in the tunnels of the maze. I've briefed him on the mystery passage and its location as well as I can."

Lane turned on his own voice function. "Sai. Lane here. Request you go up to street level and get explosives, the kind used for lunar mining."

"Do I read, 'explosives'?" Yojimbo asked. "Are we going to bring these tunnels down on our heads?"

"No," said Lane. "Get small, tightly focused directional materials—whatever somebody used to burrow these tunnels in the first place. Then rendezvous with us. We'll keep the enemy passage under surveillance."

"Agreed," said Yojimbo.

While Fay finished conferring about their location, Lane moved up slightly to listen again. He still heard no sounds from the enemy passage. If the enemy came out, he and Fay would have to withdraw ahead of them to avoid revealing their presence before Yojimbo's squad joined them.

Fay stashed her belt computer and moved up behind Lane, still whispering. "Hear anything?"

"No. Now we just wait."

"Explosives?"

"One of the jobs I did last year involved some old mine shafts and tunnels. I think that's what we're looking at here. Construction explosives will do the job for us."

"Should we move closer now?"

"No. Too much risk of being seen or heard if someone comes out. Back here we're more likely to hear them first. They won't have a reason to be unusually quiet."

"Right." She hesitated. "Do we have to maintain silence at this position?"

"No, not as long as we whisper. You want to confer about something?"

"It's personal, not military. At least, not directly. But everything becomes part of our work, doesn't it?"

"Yeah. Part of being a free-lancer. But what's on your mind?"

"You've been just a little different since Pam disappeared—or was taken, rather."

"Yeah?" Lane said cautiously. "How so?"

"It's not anything overwhelming. But you're a little more energized—more into the job."

"We have more focus."

"Yeah, but *you're* more focused, too."

"What of it?"

"It's Pam."

"My partner."

Fay laughed lightly. "You were telling me before that you and Pam sometimes wondered if this life was worth living. I bet Pam's sure it is, right now."

"Maybe," Lane said soberly. "Or else she's wondering if she should have wasted her life in a career that brought her to this point."

"But it woke you up, didn't it?"

Lane paused just a moment. "Yes, it did. If I have to live this lousy life, I don't want to lose her." He grinned in the darkness. "At the very least, she hates it as much as I do—we have that in common."

Fay said nothing else.

Lane felt closer to Pam now than he had in most of the time they had known each other.

CHAPTER 27

Yojimbo took Vic and Klaus back up to the street after conferring with Fay. Klaus led them to a black market where Yojimbo purchased the explosives that Vic and Klaus recommended. He also bought backpacks to carry them. Wearing the backpacks with the Gehenna Pukers was awkward, but soon the squad had returned down into the tunnels, their head lamps lighting the way now that Lane and Fay had the forward position secure.

As Yojimbo walked point in the tunnels toward their rendezvous with Lane and Fay, he was already picturing the problem Fay had relayed to him. Obviously, Lane had some plan regarding the explosives. No matter what it was, however, Yojimbo could not accept a simple assault up the mysterious tunnel. It was simply suicidal.

"Sai," Lane's voice whispered on Yojimbo's belt computer. "Turn off the lights, but advance straight ahead. You're coming right up to us."

"Lights out," Yojimbo said quietly, shutting his off. Vic and Klaus did the same.

In a few moments Yojimbo reached Fay and Lane.

"We have the explosives you suggested," Yojimbo whispered. "Three backpacks, filled with them. But we cannot afford to charge up an unknown tunnel. And since we do not know exactly who or what is inside it, we cannot just bring it crashing down, either."

"I don't intend either one," said Lane. "I'm sure the enemy passage is part of an old mine tunnel. They just connected it to this tunnel system by blasting through a wall; that means we can do the same. I've located a spot where I think I can blast through a tunnel wall to connect with another spot in the interior of the enemy passage."

"To create a diversion," said Yojimbo. He still felt misgivings. "I see. However, the main passage will still be very difficult to assault—probably too difficult."

"*You* create the diversion," said Lane. "With a direct assault up the existing tunnel."

"To what end?" Vic asked.

"After it starts, we'll blast through the wall and move through the tunnel wall into the new passage," said Fay. "We can take the defenders in the rear."

"What if it doesn't work?" Klaus asked. "You might not make the connection you want."

"We'll keep blasting," said Lane. "In any case, you probably won't be able to move up, so you won't be in undue danger. Just keep the enemy busy."

"Agreed," said Yojimbo. He felt this was as good a tactic as they would have. Glad to have something feasible, he unslung his backpack and gave it to Lane, as did Vic. Klaus gave his to Fay.

"Are we ready to move right away?" Lane asked. "We don't know how Pam is being treated in there."

"As soon as you say," said Yojimbo. "How much time do you need to get into position?"

"Not much," said Lane. "We only need to move up past the passage before you start. Then we'll want your squad to begin the diversion before we blast."

"Good," said Vic. "I don't want to waste any time, either. Let's move."

"We'll move up and show you the enemy passage," said Lane. "Follow me."

Yojimbo waited while Lane switched on his head lamp and walked point with Fay right behind them. No one else used their head lamps. In a few moments Yojimbo was able to look past Fay and Lane to a gaping hole in the side of a tunnel.

"All right," said Yojimbo. He turned to Vic and Klaus. "At my signal we'll rush to the opening but not enter it. Klaus, you and I will begin with our loudest noisemakers, our light machine guns. When we raise a response, be ready to shift to the incinerators fast."

"On your signal," said Klaus.

"Lane, move out," said Yojimbo. "Give me a 'sai' when you're clear."

Without a word Lane jogged forward, keeping a wary eye on the opening in the bobbing beam of his head lamp. Yojimbo watched Fay trot after him, her petite body nearly hidden from behind by the Gehenna Puker on her back. Shortly after they had passed the enemy passage, Lane turned left around a corner. Fay vanished around it, too.

"Sai!" Lane shouted back down the tunnels, not bothering with the belt computer. "Sai!"

"Sai!" Yojimbo shouted, rushing the opening with his Windrider forward. He fired, keeping the passage in sight by the light of the flame at the end of his barrel. "Sai!"

"Sai!" Vic shouted, jogging up behind him.

"I'm not going to yell that," Klaus growled as he fired his weapon just to Yojimbo's right. "That's stupid."

Yojimbo reached the edge of the passage and crouched just around its left side, pouring fire forward. Vic stood over him, his Gehenna Puker ready. Klaus took the right edge of the passage, also firing.

Shouts of surprise and rage echoed somewhere down in the strange passage.

Lane dropped a backpack of explosives onto the floor of the tunnel and checked the map of the maze once more. This was the spot. He was no demolition expert, but he and Pam had both learned some basic demolition skills as part of the Martian Banshees. Now he just had to hope he could blast through the wall without bringing the entire tunnel down.

Fortunately, he recognized the type of explosive Yojimbo had brought, though not the make; he did not waste any time looking for a brand name. He took small, hand-held cylinders of explosive charge out of the backpack and saw that they were directional. The same end that provided the blast had a soft, sticky claylike detonator that stuck to the wall when he pressed the cylinder against it.

Around the corner Lane heard shouts of "Sai!" and the chattering of two light machine guns. Obviously, Vic was waiting patiently with his Gehenna Puker. In the enemy passage roars and growls answered them, muffled, but no enemy fire had sounded yet.

Lane handed some cylinders to Fay, and they lined them in a narrow, arched shape the size of an ordinary doorway. Fay connected the malleable detonators with a thin wire. Then they both backed away.

"I'll lead," Fay declared. "The opening may be uneven. I'm smaller."

"All right. But remember, we may have to detonate several sets before we burrow all the way through. Fire it."

Fay fired her AR3000 at one of the cylinders. When the bullets struck the clay, it ignited the charge in the rest of the cylinder and blasted forward. In the same moment the wire carried the impulse to all the other cylinders, which exploded around the narrow arc in quick succession.

"Sai!" Fay slung back her AR3000 and brought her Gehenna Puker forward. Charging the smoke-filled opening, she roared the flame into the newly blown gap, even though they could not tell if the explosion had broken through or if they needed another one.

"Since when do we have a battle-cry?" Lane muttered, bringing his own incinerator into ready position. Then, as he saw her slip into the smoke and disappear, he ducked and followed her.

The serial blasts of explosives echoed down the tunnels to Yojimbo. Still leaning away from the opening as he fired around the corner, he now heard the roar of heavy machine-gun fire coming back out of the passage. Startled, wordless screams of rage and anger echoed among the solid rock walls of the enemy lair. Then heavy, pounding footsteps ran toward them up the gravel.

"Stay low," Vic ordered.

Yojimbo felt the big man swing his Gehenna Puker around the corner over Yojimbo's head. The flame roared out, lighting up the passage. Across the opening, Klaus did the same with his own incinerator.

In the same moment a giant column of flame whooshed back out of the passage.

Yojimbo winced in the heat, feeling it on his face even as he turned away. The enemy had their own black technology incinerators, even more powerful than the Gehenna Pukers, indicated by the size of this flame. Yojimbo shifted his Windrider out of the way and brought his own Gehenna Puker into position. Then he fired it around the corner, under Vic's.

Klaus maintained his flame, as well.

As Yojimbo had expected, this passage would be easy for the enemy to defend. Certainly no one on his team could charge into a breech filled with incinerator flames. He could only hope his squad faced no worse than a stalemate.

Pam had been sitting quietly next to the unconscious woman when the first sounds of light machine-gun fire reached her. It was well muffled, but still close; she felt certain that the team had picked up the haphazard signal from her belt computer. She felt for the belt computer in her jumpsuit to see if she could reach someone now that the action had started.

Suddenly, she heard two sets of footsteps approaching the door to the chamber. Hoping that whoever was coming would be distracted by the attack, she jumped to her feet and flattened herself against the wall next to the door. She felt the rush of adrenaline once more.

The lock snapped open.

A man she had not seen before, clearly another heretic, shoved Honorius inside, where he stumbled and fell. Just as the heretic reached for the latch to slam the door shut, Pam grabbed his wrist with her left hand and yanked him into the chamber, pulling with all her weight. Off balance, the heretic staggered forward.

Pam cocked her right arm back across her body to chop the man's throat with the edge of her hand in a backhand stroke. Instantly, she went blind and felt overwhelming pain shoot through her body. She swung wildly, hitting the man in the face rather than the throat, but hung onto his wrist desperately with her left hand.

The first time this Dark Gift of pain had struck her, out in the tunnels, she had been startled and overwhelmed. It hurt no less this time, but she kept her concentration better. She channeled her response to pain into clutching the heretic and threw her other arm around his torso.

They both fell, Pam on her back to bang her head on the hard floor, with the heretic on top of her. As he rolled to one side to get up, her left arm hooked around his neck. She tightened her arm as hard as she could, bracing it with her right hand, grimacing against the pain wracking her entire body and focusing her mind totally on holding her arm in place.

The man kicked, thrashed, and rolled; Pam rolled with him, putting all her energy into her stranglehold, allowing him to carry her across the cold stone floor of the chamber. The heretic made gasping, wheezing sounds, and even through the extreme pain Pam was encouraged. She held on longer and felt him slump in her grasp.

Still, Pam did not dare let go. He was weakening, but could be faking his collapse. Then, all at once, the pain in her body vanished and her sight returned. In the blue and orange glow, she saw that he had fallen unconscious, causing the Dark Gifts he had forced on her to disappear.

Nearby, a series of explosions in quick succession vibrated the rock walls around her.

Pam pushed herself up, weak and dazed from the pain she had experienced. She staggered to the door, but turned before going out. Honorius, still lying on the floor where he had been flung, looked around at nothing in particular. She decided he would be safer here in the chamber than in the middle of a firefight. However, she grabbed the heretic's ankles and dragged him out of the chamber with her. Then she closed the chamber door behind her to protect the two people inside.

The roar of incinerators reached her out here in the dimly lit rock passage, as did the continuing chatter of heavy machine guns. She glanced around the passage for a way to confine the heretic so he would not wake up and either go after Honorius and the mystery woman, or attack Pam again, but she saw nothing she could use. Finally, she dropped his ankles and left him, to move slowly along one wall. She looked for a chamber where she might find a weapon.

Several intersecting passages opened on this one. Some doorways opened on chambers like the one she had just left, except that none of the doors were closed. She glanced inside three of them, but saw no one inside and no weapons.

Another staccato chain of explosions echoed through the passage, vibrating the floor under her feet. She heard rock falling hard to the passage floor nearby. Cautiously, staying close to one wall, she moved up to see what had happened.

A door-size hole had been blasted into the passage. As smoke and dust roiled forward, Lane advanced out of the cloud in a crouch, his Gehenna Puker aimed forward. Fay stepped out right behind him, stumbling through the rubble.

"It's Pam," she called frantically, not sure if Lane could see her clearly through the smoke.

Lane saw her in the same moment and moved away his incinerator. Fay quickly slung her Gehenna Puker off and threw it with both hands to Pam. While Fay brought her AR3000 around on its strap, Pam nodded acceptance. She understood; her greater height and weight meant that she could handle the big incinerator more efficiently than Fay.

Around them the roaring of incinerators echoed down a couple of intersecting passages, making the source of the sound difficult to judge.

"Which way to the main entrance?" Lane shouted over the noise, looking frantically up and down the passages. "We have to take the defenders in the rear."

"I don't know. I was brought in blind and just got out of a locked chamber." Pam slipped on the straps of the incinerator and moved it into position. "You can probably guess better than I can."

Lane glanced around and then moved up one of the passages. Fay followed right behind him and Pam brought up the rear. The smoke and dust from the blast lingered in the air, lowering their visibility as they advanced.

Suddenly very heavy, thumping footsteps pounded toward them from a side passage.

Yojimbo, Klaus, and Vic held their positions at the main opening of the enemy passage. They could not even look around the corners because the intensity of the enemy incinerators never let up. Instead, they could only answer with their own weapons, held awkwardly around the corner of the passage without exposing themselves to the flames, turning the narrow passage into an inferno that neither side could enter.

Footsteps running up the tunnel behind Yojimbo got his attention. Alarmed, he turned and released the trigger of his incinerator, preparing to swing it around and fire behind him while Vic maintained his fire up the passage. By the light of the flames roaring in the passage, he saw two men running forward.

"Careful," Klaus warned, looking back over his shoulder. "Don't let down your guard!"

CHAPTER 28

"Friends!" The one in front held his hands forward, empty. "We're here to help." A big Purifier bounced in front of him on a strap. It was a Brotherhood weapon that combined a twenty-millimeter machine gun with an incinerator that shot synthoplasmine, a sticky flammable substance. "I'm Vitus Marius, a mortificator."

"Advance." Wary under fire, Yojimbo still held his Gehenna Puker on them, eyeing them carefully as they came up. He saw that they still kept their hands away from their weapons.

"My name is Titus Gallicus, a Senior Inquisitor." The second man carried a Bauhaus ARG-17 that fired a thirty-millimeter rocket grenade that exploded on impact. "We know you fight the Dark Legion here. We will help."

Yojimbo knew that Inquisitors were stern, unbending enforcers who sought to eliminate corruption, as they saw it, in any form. He studied them both cautiously as Vic kept up the flame in the passage. "I know that mortificators do not wear a logo. If you are a Senior Inquisitor, you should be."

"I have masqueraded as a free-lancer in order to find you. Now please accept our help."

Yojimbo noted with respect that Titus did not presume to ask him to identify his team or their purpose. Fighting the Dark Legion made them allies, at least for now. "At what price?"

"We must have the mystic called Honorius if he still lives at the end of this."

"You have been searching for him and following us?" Yojimbo asked quickly, over the whooshing roar of the incinerators.

"Yes. The last leg of our search was based on the name of one of your team, then a free-lancer's bar, and witnesses who remembered people wearing Gehenna Pukers as they came down an access hatch. I share this to convince you of our sincerity. Will you accept the deal I offer?"

Yojimbo thought quickly. Honorius could not survive in the violence of Luna City streets on his own for any length of time. Up to now, he had simply been lucky on his own. He had no plans or ambitions that anyone on Team Yojimbo had learned. The Brotherhood was the only group that had an interest in taking care of the near-helpless mystic. "Agreed."

"Stand back, then," said the mortificator. "You have a stalemate. We'll send down a rocket grenade followed by a synthoplasmine flame. If the enemy flame falters at all, we will rush the tunnel. Be ready to move up behind us."

"On your signal," said Yojimbo.

"Ready," called Klaus.

"Hurry up," yelled Vic.

Lane heard the vibrations of heavy footsteps on the stone floor and started to turn with his incinerator, expecting another necromutant. What he saw instead startled him: a monstrous entity four meters tall, thick with heavy muscles, running toward him with his arms extended. His hands were empty and grasping. Long, sharp spikes grew out of his shoulders and the sides of his head. One long spike angled forward from the top of his head. His low forehead ended in a heavy brow ridge over deep-set eyes. The nostrils of his short, pointed nose flared; the monster screamed with rage, revealing long, shiny teeth as the thunderous roar echoed off the rock walls.

For one long, shocked moment even the veteran of the Martian Banshees and countless free-lance jobs froze in place.

"Lane!" Pam screamed behind him, moving up past Fay to get a clear shot of her own. "It's the nepharite!"

Lane belatedly swung up his incinerator, realizing that Fay and Pam could not fire from their positions without hitting him. Before he could shoot the flame out, however, the nepharite swatted the gear out of his hands and knocked him aside, sending him rolling on the floor of the passage.

When Lane stopped rolling, he looked up in time to see the monster lash out at Pam and send her flying across the passage with the Gehenna Puker on her back.

Fay skipped backward, away from the nepharite's long arms, firing her AR3000. A lace of bullets slashed his right arm, tearing the flesh but not stopping him. She lowered her aim, still dancing away from him, and concentrated fire on his right leg.

The nepharite stumbled, but reached out with his left hand and simply ripped the AR3000 out of her hand. He swung it against the rock wall of the passage, smashing it. Instead of fighting with any of them, however, he jogged with a limp down the passage past her.

"Come on!" Lane pushed himself up and unslung his CAR-24. He tossed it to Fay as she got to her feet. Then he brought his incinerator back into position and started away from the nepharite, in the direction where he thought the main opening lay. "Forget him! We have to take the pressure off Yojimbo!"

"No!" Pam shouted. "We have to stop him—he's going for Honorius and the mystery woman!"

Yojimbo watched as the stern, grim-faced Titus fired his rocket grenade around the corner of the main passage. It whooshed out of sight through the flame and exploded, shaking all the walls of the tunnels. Yojimbo looked up for a moment, certain that the entire maze would collapse on them.

It did not, and the flame from the enemy incinerators suddenly stopped. Vitus fired his synthoplasmine up the tunnel, lighting it up again through the smoke and dust from the rocket grenade. Without a word, he advanced at a run up the passage.

Titus stood aside for the other three men with incinerators. Yojimbo led Vic up the passage, ready to fire as soon as the mortificator ahead was able to move out of the way. He heard Titus bring up the rear.

In front of Yojimbo Vitus fired his flame forward

again; portions of the floor and rubble at the end of the passage still burned with the sticky fuel. As Yojimbo came out into some kind of foyer behind the mortificator, he saw two dead necromutants, their bodies burning with synthoplasmine even as their own smoldering black technology incinerators still lay in their grotesque hands.

Yojimbo stared at them in some surprise.

Penyon eagerly sneaked forward through a narrow passage, following Gorong, the necromutant in front of him. This was his chance to make the ultimate heroic act in defense of his new master. Concentrating on his lone Dark Gift, he prepared to hit the first attacker he saw. In front of him Gorong turned and pointed to the opening ahead, where their passage intersected the main foyer.

Penyon slipped past him, anxious to find someone he could hit with his Dark Gift.

Vitus moved up ahead of Yojimbo, looking around carefully. The foyer opened on many different passages. He advanced, ready to fire again, searching for a target.

Suddenly Vitus hesitated, looked startled. "I can't see," he shouted.

In the same moment two figures leaped out of one of the passages. One was another necromutant, leveling a big necrotechnology heavy machine gun. The other was a human, a heretic, fixing his gaze on Vitus.

As the necromutant's fire ripped into Vitus, making him dance crazily backward, Yojimbo fired his Gehenna Puker at the necromutant, enveloping him in flame. The monstrous creature staggered forward, blazing, turning as he fell toward Yojimbo.

Firing wildly, the necromutant's bullets tore into Vic, throwing him backward. Before the necromutant could fire again, however, he collapsed in a burning heap.

In the same moment, from behind Yojimbo, Klaus incinerated the surprised heretic, whoever he was.

Titus trotted up behind them, looking down at Vitus impassively. "He fell well. So did your large friend." His voice was emotionless.

"Advance carefully," said Yojimbo, moving cautiously

forward to peer into the next chamber. It was empty. "We don't know how many of the enemy are here. But we're sure one's a nepharite." He would mourn Vic later.

Without speaking, Klaus kicked open a door already ajar. That chamber, too, was empty.

"Embodiments of evil," muttered Titus. "We must be careful not to harm the mystic."

Lane ran after the nepharite, with Pam and Fay right behind him, and yelled back over his shoulder. "Why isn't he armed? Does anybody know?"

"He must have been caught by surprise," Fay shouted. "He may find a weapon, so watch for it!"

Lane rounded a curve in the passage just in time to see the nepharite rip a door off its hinges and fling it away, to smash on the far wall of the passage.

An unfamiliar human, presumably a heretic, lay on the floor of the passage.

Through the doorway Lane saw Honorius sitting quietly, with a prone woman lying behind him. Lane dialed the width of flame down quickly and fired a long, narrow stream of fire in front of the nepharite, without hitting the two humans inside the chamber. He held it tightly in position, not sure if the monster would simply run through it or not.

The creature did not. The nepharite dodged back from the stream of flame, away from the doorway. He glared at Lane for a long moment, uncertainly.

Lane advanced obliquely, his hand on the dial to widen the flame when he had changed his angle of fire enough to avoid the open doorway. First he had to move so that he would hit only the nepharite when the flame widened, and not Honorius and the woman near him. Fay fired the CAR-24 again, still working on the nepharite's wounded right leg to bring him down.

"Fire at his head!" Pam shouted to Fay, coming up near Lane to fire from the same angle he needed.

The nepharite roared again, wordlessly, but did not try to charge them. As Pam brought up her incinerator to fire and Fay raised her arm toward his head, the nepharite suddenly ducked, turned, and ran around the curving passage.

Lane jogged after him, dialing up the flame width to maximum again. Pam joined on his right, also shooting her flame forward. Neither flame struck the nepharite. Still behind them Fay stopped firing to avoid hitting them.

As Lane hurried around the curve, he saw the huge nepharite duck into a surprisingly small opening for a creature his size and disappear into darkness, down a steeply descending passage.

Lane and Pam moved up together, sweeping the opening with both streams of flame. As they came up to the opening, however, he could see that the sharp downward incline of the passage had quickly carried the nepharite past their angles of flame. This, too, looked like an old mine tunnel.

They both released their triggers, looking into the opening. The only way to pursue the nepharite was to plunge into this unknown environment. The chance of a trap was very high.

"What are you waiting for?" a strange man shouted angrily behind them. "He's getting away!"

Lane turned to look. Pam, taut with annoyance, also spun around. Fay held the borrowed CAR-24 ready to fire.

A stranger had come with Yojimbo around the curve in the passage. He held up a rocket grenade launcher. "Get that nepharite!"

"No!" Klaus shouted, appearing around the curve behind Yojimbo and the stranger. "That's reckless. You're not being paid for that."

Pam looked at Yojimbo. "Orders?"

"We might get him, Yojimbo," Lane added quickly. "What do you want us to do?"

"Your call," said Yojimbo. "I will not order you to take that kind of risk."

Lane looked down the dark mine tunnel. The nepharite could be waiting around the first bend, or might have wired the tunnel with explosives to bring it down. If the nepharite had carried Pam down there, or one of the other team members, pursuit would have been worth the risk. Even then, the move was almost suicidal.

"No," Pam said quietly, nearly in a whisper. "This life is lousy, but it's still worth keeping."

Lane knew in that moment she was right. He looked up into her blue eyes and smiled slightly. "Yeah."

"Well?" The stranger glared at them.

Lane lowered his Gehenna Puker and backed away from the wall. "We can't risk following him."

"Accepted," said Yojimbo. "Lane, maintain surveillance of that opening and the immediate vicinity. We'll finish securing the area." He led Klaus and the Brotherhood man on up the main passage.

Fay remained where she was with the unconscious heretic lying behind her. "At least he's wounded. That's something."

"I don't want him coming back out," Lane said to Pam. "If we're lucky, that's a dead end, and he won't find a way out. Let's close this end." He reached back over his shoulder for some more of the explosives.

"Good idea." Pam helped take them out of his backpack.

Together they placed them just inside the opening. Then they backed safely away from the wall. Lane fired a quick tongue of flame at them, and the charges exploded simultaneously, bringing a fall of rock down inside the sloping passage. When the smoke and dust had cleared slightly, Lane saw that the opening had been filled with fallen rock.

Behind them Fay gave a surprised, gasping cry of pain.

Lane and Pam whirled at the same moment. Fay had fallen to her knees, clutching her abdomen with both arms. Lane's borrowed CAR-24 clattered to the floor of the passage. Behind her the heretic, who had been lying unconscious, had pushed himself up groggily to his hands and knees.

"The heretic's hit her with his pain gift," said Pam, swinging her Gehenna Puker out of her way. Moving laterally to get Fay out of her line of fire, she drew her Bolter pistol and dropped the heretic with a single head shot.

Pam moved up and helped Fay to her feet. Lane hurried to the chamber holding Honorius and the woman. A quick glance inside told him that neither had moved.

As Pam and Fay stood in the passage, warily watching for more of the enemy, Lane drew his belt computer and hit the voice function.

"Sai! You there, Yojimbo? Lane here."

"Report," said Yojimbo. His voice came through strongly.

"Have secured mystic and strange woman with Pam and Fay. One heretic dead here, nepharite's escape route sealed. We closed it off with explosives and consider him gone."

"Maintain position," Yojimbo ordered. "We've reached the end of the main passage and have secured each chamber and side passage. No more sign of hostiles so far."

"None here, either."

"We didn't tell you a minute ago," said Klaus, also through the voice function. "We lost Vic to a necro-mutant."

"We'll hold here," said Lane more quietly. He exchanged a sober glance with Fay and Pam, who had overheard them.

Pam entered the chamber where Honorius still sat impassively. Lane decided that the firefight was over. He walked with Fay into the chamber after Pam.

"For many will come in my name," Honorius said quietly to no one in particular.

Pam walked over to the strange necrotechnology computer machinery against the far wall. She looked it over for a moment, then glanced down at the motionless woman. The cap of wires leading from her head to the wall of monitors was still in place.

"Destroy it." Pam nodded toward Lane's CAR-24 in Fay's hands.

"She might need that to live," said Fay.

"If so, we'll put her out of her misery. If not, we'll free her." Pam knelt and pulled off the cap. Then she eased the petite woman over one shoulder and carried her away from the wall.

Fay fired the CAR-24 from her hip, spraying the machinery back and forth. It sparked, hissed, and popped. The monitor's blue and orange lights went dark.

Pam felt the woman's neck for a pulse. "She's still alive, so far. I want to get her out of this chamber." She turned and carried the woman out into the passage.

Fay moved her CAR-24 to one side and took Honorius by one arm. When she lifted, he rose, as cooperative as ever. Fay brought him out after Pam.

Lane followed them. Yojimbo's squad met them coming back down the passage. Their weapons swung on their straps, no longer ready to fire.

"We're secure," said Yojimbo. "You truly consider the nepharite finished?"

"He can't come back here," said Lane. "He's either on the run with nowhere to go, or maybe he has arrangements for an emergency escape. But if he shows himself anywhere on the surface, he'll be shot to pieces."

"I agree," said Yojimbo. "He is either trapped or fleeing. If the latter, he will turn up again, but without troops or a place to hide."

Klaus nodded to Fay and moved to stand next to her.

"Greetings, Honorius." Titus looked into the mystic's eyes. "Can you understand me?"

"I fear no evil," said Honorius calmly.

"If I may?" Titus glanced at Yojimbo.

"Yes. The Senior Inquisitor will return the mystic to a Brotherhood haven."

"You sure?" Lane asked suspiciously. He neither liked nor trusted the Brotherhood.

"We have agreed."

Lane said nothing. This was Yojimbo's team. Besides, he did not want to baby-sit the mystic forever, either.

Fay released the mystic's arm.

"Thank you," said Titus, taking Honorius gently by the shoulders. He turned to Yojimbo. "You know that word of this incident will only disrupt life throughout Luna City. It must not be allowed to spread."

"Yes. We operate under an agreement of secrecy ourselves," said Yojimbo. "We will honor it."

"If you agree, I will have a Brotherhood team reclaim

the remains of the mortificator and eliminate all evidence of the events here."

"That is acceptable," said Yojimbo. "Please have the remains of our fallen team member recovered, as well. Then contact me at the Midnight Star."

"Good. We will take our leave."

"Very well. Thank you for your help."

Titus steered Honorius down the passage toward the main entrance.

"This woman is still alive?" Yojimbo nodded toward Pam's charge.

"Yes. But we don't know anything about her," said Pam. "What about her, Yojimbo? You've kept your employer—the ultimate employer of us all—a secret. What's his business with her?"

"Will he take care of her?" Fay asked. "She's been through a lot already. Why should we turn her over to someone without knowing how she'll be treated?"

"My employer has no further interest in her," said Yojimbo. "She was a lead to the presence of the Dark Legion here, no more."

"Then we're free to help her?" Lane asked.

"That is correct. My . . . our employer will be satisfied with the report I will give."

"A rogue Capitol ship brought her from Venus," said Pam. "I'll check her into a Capitol hospital. If she's okay, I'll have Capitol send her back to Venus. Maybe they can find some family members to take care of her."

"Excellent," said Yojimbo.

"Come on," Klaus said to Fay. "I want to look around this place before we go. It's got some interesting stuff, but we'll never see it again after the Brotherhood gets through here."

"Yeah?"

"I'll show you the biggest stone chair I've ever seen." Klaus grinned.

Fay shrugged and walked away with him.

"My honor is restored," Yojimbo said quietly, virtually to himself. He felt a deep sense of warm satisfaction. For a moment he wished he could share his history with Mishima Elite and the moment he had first met Lord Mishima, earning his respect. However, he could not violate Lord Mishima's instruction to keep his name private without dishonoring himself all over again.

Lane looked at him curiously. "Really?"

Yojimbo smiled tightly. "Merely a personal matter. But . . . yes, really. And I owe all of you very much for your loyalty, honor, and courage."

"Aw, that's hokey," said Lane, but he was smiling.

Embarrassed by Yojimbo's compliments, Lane turned and gave Pam a quick kiss.

Pam grinned at him, turning awkwardly with the woman still over her shoulder. "So even *this* life is worth living, after all."

"It sure is." Lane nodded toward the unconscious woman. "Even hers."

"Maybe we can make life better if we just keep at it. As long as we're still here, Chung, we have a chance."

"That's right, blue eyes. That's exactly right."

FANTASTICAL LANDS

If you and/or a friend would like to receive the *ROC Advance*, a bimonthly newsletter featuring all the newest and hottest ROC books and authors, on a complimentary basis, please fill out this form and return it to:

ROC Books/Penguin USA
375 Hudson Street
New York, NY 10014

Your Address
Name _____
Street _____ Apt. # _____
City _____ State _____ Zip _____

Friend's Address
Name _____
Street _____ Apt. # _____
City _____ State _____ Zip _____